KU-582-302

# EYE OF THE SERPENT

100 cm

TULLAMORE
1 1 APR 2023
WITHDRAWN

# EYE OF THE SERPENT

Joanna Challis

CHIVERS

## British Library Cataloguing in Publication Data available

This Large Print edition published by BBC Audiobooks Ltd, Bath, 2007.
Published by arrangement with Robert Hale Limited

U.K. Hardcover ISBN 978 1 405 64008 4
U.K. Softcover ISBN 978 1 405 64009 1

Copyright © Joanna Challis 2006

The right of Joanna Challis to be identified as author of this work has been asserted by her in accordance with the Copyright, Designs and Patents Act 1988.

All rights reserved.

Leabharlann
Chontae Uibh Fhaili

Class: _____

Acc: 015058

Inv: 04193

Printed and bound in Great Britain by
Antony Rowe Ltd., Chippenham, Wiltshire

# PART 1

# The Castle of Dreams

# CHAPTER ONE

I will never forget my first sight of the Castle of Dreams.

It looked like a painting. Out of regal snow-capped mountains rose the sleek, cream-coloured towers of a dream. Surrounded by stone walls seemingly as old as time, the glazed windows of the castle radiated the dying embers of a setting sun.

Ancient, foreboding, beautiful.

'Takes your breath away, doesn't it?' Herr Reimann's teasing whisper held an awe of its own. 'I can never get used to it . . . even after all these years.'

I smiled at the attorney. Expecting a quaint country manor or a hillside lodge, the *schloss* did indeed take my breath away.

We crossed a bridge of stone up to the castle where the enormity of my interview with the Count dawned. What if he found me unsuitable? Would he pay for my passage home?

A pair of rusted wrought-iron gates opened. I studied the grim face of the old man guarding the gate. 'Who is he?'

'Old Josef,' Herr Reimann replied. 'The gatekeeper.'

Reaching a courtyard of weathered cobbled stone, two liveried footmen emerged to help

3

us alight.

Guided inside the almost humble doorway, we were asked to wait in the parlour. Could one call it a parlour? It looked more like a cathedral to me with its painted high-domed ceilings, burning candelabras and gold embossed scarlet standards. Herr Reimann pointed out the family crest of the sword and the serpent.

Footsteps creaked along the wooden floors.

'Fräulein Brown?'

A stout woman of middle age approached, her hair rolled up in the old style. 'Elfriede will show you to your usual quarters, Herr Reimann. I will take the English *fräulein* to a room.'

'A' room, not *her* room, I noted. Evidently, Frau Vetsera had already dismissed me in her mind. 'Have you lived at the castle long, Frau Vetsera?'

'All my life,' came the gruff answer.

I remained silent as I followed her upstairs and down a long corridor of glazed windows overlooking the mountains. Suppressing the urge to linger at the spectacular sight, we finally reached the room allotted to me.

It was a cramped chamber, redeemed only by the view.

'There is a water-closet next door,' Frau Vetsera informed me. 'The fire is lit once daily. The Count wishes to see you before dinner. I shall return to collect you in an hour.'

The door closed.

Unbuttoning my dress, I opened the tiny window to inhale the sweet mountain air. The light was rapidly fading. I supposed it grew dark earlier in the mountains and this would explain why the Count dined so early. I glanced at the clock ticking on the mantel-piece above my fireplace. Five o'clock.

I rummaged through my trunk for something suitable to wear. I wanted to look professional. At length, I decided on a grey gown that had once served Emily, my former charge, as a riding habit.

As much as I tried, I could not conceal my youth. Pinning up my rebellious honey-coloured curls, I put on my spectacles. Granny said I looked at least 28 in them.

Frau Vetsera arrived ten minutes early. By the disappointment lurking on her lips, I knew I had prepared myself wisely.

Frau Vetsera did not carry a candle for the entire castle glowed with light. Even the set of towers across the ridge of the mountain-face, the highest point of the *schloss*, radiated a golden colour. I imagined the castle must look beautiful at night to those dwelling below in the valley. If I wanted to see it, I must first survive this interview.

The uncertainty of my position unnerved me. I concentrated on the castle instead, wondering which part my charge lived in and whether I would meet her tonight.

We eventually came to a stop outside a half-open door. Inside the brightly lit room, I glimpsed a hand scribbling across a desk.

'Thank-you, Helga. Show the young lady in.'

Helga, I almost laughed. The name suited the grim-faced housekeeper.

Hunting scenes and ornaments filled the large, cosy room. Distinctly a male's room with its array of weaponry and scent of leather-bound books and cigars, I shuddered at the wolf's head mounted on the wall. Two lounge-size sofas adorning the open fireplace leant a degree of warmth to the room, their ornately gilded legs matching those of the desk. And on a high-backed chair of scarlet velvet sat the man who held my future in his hands.

I started forward, shock replacing my nerves. 'Y-you . . . the coffee house in Vienna!.'

A half amused smile met my outburst. 'I sincerely regret I did not meet you at any Viennese coffee house, *fräulein.* If I had, I would not have forgotten the incident.'

The cool, precise way he spoke contradicted the glimmer of his dark eyes. On closer inspection, I realized he was not the stranger I had met in Vienna but another man, dark-haired and older. I could only attribute my error to a trick of the light.

'I hope this news does not disappoint you?'

I was about to say 'no, sir', when I recalled a mere 'sir' might offend a count. I couldn't remember how to address a count. Was it your grace? Your lordship? Your eminence?

'Do sit down, Miss Brown.'

The chair relieved my humiliation. 'I must apologize, my lord. Under the light, you appear remarkably like the man I met in Vienna.'

He raised a cynical brow. 'And did this stranger approach you, or did you approach him?'

'He approached me, my lord. He offered to buy me a coffee.'

'I see . . . and did you happen to learn the name of this kindly stranger?'

'No, I did not, my lord.'

To my astonishment, the count began to smile. He looked handsome and younger when he smiled and the likeness between him and my stranger suddenly dawned. 'Is he . . . your brother, my lord?'

The smile disappeared. 'No. I believe the man you met would be my cousin. Cousin Karl likes to play practical jokes.'

I felt the great fool.

The Count observed me through pensive, dark eyes. 'You are younger than I anticipated . . . do you always wear spectacles?'

The question caught me off guard. 'I use them mostly when reading.'

'You intend reading the menu at dinner?' He relaxed against his chair. 'Glasses don't suit you, Fräulein Brown. I suggest you only wear them when you must.'

I removed the spectacles. 'Yes, my lord. Does that mean . . . ?'

'You can stay? You come highly recommended, Fräulein Brown, and I am eager to see results.'

I handed him my references.

'. . . excellence in German. You are something of an enigma, Fräulein Brown—a German grandmother, English parents and a curious name . . . Cristabel. It will be interesting to see how you perform, Fräulein Cristabel.'

I refused to allow his mocking tone to unease me. 'May I ask a few questions, my lord?'

'Ah, so there is the connection. The inquisitive Englishwoman.'

'I have been told little about the post and my charge.'

'Which one do you want to discuss first? The post? Three-month trial, one to two-year term and, if you manage that milestone, you will be handsomely compensated. If you are successful, we'll set a nominal salary, say two hundred pounds?'

Two hundred pounds! Some governesses only earned thirty pounds a year!

'This does not please you?'

If I didn't have my family to think of, I never would have accepted such an outrageous sum. 'It is very generous of you, my lord.'

'Any other requests?'

I read the cynicism in his eyes. 'Yes. When the amount is payable, could you please send it to England, to my family? They are the ones in need of it.'

The coldness left his face. 'Consider it done. You are not a squeamish English miss, are you?'

'I always try to be honest, my lord.'

'Then promise me something, Fräulein Cristabel.'

'Yes, my lord?'

'Never lose that quality.'

## CHAPTER TWO

After the interview, at which I learned nothing about my charge, Frau Vetsera announced dinner in the great hall.

The great hall. I couldn't wait to see it.

'In many ways,' the Count guided me, 'the *schloss* is still a functioning medieval castle. Perhaps you have noticed the differing periods where my ancestors performed their renovations and added their extensions?'

'I have only seen a little of the castle,' I replied, 'but I am enchanted by what I have seen.'

'Enchanted,' he murmured. 'I am pleased you like our home.'

9

The Count's manner surprised me more than the great *schloss*. I felt overwhelmed by the almost guest-like way he welcomed me into his home.

'Tomorrow,' he said, 'I shall give you a proper tour before you start your duties. It is a large castle and we can't have you getting lost, can we?'

Frau Vetsera followed at a discreet distance. I didn't like her proximity, or how her gaze searched my face when the Count addressed me.

The great hall formed the body of the old castle on the ridge. I complimented the Count on how well lit the castle was at night.

'It is an old custom, Fräulein Brown. The castle is something of a lighthouse in these dark mountains. Its presence gave strength to the folk who dwelt below in the valley in the old days and the tradition has continued.'

'And there is the issue of safety,' I said.

He smiled. 'How astute you are, Miss Brown. Yes, a few have fallen to their deaths. It's a penalty for living in the clouds.'

We had stopped to view the valley in the moonlight. Beyond the castle walls lurked a steep decline, made more dangerous by the deceiving presence of the pine trees. The trees gave the illusion one could recover balance if they slipped and fell down the mountain.

I wanted to ask the Count how many had fallen to their deaths, however, I didn't wish to appear morbid or remind my new employer of past fatalities for which he might feel responsible.

Stepping into the great hall was like stepping into the past. A long beautifully carved cedar table with high-backed scarlet velvet chairs dominated the massive, high-ceilinged room where large round chandeliers still hung from the vaulted ceiling. Turkish carpets replaced medieval rushes on the stone floor, adding warmth and texture to an otherwise sombre atmosphere.

Herr Reimann lounged by the fire, talking to a girl.

'Liesel,' her father called, smiling, 'here is your new English governess, Fräulein Brown.'

The sullen girl rose to her feet. Under the light, I recognized the regal hauteur in what could be a pretty face. She had dark hair and her violet eyes regarded me with open contempt.

'Fräulein who? She looks too young to be a governess.'

'Liesel,' her father warned.

His crisp tone prevented any further outbursts and during the course of dinner, my charge remained stubbornly silent.

I supposed coming to live in such a magnificent castle must have its drawbacks. Liesel promised to be a difficult pupil.

\*       \*       \*

I awoke late the next morning.

Horrified, I dressed and sped down to the Count's study.

Standing behind his desk, he waved away my apologies. 'You are tired after your long journey. I hope you had your breakfast?'

I assured him I wasn't hungry, but my stomach betrayed me. He smiled and rang a bell.

A maid soon delivered a tray of coffee and sweet pastries.

'Eat,' the Count insisted. 'The tour can wait.'

Count Maximus von Holstein was nothing like I expected. A widower, they said. My mind had conjured a vision of a balding squire of 52, not this attractive man sipping coffee opposite me.

It was a memorable morning, made so because of the absence of Frau Vetsera. As we progressed from room to room, I wondered if my predecessors had benefited from the same personal attention.

The answer arrived when we reached the schoolroom. The airy sizeable room invited and I smiled at my pupil.

She stood by the bookcase, tapping her fingers.

Once the Count left, I attempted to melt her defiance by asking about the castle.

Liesel crossed her arms. 'Why have you

12

come? I know English. I do not need you.'

'Show me then.'

She tossed her hair over her shoulder. 'I do not have to answer to you. I know why you have come. You are too young and pretty to be a governess. Do you think I am a fool? You are the fool. Nobody will ever replace my mother.'

I sighed. 'I came here to perform a task. It is what I do for a living.'

'I do not believe you. You wanted an adventure. I can see it in your eyes.'

'Yes.' I tried a new tactic. 'I suppose I did. England can be dull at times. Have you been there?'

'No, and nor do I desire to. Nothing compares with the mountains.'

I smiled, glancing out of the window. 'At least we agree on something; it is a start, don't you think?'

She wrapped a ribbon around her arm. 'Do you know what happened to the last governess Fräulein Suski?'

I recognized the ploy.

'They found her at the bottom of the mountain.'

I remained unmoved. 'She tripped?'

Liesel sent me a weary look. 'Are you so cold-hearted?'

'I am not easily frightened.'

She examined me with a curious eye.

'We'll speak in English from now on,' I directed.

13

We began our first lesson on that chilly and awkward October morning. Liesel showed intelligence in her grasp of the language, however, an hour later she could be as vague as a scatterbrain.

'It's very odd having a pretty governess. Mama never approved of pretty governesses.'

'When did your mother die?' I broached.

Her face paled. 'Last winter. Shall I read this page now?'

She did not want to talk about her mother's death. She was a strange girl, pliable one minute, cold the next. Relieved to learn of her music, dance, and 'etiquette' lessons during the week, I asked her what I might do in my spare time.

'Oh,' she said, 'there's the library, and if you're bored, you could always visit Aunt Gisela.'

'Aunt Gisela?'

'My great-aunt. She's an invalid.'

'Is she very frail?'

'Frail?' Liesel laughed, hurling aside her book. 'Come, you should meet her. Aunt Gisela likes meeting new people.'

Liesel's excitable nature led me through the corridors to Aunt Gisela's chambers in the left wing. Pink curtains hung at the windows, matching the pink woven in her tapestry-covered antique gilded chairs and the pink floral arrangement of her bedspread. Though a large room, it was cluttered with tables full of

14

books, small picture frames and general bric-à-brac. And in the midst of it all, lying outstretched on what appeared to be a sofa, smiled the fattest woman I have ever seen.

'So this is the girl, eh? Liesel dear, pass me that eyeglass, would you? My, she is pretty. Mustn't have any experience.'

Experience I had in the form of one charge. Miss Emily Munroe had caused me trouble from day one. Even now, I doubt if she knew what I'd sacrificed on her behalf. No . . . I would not think of Lord Hugo now.

'And young.' She chuckled and the rumble brought out a thin, haggard-looking woman.

'It's all right, Ingrid.' Gisela waved her hand. 'Miss Brown will take tea with us tomorrow when the baroness arrives for Liesel's instruction.'

I felt the day ended on a successful note. We hadn't covered much in the programme I had prepared earlier that morning but Liesel showed a natural interest in new people and I planned to develop the interest by becoming interesting to her. To do so, I had to find out her likes and dislikes and that would take time.

Time I did have. I returned to my room to wash and dress before dinner. I had half-written my letter to my family and sat down to finish it before I went down.

I opened my writing case as usual, startled when a note slid on to my lap. I recovered it with a smile. Granny. She always liked to hide little notes here and there.

*Dear Cristy*
*I have something special for you. You will find it wrapped in the gown I altered before you left. It is a very special piece, sacred to me, and the time has come for me to pass it to you.*
*You will be wondering where I got it. I found it in the mountains as a girl and have kept it carefully hidden all these years. As you are in my homeland, perhaps you might like to trace its origin as I never had a chance to.*
*Your loving grandmother, Frieda*

Intrigued, I hunted through the closet and located the hiding place. There, in a concealed pocket, lay Granny's present. I couldn't believe I hadn't noticed it before, but the heavy material of the gown provided a perfect enclosure for the piece.

I slipped my hand in and drew it out. It was a bracelet, very old with a serpent's head. Emeralds glittered as the eyes of the serpent and roughly cut diamonds served as scales in the three-loop design. Beautiful and deadly, it looked like an item one would find in an Egyptian tomb. I put it on to my wrist, surprised by how snugly it fitted. It was almost as if it belonged there.

How had Granny come across such an item?

Surely not lying in the field? A terrible thought came to me. The serpent insignia loomed everywhere in this castle. Could the bracelet have been lost by the von Holsteins?

No. I refused to believe this bracelet had any connection with this house. It was ludicrous. Serpent designs were used in many houses. Even so, I felt uneasy as I hid it away.

Somehow I finished my letter, laden with questions for Granny.

I groaned, knowing I'd have to wait for the answers.

*     *     *

I was strangely restless that night. The rain pelted against the windows, preventing me from falling back into a dreamless slumber.

I lay there listening to the rain when the moan first startled me. It sounded like a whisper, yet the wind carried it. Determined to find the source of this fancy, I slipped out of bed and went to the window. The rain had reduced to a silent drizzle and above, a full moon struggled to shine. I had a theory about full moons and their involvement in odd events. I pushed my forehead against the glass, listening intently.

There it was again. A faint moan . . . a cry. I waited for it to return, but it did not and by the time I returned to my bed, I wondered if I had imagined it.

17

# CHAPTER THREE

I decided to seek out the Count the next morning.

As I lingered in the corridor, wondering how to phrase the matter concerning me, I saw the baroness arrive. A tall woman, elegantly enveloped in a light, fur-lined cape, she alighted from her conveyance and glided into the parlour where Liesel skipped over to hug her.

'Ah, dear child! Will you never learn?'

I could not hear Liesel's reply.

The baroness laughed, her long nose and lively eyes now apparent. I thought her charming, an excellent choice, for she did not pander to Liesel's whims. Liesel considered her an equal and an equal must be respected. A dependant (like me) could be treated with contempt and indifference, but a former star of the court had to be admired.

When they disappeared, I took a deep breath and knocked on the door to the Count's study. I waited for the brusque 'come in' before quietly entering the room.

He was stoking the fire. 'What is it this time, Frau Vetsera?'

'It is not Frau Vetsera, my lord.'

The irritation immediately left his face. 'Miss Brown! What a pleasant surprise. Please, join me. We have fresh coffee and our version of English scones.'

I grimaced, unprepared for such a warm welcome. 'I'm having tea with Lady Gisela but coffee would be nice.'

He poured it himself. 'And what do you make of our Aunt Gisela?'

'Charming . . . warm . . .'

'Fat?'

'She is . . . amply clothed.'

His laughter echoed through the room. It was spontaneous and very magnetic. 'Amply clothed . . . how diplomatic of you. Is that another polite English expression of yours?'

'We English are not always polite. In fact, we can be quite ill mannered at times.'

'I can't imagine *you* ever ill-mannered, Miss Brown.'

'Then you don't know me very well. I have come about the dinner invitation, my lord. I think I should I take my meals in my room.'

'Did Liesel persuade you?'

'No; however, I do feel this is the best course of action. In England, the rules are very strict. We governesses operate in a kind of limbo—we are neither family nor servant.'

'A lonely existence.'

I shrugged. 'It is part of the job.'

'And you enjoy this kind of life?'

'Especially if it involves castles as magnificent as this one.'

A sad smile lingered on his lips.

'Magnificent castles do not always bring happiness, Fräulein Cristabel. Perhaps you would do better to return to England . . . and marry.'

'Marry!'

He raised a brow. 'Is the state distasteful to you?'

'Very much so. I prefer to be independent.'

'You are young. Perhaps too young to know what you want in life—'

I resented the judgement. 'Are you afraid I cannot fulfil my obligations?'

'. . . and honest. Honesty can be very rare.'

'Only in the dishonest.' I grinned. 'And I am quite adamant about taking my meals in my room.'

He leaned back in his chair and considered me. I found it unnerving that my employer should be a male and a handsome male too. I was used to demanding females; if the Countess had been alive, I would be addressing my concerns to her.

Something else concerned me. The relationship between the Count and his daughter appeared strained and perfunctory. This might explain why he'd forgotten to mention her other lessons to me. Liesel only came to his attention when there was trouble and it occurred to me as I sat there that Liesel probably behaved badly to get attention—attention from her father.

Though he may have guessed my motives,

20

he did not mention Liesel again. 'You shall, of course, join us every Friday with Aunt Gisela. Fridays are special here and it would be an honour to include you at our table.'

I stood up. 'Then I should be honoured to attend, my lord.'

The formality returned and, as I walked to Lady Gisela's room, I wondered if I had conjured the little tête-à-tête with the Count. Heat flooded my face whenever I thought of him. If I had known my employer was to be as handsome as he was contrary, would I have still come?

I knew I would have. However, there was a danger there and it behoved me not to encourage any special attention. Special attention. I almost laughed. I was beginning to imagine things were there that were not there.

Lady Gisela proved a welcome diversion. In preparation for the event, she had sent to the kitchen and it seemed the kitchen had come to her. I could not believe the abundance of the food on display. Pastries, strudels, jam scones and biscuits replaced the usual pile of books on the many tables scattered about the room. I now understood the cause of her three chins.

I liked Lady Gisela. She made me feel more welcome than anyone else had and she had the knack of imparting knowledge without sounding like a chronicle. In fact, I came to think of her as a chronicle because, despite being incapacitated, nothing in the castle

21

escaped her attention.

'. . . so the baroness is here again. A very *cultured* woman . . . like a piece of cheese.' She glanced at me archly. 'Hope you haven't come here to catch Max for I should warn you, he won't be entrapped again. He's destined to be a widower for the rest of his life.'

'Lady Gisela—'

'Ah, I'm only teasing! No need to become hoity-toity over it. I can only say this to you for you are the prettiest of the lot. Probably thrown Max into a quandary—he distrusts beautiful women.'

'I fear you exaggerate my looks, Lady Gisela.'

'You have such pretty hair. Why do you pull it so tightly? To make yourself unattractive?' She chuckled. 'It doesn't work, my dear, for one would have to be blind not to notice you, even in those drab grey skirts and puritan blouses you like to wear. Now, what are you going to wear this evening? Do you possess *any* nice dresses?'

'One or two,' I answered noncommittally.

'But you feel more comfortable in your drab uniform?'

'Y-yes. I feel it is inappropriate for one to dress above one's station.'

'Why? Is the dress encrusted with jewels?'

'No, but—'

'I won't hear of it. Now, Max tells me you met Karl in Vienna. What do you think of

Cousin Karl? Having seen you, I've no doubt he'll be dashing up here as soon as he can manage it. It'll be nice to have some handsome and lively people about the place again . . . just like the old days.'

I could have asked her then about the late Countess but I did not want to appear impertinent. And I especially did not want to sound like a contriving adventuress who had designs on the Count or indeed any male member of the household.

Lady Gisela's comment remained with me the entire afternoon. Liesel had pleaded a headache after her 'session' with the baroness and begged to retire. I lunched in my room and later visited the library.

Another grand room, floor to ceiling filled with books.

'The count prizes his books,' Frau Vetsera said behind me.

I jumped.

'Forgive me for startling you, Fräulein Brown.'

'I wasn't aware you followed me.'

Her bland face did not register my cool tone. 'Some of the books are very fragile.'

I gave her a weary look. She had come here to spy on me.

Ignoring her, I selected a book without reading the title and sat down in one of the cosy armchairs by the fire. I could sense her outrage and a tiny smile danced on my lips.

She could not command me as easily as a housemaid.

The hours slipped away in delightful discovery. When the clock struck six o'clock, I returned to my room to dress for dinner.

Despite Lady Gisela's encouragement, I chose a modest skirt and cashmere blouse, making a slight concession with my hair. Pinning it up loosely, I permitted a wisp or two to fall about my face.

I studied the result in the mirror. The navy skirt enhanced the blue of my eyes. I twisted about, attaching Granny's brooch to my blouse and dismissing the painful event associated with it: the night Lord Hugo had declared his love for me and my subsequent rejection of him. No . . . I did not regret my decision. Emily loved Hugo. How could I have stolen him from her?

Emily. She would be delighted to hear about the *schloss*. I must write to her when I next had an opportunity.

I found Liesel's room without any difficulty. It was the highest room in the *schloss*, in the tower attached to the great hall.

I climbed the seemingly endless spiral stairs, passing one or two pleasant sitting-rooms until I came to the glass door at the top. The door was in the French fashion and heavy curtains in scarlet with the family crest embossed in gold prevented one from seeing into the room. Before I could knock, a serving woman I had

24

not seen before walked through the curtains to open the door.

Keys jingled on her hip. I smiled at the old, hard face but received no response. She merely stared at me, her little brown eyes darting perceptively over my person.

I was unprepared for the beauty of the room. Light flowed in from the large bay windows, each framed by the scarlet curtains and fastened to the wall with a golden cord held by the mouth of a serpent. I vaguely noticed the large four-poster, hung with transparent white material, the painted mural around the fireplace, the Louis XIV dresser laden with exquisite bottles and silver-backed items, and the Turkish carpets on the floor. My attention was drawn to two things—the face of the serpent on the wall and the portrait of the woman above the fireplace.

'That's my mother,' Liesel said, emerging from a concealed water closet. 'She's beautiful, isn't she?'

I studied the woman in the portrait. It was a traditional sitting and the stark plainness of the Countess' attire emphasized her beauty. Somehow, I had imagined her extravagant, bedecked in a vibrant-coloured gown, jewels glittering from her neck and earlobes. To see the pale, black-haired beauty staring back at me, her large unusual violet eyes peering into my soul made me shiver. There was a mocking glint reflected in her eyes and in the curve of her mouth as though she had assessed me and found me wanting.

'She is . . . very beautiful,' I managed to say at last.

'She was too young to die. They say it was an accident but I don't believe them.'

'What do you believe?'

Liesel lifted her shoulders. I noticed she had selected a gown very similar to her mother's to wear this evening. Her immature figure did not suit the black velvet, nor the diamond studded combs in her hair. However, I could not say anything. Here was a girl who mourned the loss of her mother and wearing adult clothes in tribute to her could not be a crime in those circumstances.

'I believe . . .' She smiled. 'You're not wearing an evening gown. Don't you have any?'

'I am not eager to dress above my status.'

'Oh, who cares about that? You'll look silly if you go dressed like that.'

I glanced at the clock. 'I don't have time to change.'

She sat on the edge of her bed and studied me. 'I heard you asked to have your meals sent to your room. Why?'

'Because I did not feel it was my place.'

'Aren't they kind to governesses in England?'

'In England, we have a very different system. Governesses do not dine with the family.'

'You did it for me, didn't you? You felt I would be pleased to have my father to myself.'

I was astounded by her perception.

'You needn't answer. Your face betrays you. You have a very expressive face, Fräulein Brown.'

'Please call me Cristabel.'

'Miss Cristabel,' she tried in English. 'Papa says you will join us every Friday. It is our family evening and one does not wear skirts and blouses to an evening dinner party. Surely you have the same etiquette in England?'

Rather than wait for me to respond, she grasped my hand. 'Come with me.'

She pulled me down the narrow spiral stairs to the sitting-room I had passed earlier. On my way up I had not noticed half the area had been devoted to a dressing-room and the opulent array of exquisite gowns, fur coats, riding habits, hats and shoes left me speechless. It was a dream wardrobe and the dreadful suspicion descended on me as Liesel began rifling through the evening gowns.

'Liesel, I cannot borrow your mother's gowns.'

Arching a brow, she pulled out one in deep blue. 'Why not? You would look superb in this and it would be funny to see Herr Mendel grovel over you.'

'Herr Mendel . . . the castle steward? Is he back?'

'Oh, yes.' Liesel nodded, a secretive smile on her lips. 'He's handsome too and you needn't worry about joining us at dinner. He always dines with us so your removing yourself to your room only suits your own vanity. I am never alone with Papa.'

She uttered the statement so dispassionately, I felt pity for her. To have lost one parent was unfortunate, but to have lost both was a disaster.

She was a child really and her mind seemed younger than her fifteen years would suggest. Perhaps being an only child slowed her development. Also, an only child often suffered acute loneliness.

'You don't have to pity me, Fräulein Brown—I have Frau Bruns, don't I, Oma?'

Frau Bruns, the woman who had opened the door for me, now stood protectively near Liesel.

'Frau Bruns was my nurse since I was a baby,' Liesel explained. 'She takes good care of me, don't you Oma?'

I recognized Oma as a pet name, though I didn't consider it appropriate for Liesel to use since Frau Bruns was not her grandmother.

Frau Bruns wisely made no comment. Liesel thought it terribly amusing and I believed she expected me to upbraid her for calling a servant 'Grandmother'. But I would not pander to her silly games, nor would I consent to borrow any of her mother's clothes. She seemed the kind of girl to have a mischievous reason behind everything she did and said.

She tried once more to change my mind but I was adamant. When she realized I would not bend, she shrugged and Frau Bruns reminded us of the time.

As we walked along the silent corridors toward the great hall, I kept seeing the face of the serpent in Liesel's room.

It was the face on Granny's bracelet.

## CHAPTER FOUR

Light, flirtatious laughter drifted from the great hall.

I paused to listen and would have queried Liesel about it had she not skipped on ahead.

The laughter did not belong to Lady Gisela and ceased the moment I arrived. I was vaguely aware of the group sitting by the fire, Lady Gisela and a man I did not know on the left, and the Count and a mystery woman on the right.

The red-haired woman studied me with contempt. Obviously, my simple outfit failed to meet her standard of elegance and I wished I'd stayed in my room. There was something possessive and alluring about the pouting woman. She was not conventionally beautiful, however, her air of sophistication and *savoir-*

*vivre* gave her confidence and I wondered who she could be. A relative?

The Count was introducing me to the man sitting beside Lady Gisela. Herr Mendel, the castle steward, surprised me as much as the presence of the woman. I did not expect him to be so young or so good-looking.

'You are very welcome, Fräulein Brown.' He stood and bowed, his dark eyes appraising me. 'I hope we shall be good friends.'

He spoke flawless English, as did the redheaded woman who left her seat to meet me.

'Miss Dara Quinn.' She curtsied, a degree of mischief in her voice.

'You're Irish?' I blurted out.

'Why, yes,' she grinned. 'Does it surprise you?'

I had a thousand questions on my lips. An Irishwoman in the mountains? Did she live nearby? What was her connection to the family?

'Dara lives on the other side of the mountain,' the Count explained, and I watched Miss Quinn gaze at him in open admiration.

'Oh,' I said, 'how far is it?'

'Just through the woods,' Dara smiled, 'in a cottage. You should come visit me some time. I like company and the mountains can be very dull.'

She looked at the Count again and I thought: his mistress? Would he include his mistress at his table with his daughter? No . . . he wouldn't. Lady Gisela wouldn't allow it. She must know who this Dara is; I would have to visit her at a convenient time and find out.

No further details became apparent during the course of the dinner. Miss Quinn spoke of her homeland and her little cottage and skilfully diverted any personal requests for information. She did, however, show some surprise at my youth and asked how I had come by the post.

I felt my answer being absorbed by all and especially by Herr Mendel. Liesel watched him with a little smile as he found it difficult to pry his gaze off me and this disconcerting fact led me to beg for an early retirement.

'Fräulein Brown, I must ask you to stay.' The Count said, as he caught me on my way out.

The light touch of his hand did indeed stop me. I turned around slowly, shaken by the impact. There was something so very compelling about him, a magnetism that transcended all my limited experience with men. 'M-my lord?'

'Fräulein Cristabel, you have not yet observed our folk music and Liesel would want you to be there. She adores music.'

I raised my eyes to meet his. What was it about him? My throat burned with an uncomfortable dryness at the mere proximity of him. 'I don't know,' I managed to say at last.

'I am rather tired.'

'Please . . . stay.'

The low murmur chased away my fatigue. He was actually asking me to stay. Elated by the personal request, I nodded and joined the others in the music-room.

Liesel turned in a beautiful performance. I kept my gaze fixed on her, conscious of the speculative glances thrown in my direction from Herr Mendel and Dara Quinn. I could guess at their interest in me. Herr Mendel didn't get an opportunity to meet many young women on the mountain and I looked nothing like my predecessor. Miss Quinn regarded the fact as one would a rival and I understood she had set her cap at the Count and determined to win him.

I could not read anything in the Count's face. In fact, he often seemed detached from the company, a bored spectator, and one could never quite tell what he was thinking. He did not wear his 'emotions on his sleeve', as my mother would say.

I experienced a sudden pang of loneliness that night. I would not see my family for an entire year and the realization finally hit me. When Liesel's performance ended, I asked the Count if I might retire and this time he did not detain me.

Silence accompanied me from the room and I had no doubt where their discussion would lead the moment the door closed behind me.

\*        \*        \*

Alone in my room, I unwrapped Granny's bracelet. I had to make certain the face of the serpent matched the one in Liesel's room. Could I have imagined it?

No, it was the same, uncannily the same.

I knew then the bracelet had a mysterious connection with this family.

And fate had sent me here.

\*        \*        \*

Two weeks passed and I began to settle down to life in the castle. Liesel seemed to accept I wouldn't be leaving and had the courtesy to attend the schoolroom each day. On the mornings of her other lessons, I went to visit Lady Gisela who readily informed me Ingrid 'could not read at all'.

'I simply must hear that lovely voice read,' Lady Gisela commanded, pointing to the book on her bedside table.

So that was how I came to be in Lady Gisela's company for three mornings of the week. I didn't mind the arrangement as Lady Gisela proved to be a library of information about the *schloss* and about the people who inhabited it.

'The von Holstein family have dominated these mountains for generations. The name is

33

as old as the stone used to build this castle.'

We had stopped reading to enjoy the tea and scones sent up from the kitchen. Food continually arrived at Lady Gisela's apartments and I was amazed at the amount she consumed.

'I adore food,' she admitted, 'it's my love. We all must have a love and food is mine. I never have to worry because my love is always faithful.' She grinned at me. 'You are wondering if some tragic event caused me to turn to food, but there is no such excuse in my case. I was born plump and plump I intend to remain, well, perhaps not so plump. It inhibits me from walking which is a nasty consequence.'

'Did you walk often, Lady Gisela?'

'Walk? I used to hike the mountains! I am still the best in the family—no one has beaten my record—well, Max has, but Max is not a female so he doesn't count. Liesel intends to break it, but Max won't allow it because of Malena.'

'The Countess?'

'The *late* Countess. She died up in the mountains. Max had to bring her body back. It was a great tragedy at the time. Nobody understood what possessed Malena to go up there alone in such weather. One could almost call it suicide.'

'And was it suicide?'

A little smile rested on Lady Gisela's lips.

'Who will ever know now that Malena is dead?'

We sat there in silence with the only sound the clink of the teapot until Liesel arrived.

'The weather is closing in,' she said, 'so the Baroness left early today.'

Liesel came to sit by me and when Lady Gisela's attention diverted, whispered something in my ear. She said she had a surprise for me this afternoon.

Curious, I went up to her room after luncheon.

'Let's go,' she said, tossing me a woollen wrap.

We went outside and walked through the cobbled stone courtyard to a small gate on the other side.

'This gate leads to the other side of the mountain.'

'Is that where Miss Quinn lives?'

'Dara,' Liesel sneered. 'Watch your step, it's slippery around here.'

I shivered, thinking of Fräulein Suski tumbling down the mountain. It could easily happen if one didn't take care and I wondered if the same thing had happened to Liesel's mother. Had she fallen, or had she frozen to death?

The unpleasant thought carried me to a small clearing in the middle of the woods. It was a peaceful place with the aromatic pine trees, the windless day rendering them silent observers of the small tombstone below the grave of Liesel's mother.

'Mama loved the woods,' Liesel murmured, sinking to her knees to tend the flowers on the grave. 'We thought it best to lay her here rather than in the chapel. Soon it will be winter . . . Have you seen the snow before? Do you ice skate or hike?'

I shook my head.

'I like hiking but Papa won't allow it.'

'Perhaps he is afraid something might happen to you.'

'I don't think he really cares. Sometimes he acts as if I don't exist.'

'I'm sure that's not true.'

She glanced at me. 'Are you? But you don't know him as I do. Sometimes I think he was happy when Mama didn't come back.'

I knelt beside her, reading the words engraved on the slightly weathered stone: *Malena, Countess von Holstein, died December 24, 1871*—almost a year ago.

'The night before Christmas they found her. I watched them carry her.'

I tried to imagine the child Liesel, staring down at the mother she had known as vibrant and beautiful. The still mask of death had snatched away her childhood and forced her into an early womanhood. The transition hadn't been smooth, (as one could see from Liesel's bad behaviour), however, now I understood her better. She didn't want to lose her mother and this is why she lived in her mother's apartments. She wanted to keep the memory of her alive.

The Count did not. Perhaps he considered it too painful a subject and thus ignored it. Or perhaps there was a truth in Liesel's strange comment: *I think he was happy when Mama didn't come back.*

By saying such, was Liesel suggesting her father might have arranged or contributed to her mother's death?

I laid a gentle hand on Liesel's shoulder and said we should go and dress for dinner.

'Dinner,' she echoed, dragging herself off the ground. 'Is it Friday again? Then Dara will be there. I hate Dara. She tried to be nice to me after Mama died. She only does it to get close to Papa. She wants him . . . she wants to be the next Countess von Holstein.'

'I'm certain that was not her original intention.'

My voice lacked enthusiasm.

Liesel's violet eyes burned with rage. 'She's a conniving adventuress. You don't know who she is, do you?'

'I thought she must be a relation of the family. A poor cousin perhaps?'

'A relation?' Liesel laughed. 'Oh yes, Dara is a relation of ours, but she's no blood relation.'

'Oh?'

'She is my father's mistress.'

*     *     *

*She is my father's mistress.*

Those words taunted me as I walked back to my room. I checked my face in the mirror. It was flushed with an emotion I couldn't describe. Anger? Disbelief? Envy? Was it true? Could such a man be tempted by an artless piece like Miss Quinn? I stopped myself short on that deliberation. It was none of my business and *would* be none of my business.

Poor Liesel. She obviously felt threatened by the presence of Miss Quinn and I questioned her father's wisdom in inviting the Irishwoman here. True, it was only once a week, but surely, he should be more discreet?

It would be interesting to learn what Lady Gisela thought of the elusive Miss Quinn. I decided to see her before dinner.

I washed and after a lengthy deliberation, selected one of my better evening gowns. Another of Emily's cast-offs, the forest-green velvet suited my skin and brought out the colour of my eyes. Pinning up my hair, I added a small turquoise comb.

'Lovely,' Lady Gisela chortled when I arrived at her apartments. 'Out to capture a husband, are we?'

'Lady Gisela.' I gave her my widest smile. 'I can't imagine what you mean.'

'Is it Ernst Mendel you're after, or our Max? If it's Max, you'll have to fight the Irish

38

dame for him.'

'Who is she?'

'Ah, an interesting question. Who is anyone?'

She refused to say any more, seeing Ingrid wheeling out the chair. It was quite a production to move Lady Gisela from room to room. I asked Ingrid if she was joining us but she said no. She preferred to spend the evenings alone and I understood her needing to be apart from Lady Gisela occasionally.

Liesel waited for us outside the great hall. She smiled, noting my dress, and kissed Lady Gisela on the cheek. There was a high colour in her face.

Herr Mendel made a special effort to solicit my attention. I suppressed a groan and answered all of his polite questions.

The Count sat next to Dara Quinn. There was a strange aura about him, perhaps because mystery enshrouded his personality and I could not read his character as easily as the others.

Or so I thought.

'Isn't our little English rose pretty?' Lady Gisela beamed to Dara, anticipating entertainment.

Dara's cool gaze swept over me. 'Miss Brown does not think it inappropriate to dress above her station?'

I smiled at her attack. 'One must be prepared for every occasion.'

39

Dara smiled sweetly. 'How nice it'll be to have some more company in the winter months. The winter months can be very lonely and monotonous. We must all be a family to one another, mustn't we?'

Her eyes softened toward the Count.

During dinner, I agreed with Liesel's summation of Dara Quinn. She dominated the conversation and I thought she is already acting mistress of the castle.

It was an uncomfortable evening. Rather than join the conversation, Herr Mendel preferred to stare at me openly.

When the time came for us to retire to the music-room, I went to assist Lady Gisela at the first opportunity. The Count had wheeled her in and Miss Quinn soon found a pretext to call him to her side.

Liesel played the pianoforte, striking the keys louder if Dara raised her voice. She was fighting for her father's attention and her father couldn't see it. Or refused to see it. Why? Did Liesel remind him too much of his dead wife? I thought of the woman in the portrait. The beautiful planes of Countess Malena's face held a secret.

Liesel's performance ended and I did my best to direct the conversation back to her. 'I have never heard anyone who can play so exquisitely, or with such depth.'

Dora set down her tea cup and swished to the pianoforte. 'Shall I sing for you all? This is a Spanish love song I once sang in the *Opéra Royal.*'

So, she'd been an opera singer before her elevation to mistress. I saw Liesel roll her eyes but she played and Dara sang beautifully, absorbing the praise afterward.

I returned to my room that night, pondering over the bizarre mix of this household. Herr Mendel was only a steward and yet he dined at the table as though an equal. Frau Vetsera, who could be considered on a level with Herr Mendel, did not eat with the family. Lady Gisela could not be termed 'ordinary' in any sense of the word; Liesel continued to amaze me with her constant mood changes and Dara the opera singer: was she the Count's mistress or not?

The Count baffled me the most. Including one's mistress at one's table may be considered bad taste in England, but perhaps it was acceptable behaviour here. Lady Gisela seemed to accept Dara. This confirmed the Irishwoman had some connection to the family.

The Count gave no hint about his relationship with Miss Quinn. He treated her with the attention and affection one might show a guest but nothing more. Whether this was his method of concealing her status who could say?

I considered it very rude of him. Surely, he must know the suspicions of the household?

His daughter? To leave Miss Quinn's position unconfirmed frustrated all concerned, including myself.

However, it was not a simple matter and certainly none of my business. I had been engaged to teach Liesel English, not to pass judgement on members of the household. The Count would do as he pleased, as previous Counts had no doubt done before him.

This became clear the following morning when Liesel showed me the portrait gallery.

'The paintings are priceless,' Liesel began, stepping into the long, narrow chamber. 'Some of them are hundreds of years old . . . like this one of Count Rudolf in the tenth century.'

'Rudolf von Holstein,' I read the plaque below. 'Rudolf . . .'

'There are many Rudolfs in the family. My late uncle was a Rudolf.'

'The uncle who—?'

'Would have inherited,' Liesel finished with a sad smile. 'I liked Uncle Rudolf. He was always nice to me.'

We proceeded along the passage, she pointing out various ancestors and their rank of importance. 'How did your uncle die?'

'In a shooting accident. He had a faulty gun and it misfired.'

'So it happened here?'

'No. In the Outten's forest on the other side of the valley.'

'You speak of it as though it were nothing.'

She shrugged. 'Accidents happen all the time in the mountains.'

I thought of Fräulein Suski and shivered. 'It seems a dangerous place to live.'

'It is only dangerous when one isn't aware of the dangers.'

I wondered how this applied to her Uncle Rudolf, the man who should have inherited this great castle. We paused by his portrait. He looked very much like the Count with his dark hair and blue eyes, however, there was joviality to his character the present Count did not possess.

'The paintings have survived the ages,' Liesel informed me, 'because the castle has never been taken. Papa said you wanted to know why it's called the Castle of Dreams?'

I nodded and stared at the painting before us. A knight on horseback, perhaps early Middle Ages, with his sword drawn and bloody. It struck me for it did not follow the other paintings of the time. I read the caption below: *Conrad, Count von Holstein, before the battle* 'The battle?'

Liesel's eyes began to glow. 'It was a revenge killing. The Turks had captured his bride and the Turkish Sultan had luck and numbers on his side. They slaughtered Conrad's army and only he and a few faithful friends managed to escape.'

'What happened to the bride?'

'That is where the story gets interesting.

Escaping her Turkish captors, she walked on foot for days in the mountains and didn't stop until she reached the *schloss*. She thought Conrad was dead and ran up to the tower and threw herself over the battlements. She loved Conrad and who could blame her when you look at him?'

I studied the handsome, proud face in the portrait. Long black hair flowed behind him and though he'd been painted in the heat of war, his blue eyes displayed a haunting beauty that could only have come from the very deepest love. As I gazed into his eyes, the Count's face emerged. I must have imagined it and looked away quickly.

'They say Conrad didn't speak for days. He locked himself in the chapel with the dead Elaina and refused to come out.'

'He joined her in death?'

'He had Elaina painted first, to preserve her likeness.'

'Where is her painting?'

'It disappeared a few years ago. It was a miniature.'

'Did you ever see it?'

She nodded. 'It was stolen from my mother in Vienna. She loved to wear it as a locket. She liked the emeralds in it.' Liesel leaned closer. 'Do you want to see the spot where Elaina plunged to her death? Come, I will show you.'

I was led along, partly out of startled curiosity. Why had I seen the Count's face in that painting of Conrad?

The day was crisp and the clouds hugged the peaks of the mountains. The beauty entranced me.

'The clouds are very deceiving, aren't they?' Liesel whispered, drawing me closer to the edge. 'Like a bed of feathers; one can almost believe it is a bridge to Heaven.'

I stared at her. 'You're not suggesting Fräulein Suski met such a fate?'

Liesel shrugged. 'She knew the dangers, but something lured her out here. If you listen closely some nights, you can hear Elaina calling in the wind.'

I wanted to reject the legend as nonsense, my practical English heritage demanded it, but instead I found myself drawn to this haunting tale of two lost lovers. I too had heard an eerie cry at night and had dismissed it. But dare it be true?

Had Elaina called to me?

# PART 2

# Murder at the Lake

# CHAPTER FIVE

The tale of Conrad and Elaina continued to distract me. I lay abed, restless, listening to the groan of the wind. Of course, it was ridiculous to think Elaina's ghost haunted the clouds, luring any to their deaths. I blamed the capricious weather for creating this fantasy.

The thought didn't occur to me until the next day. The Countess had mysteriously disappeared in the mountains on Christmas eve. Had the illusion drawn her to her death? It was certainly feasible, considering her daughter's preoccupation with legends of the past. Didn't Liesel say her mother loved to wear the miniature of Elaina? It must have been an exquisite piece and a sad loss to the family when it disappeared. I suppressed a sudden desire to show Liesel Granny's bracelet. I'd convinced myself the bracelet had no connection with the von Holstein family. A mere coincidence.

My reasoning had a motive. I refused to surrender the bracelet. I liked the aura of mystery attached to it. Besides, the bracelet had been given to me in trust.

\*     \*     \*

In spite of myself, I was growing fond of my

eccentric pupil as we swept into a rainy December. Her loneliness and eagerness to reclaim her father's attention inspired my pity.

'Please no more English today,' Liesel sighed, shutting the book in her lap and mischievously swinging a key. 'I want to show you something in the library.'

Once there, she opened a locked cabinet and removed the ancient manuscript bound in leather. 'One of our ancestors believed the tale of Conrad and Elaina should be recorded so he captured a monk and forced him to write the account.'

'How barbaric,' I smiled.

'Yes, we von Holsteins are unafraid to use whatever methods we wish to achieve our design,' the Count murmured from the doorway.

Startled, numbed, and fascinated all at once, I slowly raised my gaze to his face. He stood there with such effortless grace, his hand casually inserted in the pocket of his long, grey coat. 'Raiding Frau Brun's room again, are we, Liesel?'

Liesel's face reddened.

'My lord,' I explained, 'Liesel and I have been discussing the tale of Conrad and Elaina these past few days.'

'Opening forbidden cabinets was your idea, then?'

'I encouraged it.'

He grinned at my diversion. 'I did not know

you could read Latin, Miss Brown?'

'I cannot, my lord.'

'Then how do you propose to read the account?'

I took the manuscript from Liesel, intending to put it away when the Count touched my shoulder.

'Perhaps you will allow me to read it?'

The brief touch of his hand on my shoulder stirred a response in me I did not want to analyse. Though I had shared a few kisses with Hugo, I had never experienced a heated desire for so much more. What did this Max von Holstein have over me? Since our first meeting, a minute did not pass when I did not think of him.

He motioned us to the fireplace. By Liesel's face, I could see this didn't happen every day. I joined her on the rug by the fire while the Count commandeered an armchair and began.

His deep, melodious voice held me prisoner. Enchanted by its power as much as its content, I listened to the account, hoping my unease would go unnoticed.

It did not. When Liesel rushed off to heed a call of nature, the Count closed the book and put it aside.

'What do you think of the legend, Miss Brown?'

Aching to rub the painful prickles in my feet, I gave him a brittle smile. 'Haunting, unforgettable.'

'I agree; yet some would dismiss the tale as pure fantasy.'

'I believe it was real,' I said, with unexpected force.

'You look uncomfortable. Are your feet paining you?'

I couldn't stop the colour rising in my face. 'Y-yes.'

In one swift movement, he left his chair. 'Would you permit me to help you?'

'Ah . . .' What else could I say? Swallowing deeply, I allowed those deft hands to remove my shoes and gently massage the flesh beneath my stockings.

'You are shocked.' He smiled. 'I forget the English are so very formal.'

'And you are not?'

A devilish smile lurked on his lips. 'It is an inherent quality we von Holsteins possess—a wicked disregard for convention.'

'And are you wicked?'

I couldn't believe my own words. Here I was on the floor, engaging in a flirtation with my employer. If I wasn't careful, I could see myself heading into unknown danger.

'Very wicked,' he answered, his hands replacing my shoes where they belonged. 'You have beautiful feet, Fräulein Cristabel.'

I could only gape at him.

Silence fell between us. His fingers reached out to graze my face and I closed my eyes, revelling in the forbidden, delicious feel.

His face hovered so near mine. Daring to meet those deep, unfathomable eyes, I waited for him to kiss me. I almost believed he would, but somewhere there, his face stopped its descent and moved away.

Disappointed, I regained my balance and my wits before Liesel returned. Innately relieved she had not discovered me on the floor with her father, I retired to my room for a reflective luncheon.

Max von Holstein.

I was beginning to think a great deal more than I should of him. The low timbre of his voice, the feel of his hands on my feet, the depths of those dark, unreadable eyes . . .

I recalled the slow precision of his gaze evoking unknown responses within me and sighed. That was the most frustrating part. An unmarried woman has limited experience unless she chooses to join the ranks of a lesser society. I wished I had at least *some* inkling into the unknown world of passion. I had observed it in others, of course, yet, nothing could substitute for real experience.

Shocked at the thread of my own thoughts, I set down my tea cup in an act of determination. No matter how mesmerizing those dark, unreadable eyes were or how *alluring* the Count proved to be, I should not and *would* not let him overtake my mind.

Yet, I wanted to know everything about him: his wife, his thoughts, the heart he kept carefully hidden. Why? Did it bear scars from some woman? His wife? Dora? Or someone else?

Groaning, I stormed to the window to appreciate the view. Years ago, I never would have believed I'd be in a castle as grand as this one, watching the snow fall like teardrops across the mountains.

The time of year increased my homesickness. The first Christmas without my family, I imagined would be a lonely one, without Granny's folklore, my mother's special pudding and Tommy fighting me for the last toffee apple.

It would be my first Christmas in the Castle of Dreams.

And the anniversary of the Countess's death.

*       *       *

The next morning, Liesel sped into my room.

'Quick, miss, get up! We're going to town today!'

I would have smiled at her rendition of the English 'miss' had I not been so startled. Waking up people in this fashion happened in my village at home, but not in the prestigious castle on the mountains. Once recovered, I welcomed the loss of formality and hurriedly dressed as Liesel skipped around the room.

'Papa's given me money.' She jingled the

bag of florins before me.

And I've lots of presents to buy.'

I did not remark on her flooding back to German. This was a festive season and there would be time for English lessons later. In fact, I had an entire year to complete my assignment and Liesel had already showed rapid progress in the two months I'd been here. Two months! The days seemed to pass so quickly in the mountains.

At Liesel's reminder, I selected my warmest attire for the day. The modest ensemble didn't look as attractive as Baroness Outten's furs and Russian hats but would achieve its purpose and keep me warm.

I will never forget my first ride in a sleigh. I knew the morning would forever be imprinted on my mind the moment I stepped into the courtyard, the Count standing by the open sleigh door. The pale sun glistening on the snowy mountains, snowflakes falling from the trees, the castle towers ensconced in white pristine cloaks, standing proudly from the misty grey clouds threatening to obscure them. The beauty caught at me, no doubt glistening in my eyes.

'You look radiant, Miss Brown,' the Count smirked. 'Do you care to supply the reason?'

I climbed into the sleigh with a dismissive laugh. 'I like to save these memories for a rainy day. When I am an old woman, I shall have something to remember.'

'You, old, miss?' Liesel turned up her nose in disgust. 'I can't imagine you old at all.'

'Nor can I,' the Count said, taking the seat beside his daughter, his gaze fixed on me. 'What an enigma you are, Fräulein Cristabel: one minute the prim governess, the next a dreamy-eyed schoolgirl. What further delights await us, I wonder?'

The cool air did not prevent the heat flooding my face. Smiling at his insinuation, I replied, 'One could say the same about you, my lord.'

The sleigh began to move, the brightly coloured bells jingling around the horses' necks. We passed one-armed and one-eyed Old Josef who sat at his post inside the gatehouse, silently watching us pass. I imagined nothing in the goings-on of the castle escaped his attention.

I was a little nervous as we slid across the bridge and the Count must have noticed my apprehension.

'You can trust Hans, Miss Brown. He could do it blindfolded.'

He looked distinguished and handsome today in his long black coat and Russian-style hat. In fact, he almost could be mistaken for a Russian.

'Your scrutiny disturbs me, Miss Brown. Please advise which aspect of my apparel offends you?'

I lifted a brow, hardly knowing what to

reply.

'There shall be no formality today,' he said firmly. 'Today, we are simply good friends going shopping and good friends are free to voice their criticisms.'

'There is no criticism, sir.'

'Sir! I said *no formality.* My friends call me Max. Go ahead and try it. I promise it sits easily on the tongue.'

'Perhaps in England you would be Sir Max?' Liesel suggested.

'Sir Max,' I tried tentatively.

The Count smiled. 'You see, it is not so difficult, is it?'

It continued this way during the day and by the end of it, I found myself calling him 'Sir Max' with ease. We stopped by the village at the bottom of the mountain to watch the children and the adults throw snowballs at an ugly-looking creature with a long red tongue and bulging eyes, cowbells clanking around its neck.

'Krampus Day is one of our customs,' the Count informed me. 'The evil spirit in the fur is Krampus. The purpose of the custom is to remind children to be good.'

'I can't see how that works,' Liesel said, asking to join the children.

Her father said no. 'Krampus Day is for the villagers, not for Liesel von Holstein. Wouldn't you agree, Miss Cristabel?'

'I agree in theory,' I replied, 'but I must

confess I am as guilty as the villagers. We used to do something similar in our village back home.'

The Count raised a brow. 'And you partook of this venture?'

'Yes, of course. It was fun.'

'And when did you stop?'

I hung my head in shame. 'I haven't. I did it last year.'

He glanced at Liesel, the offer of mischief in his eyes. 'We should endeavour to make Miss Cristabel feel at home in the mountains, shouldn't we?'

Liesel's eyes danced. 'Oh, yes! Once she's hit Krampus, she'll feel better.'

She jumped out of the sleigh, pulling me with her. Fortunately, the Count caught my hand before I tripped into the snow. He drew me to my feet as Liesel thrust a fresh snowball into my hands.

I was about to throw when one of the villagers snatched Krampus from his post and began running through the streets. I saw Liesel's look of disappointment before the Count suggested we join the mêlée. I managed to hit Krampus twice and an old man once. I'd never experienced as much fun in my village and I knew this was because of him—the Count.

After we expended our energy chasing Krampus through the streets to the astonishment of the locals, Hans drove us into town where we separated to do our Christmas shopping. Ignoring my protests, the Count gave me a bag of florins. The generous amount allotted alarmed me. However, the Count said 'the money was for members of his household so why shouldn't it be spent?'

I went through the list of names and eventually selected appropriate gifts for Liesel, Lady Gisela, Ingrid, Frau Vetsera, Herr Mendel, Dora (with a roll of the eyes) and one of the housemaids who had been kind to me.

That left only the Count. And what could I get the man who had everything?

I didn't like the difficulty of my task. I perused the stalls and shops once more, searching for the perfect gift. It couldn't be something personal and I didn't have enough florins left for it to be something expensive. And whatever I chose, I knew it would be dissected by members of the household.

In despair, I went into the bookstore. A bookstore always cheered me and the friendly face of the shop assistant did something to alleviate my present concerns.

'Can I help you, *fräulein*?'

I confessed my dilemma.

The shop assistant toyed with the curl of his moustache. 'Ah, you are in luck, *fräulein*. Something very special came in yesterday.' Disappearing behind the counter, he produced a newly wrapped book. 'Fresh from the printers and an entire chapter devoted to one of our own legends: Conrad the Warrior.'

I perused the title: *A History: Medieval Warfare.* It was the perfect gift.

I exited the shop, triumphant.

The Count detected me from across the street.

'You look pleased with your purchases,' he said to me on the way home.

I couldn't stop smiling. 'Yes, it has been a most successful day.'

'I couldn't agree with you more.'

The warm words were spoken so briefly I might have imagined them. I felt the colour rise to my face and quickly turned away. I prayed the chill in the air would silence the memory of his caressing voice.

\*       \*       \*

The festive season brought a change to Liesel's routine. Her other lessons postponed, she ran to my room to report another event.

'My cousins are here, miss! Sibylla has gone straight to bed—she hates long journeys—but Karl is having coffee with Papa so come down and meet him.' Her eyes twinkled. 'I think you'll like him.'

And there, standing jauntily in the drawing-room, was the man I'd met in Vienna.

The Count lifted an amused brow. 'I believe you two know each other.'

The Count's Cousin Karl was taller than I

remembered with his crisp white-blond hair and beautifully sculptured face. He pressed my hand warmly. 'So we meet again, *fräulein*.'

'What do you mean *again*?' Liesel demanded.

'Liesel,' Karl touched her cheek, 'you grow more beautiful each day.'

I had never seen anyone charm Liesel and the effect left one amazed. She clearly adored her cousin.

The Count's face sobered. 'How is Sibylla coping after the accident?'

Karl shrugged. 'As well as can be expected. It was a great shock to her . . .'

I realized I should not be here. They were discussing family matters. I announced my departure, saying Lady Gisela had long expected me (a half truth) and retreated to that lady's domain.

It occurred to me as I walked there that Lady Gisela might know about the accident.

'I've seen Sibylla,' she beamed, 'such a dear girl, poor thing, and what do you make of Karl?'

'Very handsome,' I conceded.

Lady Gisela gave me one of her winks. 'They're twins, you know. Inseparable. Poor Sibylla lost her husband three months ago.' She shook her head. 'They say the prince was intoxicated and fell out of his villa window. It's all very tragic but she'll recover,' Lady Gisela went on merrily, 'and marry again. It's what young people do. I keep saying to Max he should take another wife but the word marriage doesn't agree with him.'

'Why?'

'Oh, who can know Max's mind? He never used to be so secretive. I suppose Malena's death affected him more than we thought.'

I sat back to absorb this information. I had to tread carefully, particularly with Lady Gisela for I did not want her to detect my interest in the Count.

'Aunt Ela?'

A young woman entered the room and I recognized her immediately. Sibylla, the Princess of Strecken-buriltz, was tall and slim and possessed the same unusual white-blonde hair as her brother. And there the likeness ended, she inheriting none of her brother's beauty with her irregular face, eyelashes and freckly skin.

Lady Gisela introduced us. I curtsied to the princess.

'Very pretty,' she remarked, as though I were a painting on the wall. 'Wherever did Max find her?'

I decided it would be best if I returned to my room.

Lady Gisela winked. 'And don't forget, tonight is the feast of St Nicholas. Be sure to wear your best dress.'

*     *     *

My best dress.

Dare I wear it? I recalled the day when Emily had tossed it to me. 'The colour doesn't suit me and it makes me look like a frog.' Whether or not she believed it would make me look like a frog too, she insisted I take it and now I was glad she had made me do so. Granny's expert fingers had transformed the sea-green silk ball gown into an elegant evening dress with a bustle and short train. The design was long and fitted, the sea-green silk trimmed by Granny's delicate white embroidery on the neckline, waist and sleeves.

After a brief deliberation, I slipped it on and loosely pinned my hair, permitting one curl to fall on my shoulder. Lamenting the lack of a necklace, I remembered the bracelet.

Drawn to its almost forbidden beauty, the stones glittered beautifully on my wrist, tempting one to commit the sin of wearing it. How could a simple governess afford such a valuable jewel? They would think it stolen and worse—*stolen from their own collection*—if, indeed, the bracelet had belonged to this family. Hadn't I convinced myself there might be a dozen families in Europe who used a serpent as part of their insignia?

I swiped the bracelet from my wrist as though the serpent had bitten me. There was something uncommon about the piece: it held a power, an enchantment of its own. I was thinking fancifully living in a fairy-tale castle inspired such fancies but could there be a connection between the von Holsteins and Granny's bracelet?

The thought terrified me. I felt like a thief. The bracelet's beauty forced one to desire things one oughtn't.

They were assembled in the drawing-room. I could hear their chatter before I walked in: Dara's high-pitched drawl, the sharp, no-nonsense voice of Lady Gisela and the smooth, attractive tone of the man who had deceived me.

Baron Karl von Lichtenburg must have thought it a great joke: escorting me around Vienna that afternoon, pretending to be a common soldier whereas, in fact, he was the heir to the castle. I noticed the appreciative glint in his eye when I entered, further proof of his libertine activities.

Silence ensued through the room, broken gratefully by Lady Gisela who complimented me on the 'excellent' choice of my gown.

Dara raised a thin brow in surprise. 'I never knew a governess to possess such an exquisite gown. Your previous employers must have been very generous indeed.'

I coloured at the insinuation. 'Miss Emily Munroe, my former pupil, was indeed generous with her cast-offs.'

Dara chuckled. 'I don't believe the gown you are wearing could *possibly* be a cast-off,

Miss Brown.'

'I have to agree,' Karl smirked. 'The gown has rather startling provenance.' He glanced at his sister. 'Paris?'

The Count strolled toward me. 'Miss Brown.'

I froze at the English pronunciation of my name. I had overstepped the boundary by dressing out of my station. I would be dismissed, never to return, never to discover the secrets of the castle, or the origin of Granny's bracelet.

I willed myself to look up at the Count. Those cynical blue eyes seemed to pierce my own with their intensity. 'Yes, my lord?'

'Miss Brown,' he repeated, his face matching the gravity of his tone, 'would you allow me to escort you to dinner?'


# CHAPTER SIX

I wasn't the only one shocked.

As I left the room on the Count's arm, I saw Dara standing there, hatred brimming in her eyes. I had never seen such a look and it frightened me. Was it true? Was she his mistress?

She evidently suspected me. With her barbed insinuations, she wished to injure my reputation and in turn, the Count's opinion of me. She'd planted the doubts and the others did not know what to believe.

As the evening progressed, I couldn't say whether the Count had done me further harm by rescuing me from what could have been instant dismissal in another household.

I pointed this out as we walked to the great hall. 'My lord, was that wise?'

He smiled. 'Would you have considered a dismissal wise?'

'I don't know . . . perhaps.'

'Do you always adhere to convention?'

'Naturally. It is what we English do.'

'But you have German blood and we Germans tend to do as we please.'

I laughed. 'You sound like my grandmother.'

'I should like to meet her one day.'

He said the most outrageous things. I hugged the comment, knowing the impossibility of the lord of the castle sipping tea at our humble home.

We did not speak again. He seemed preoccupied with his own thoughts and I remembered the importance of this month: December. His wife had died last December.

The dinner went tolerably well. I spent my time wedged between Herr Mendel and Lady Gisela. The other end of the table was infinitely livelier, Dara amusing the company with tales from her homeland. She would no doubt remain the focus of attention when we later retired into the music-room. I felt I could not endure her voice for another moment and so when the opportunity arose, I asked the Count if I could retire.

'Retire? Are you unwell, Miss Brown?'

'I have a headache.' I considered the excuse true enough for Dara did indeed give me a headache.

'Then we shall miss you.'

I didn't trust myself to look into his face. Those warm, caressing words carried me upstairs to my room.

As I continued through the darkened passages to my room, I experienced a sudden urgency to see the portrait of the late Countess. I went up to Liesel's room, encouraged by the silence. The servants usually ate at this time so I should not encounter any of them.

Lighted torches flickered across the wall, illuminating the steps as I climbed. At the top, I caught sight of the portrait emblazoned in light. I stood there for a moment, mesmerized by the haunting, mysterious beauty, wondering at the secret suggested in her eyes and in the faint curl of her upper lip until a voice startled me.

*'Fräulein?'*

It was Liesel's nurse, Frau Bruns. I stared at the old, lined face, thinking of an appropriate excuse.

'You came to see the portrait?'

I nodded and she smiled.

'Princess Malena was like a daughter to me. I can see you are confused, Fräulein Brown. You wonder why I am not like the other servants in the castle, why Liesel calls me Oma. I was a baron's daughter and serve the royal line. I nursed the princess and came here to the castle with her.'

'Liesel's mother died in the mountains, didn't she?'

The little brown eyes hardened. 'She did not kill herself. I know my Malena. She loved to laugh and have a good time. Somebody else killed her—*he* didn't want her anymore. There was a big fight on the night of her death.'

'You speak of the Count? You think he murdered her?'

She wouldn't say. She merely stared up at the portrait in holy reverence.

I left her there, the question burning inside me: did her suspicions hold any truth?

\*　　　\*　　　\*

The next two weeks passed quickly. I was often on my own as Liesel liked to spend her time with Karl and Sibylla. Though sometimes grudgingly invited along, I preferred to give her the liberty she needed.

I occupied my time in various pursuits. I continued to read to Lady Gisela every afternoon, and in the mornings I also liked to take a brisk walk in the woods beyond the castle. On one of these mornings, I met Karl in the courtyard and he insisted on accompanying me.

We had walked a little way when he murmured, 'You are still angry with me for deceiving you.'

I pressed on. 'Where does Miss Quinn live? I have been searching for her cottage and I can't seem to locate it.'

He lifted a brow. 'You are curious about her.'

'She asked me to visit. I thought it only proper that I should accept the invitation.'

'Proper.' He smiled with a faint grin. 'Yes, the English are always very proper.'

I compressed my lips to prevent a smile. He was an attractive man and possessed enough charisma to charm a saint. A dangerous asset and an enjoyable one. I had decided to dislike him, but by the end of our morning found I couldn't.

'There is a hidden entrance,' he confessed conspiratorially, 'but as we are invited, I will divulge the family secret.'

He pushed through the thick copse to reveal a small iron gate.

I looked at him in surprise.

'I know. You would never have found this gate on your own. That is the purpose of it. It is not meant to be found.'

I wondered at the meaning behind his words

as we walked further into the thicket. I could see a glimmer of yellow up ahead.

'There is the cottage. It's cosy; you should like it and its drawing-room has a spectacular view as you will see.'

As I entered the charming, yellow-washed cottage, its windows framed in wood and its interior decorated with delicate floral curtains, I remembered how easily I could have been mistress of such a cottage. I could have married the local doctor back at my home village.

A maid led us to the drawing-room where I warmed my hands by the fire and gazed out of the window. The view startled me.

'Do you like it?'

Dara Quinn had entered the room, dressed in a simple woollen gown. 'I wasn't expecting visitors today, but you both are very welcome.' She turned to the maid. 'Heidi, please bring us some tea.'

'You are very kind, Miss Quinn,' I said.

'Oh, do call me Dara. It is so lonely on the mountains it seems silly to address each other by our proper names . . . and titles.'

I registered her meaning and ignored it. 'Baron von Lichtenburg was kind to show me the way here. I confess I never would have found it otherwise.'

Dara smiled. 'I should have given you the directions. Do you like it?'

I could see she was proud of it and who

wouldn't be? 'It's lovely,' I replied.

'It's small and poky but it's home. The fires keep us warm in winter and the mountain air keeps us cool in summer. So it is quite perfect.'

'Do you miss Vienna?'

'You must,' Karl grimaced, 'and Vienna misses you, Dara.'

Her eyes sparkled. 'I suppose I do miss it sometimes. But I am quite content here. I have all I need.'

Did that include the Count? She must be his mistress. Why else would she live out here all alone?

After an enjoyable pot of tea and a selection of Austrian biscuits, we prepared to leave. I was standing by the door when I heard a noise, and turned around to see a little boy sitting behind a shrub in the front courtyard. When he saw me, he froze in alarm, but made no move to rise and run away. A glimmer of light shone on his dark hair and luminous eyes pleaded with me not to betray his presence.

I turned away as Dara came out on Karl's arm.

'Thank you so much for visiting,' Dara cooed. 'Do come any time. It is always just me and Heidi.'

Did she mean to say someone else? The boy? Her son?

I pretended I hadn't seen him. Poor little boy! I felt sorry for him, living in such a remote place with no children of his own age

71

to play with. Why should his existence remain a secret?

Unless he was the Count's son. Yes, that would explain Liesel's fear of Dara's presence in the household. If the Count should marry his mistress and legitimize his son, Liesel would be thrust out of the picture. And so would Karl, as the Count's heir.

I tried to recall Dara's reaction. She behaved as a perfect hostess: warm, friendly, entertaining, but had there been fear behind those bold eyes?

I found it difficult to read that afternoon.

Lady Gisela noticed my lack of enthusiasm. 'Are you *ill*, Miss Brown?' She put up her eyeglass. 'You do seem a little pale now that I look at you. Or did you encounter a ghost on the way?'

She chuckled vivaciously. 'Ghosts *do* live here, you know. I have one who visits me frequently. A pretty one, to be sure. Sometimes I fancy it is Elaina walking the corridors at night, luring her next victim to their death.'

'Lady Gisela, you don't really believe—'

'Oh, yes, I do. That unfortunate governess, Fräulein Suski, succumbed to the allurement as did Malena, I daresay. She was in an odd state of mind the morning she disappeared. I do believe our Elaina charmed her to fly to the mountains.' She examined me frankly. 'You English don't believe in ghosts, do you?'

'I have never met one,' I answered.

'You consider us fanciful.'

I shrugged. 'I can only venture to say I believe ghosts are conjured by our own imagination and fear.'

She did not seem to hear what I had said.

'It was such an ugly business . . . how could they even suspect Max of killing his wife? The inquest proved his innocence, but they still talk about it, you know. They whisper in the shadows. Tell me, Fräulein Brown, do you think our Max is a murderer?'

I hoped the colour didn't flood to my face. 'I-I hardly know him.'

Lady Gisela winked. 'Don't be so coy. You have some influence. I've never known any of the other governesses to interest him as much. So you went to Dara's cottage, did you? You found it on your own?'

I told her Karl had escorted me.

'Oh, did he?' She suppressed a chuckle. 'And how did our Irish lass receive you?'

'Very warmly.' I wondered if she knew about the child. 'It's a beautiful place but it must be lonely for her.'

My words seemed to amuse Lady Gisela. 'Lonely. Hm . . . that is a new word for it.'

Before I could ask what she meant, Ingrid came in with a fresh pot of coffee. It signalled the end of our discussion and I left somewhat disappointed.

I found Liesel in her room with her cousin,

Sibylla. They both eyed me unappreciatively as I entered.

The princess regained her composure first. 'Miss Brown, do come in. Liesel and I have just been discussing when *Christkindl* will mysteriously arrive to decorate the tree. It must be tonight or early in the morning for he has not shown up yet.'

Liesel grinned in excitement. Sibylla was doing her best to keep her young cousin's mind occupied in light of the anniversary of Countess Malena's death tomorrow. I was grateful for her efforts for Liesel's passionate devotion to her mother's memory could not be described as healthy and would not help her regain her father's love. Especially considering the circumstances of the Countess' death and the suspicion involving the Count. He had been acquitted of the crime but the reminder of the affair must be as painful to him as it was to his daughter.

I wanted to know more about it. I knew I shouldn't be so inquisitive or interested in such a macabre affair but I couldn't seem to help myself. I didn't want to be remembered as 'another governess.' I wanted to be remembered for making a difference. I wanted to see Liesel and her father reconciled. I wanted . . . to capture the Count.

There, I'd admitted it. I could not rid my mind of the memory of his hands caressing my feet. Since that day, Max von Holstein had stirred rebellion in my soul, hidden desires a young lady should not possess. Or if she did, they should be kept secret.

My fascination with the Count grew daily, to the point where I wondered if I suffered from a form of infatuation. It was an interesting turn of affairs. Back in England, the young men had been infatuated with me and now here I was, captivated by a brooding widower with a possible mistress and son in tow.

It presented a challenge, one I relished.

I didn't stay long in Liesel's room. Liesel seemed content with her cousin's company and did not want her governess hanging about. There was no sign of Frau Bruns and I wondered if she regretted what she had confessed to me the previous night.

I went down to the library and, as I perused the vast array of books, searching for something new to read, Frau Vetsera stepped before me.

'Ah, there you are, *fräulein*. The Count wishes to see you in his study.'

I nodded, suppressing a smile.

He was sitting at his desk looking out of the window, his necktie half undone around his neck. His thoughts seemed far away. Troubling, unpleasant thoughts? I wished I knew. 'You sent for me, my lord?'

He looked at me in confused surprise before his brow cleared. 'Yes . . . yes, I did. Please sit down, Miss Brown. I thought you might be able to provide some assistance this eve in decorating the tree. Last year the duty was left to me and I'm afraid I made a poor job of it.'

Last year, I thought. The night before his wife disappeared, he'd been decorating the tree. The reason why one usually made a poor job is lack of concentration or attention. Evidently, his mind had been engaged with 'other matters.' Did those other matters concern his wife?

I replied I would be delighted to help and watched a smile pass his face.

'Delighted to help. Do you really enjoy helping people?'

'Why shouldn't I? Especially if a kindness has been done to me in turn.' I lowered my eyes, my traitorous mind flooding back to the library.

'Kindness,' he echoed. 'Do you believe kind people still exist in the world?'

'The world would be a very dark place if one didn't believe it.'

'I admire your confidence.'

'It is easily acquired where one has faith.'

He laughed. 'How ever did we manage without your English conviction?'

'I would say you managed very well.'

'What would you say if I said we managed very poorly before you arrived?'

'I should hardly believe it. I have only been here three months, scarcely long enough to have made any impression.'

'My dear Miss Brown, you have made more of a difference than you will ever know.'

I felt his dark-blue eyes scrutinize me with a depth I couldn't identify. It didn't last, vanishing the moment Sibylla and Liesel entered the room, an amused Karl behind them.

'Ah, here she is . . . with Cousin Max. I never knew you had an eye for pretty governesses, Cousin. Sorry to have interrupted your private *tête-à-tête*.'

'There was nothing private about it,' the Count insisted. 'As you can see, Herr Mendel is in the room.'

Horrified, I followed Karl's glance to where Herr Mendel sat busily writing. What I had thought a 'private' conversation with the Count evaporated before me. Chiding myself for a fool, I smiled at Karl when his quizzical gaze rested on me.

'Miss Brown, I suddenly feel the need to exercise my English. Would you care to take a stroll with me outdoors? A little fresh air is always advisable.'

I glanced at the Count to judge his reaction but Sibylla had engaged him in conversation.

Karl lifted a brow. 'Unless you have other commitments?'

I ignored his smiling insinuation. 'I have no present engagements, Baron von Lichtenburg.'

We decided to take a turn through the

arbour. I asked him what he knew about Fräulein Suski.

'Fräulein Suski?'

'The governess who fell.'

'Oh that. The unfortunate woman had poor eyesight, I believe.'

'You dismiss her as nothing.'

He shrugged. 'She was a silly woman. She never should have been out in the dark without her glasses.'

'Perhaps if she had been a "pretty governess", you might have felt differently.'

'Ah, so you object to my calling you a "pretty governess". Most women would be flattered.'

'I am not like most women.'

He studied me objectively. 'No, you are not. You are not at all what I expected.'

'What did you expect? An old maid?'

His lips twisted. 'Something like that. Now why are you using your venom on me? I have done nothing to deserve it.'

I wished he would go away. He prevented me from deliberating about the Count. 'I find your English needs no further exercising and it's getting chilly,' I said, 'I'm going in.'

He caught my elbow. 'One moment, Miss Brown. You cannot deceive me. I am on to your game.'

'My game!' I laughed. 'Would you oblige me by telling me what my *game* is, exactly?'

'To capture the Count. There is no point in you denying it. Why else would you put up with my naughty niece?'

'A naughty girl can be managed.'

'And you have elected yourself as her saviour . . . and Max's.'

'Your insinuation, Baron, is not only ridiculous but offensive.'

He grinned. 'We shall see. I regret to find Cousin Max is ahead of me in the game. I had hoped to woo you for myself.'

'I will forget this conversation.' I turned on my heel. 'I advise you to do the same, Baron von Lichtenburg.'

\*          \*          \*

I joined the Count in the Christmas room an hour before dinner. He was standing halfway up a ladder and seemed surprised to see me.

'I didn't think you would come. Frau Vetsera has been helping, but she is too old to climb these ladders.'

'I'm sorry I'm late. I had an—er—encumbrance.'

He laughed. 'I don't think Cousin Karl will enjoy being termed an encumbrance. Women usually encumbrance him.'

'Yes, so I gathered.'

He came down from the ladder and opened a box. 'Are you saying you find the Baron's attentions repulsive?'

'I do.'

'But he is generally revered as a great

catch.'

'In his own eyes, no doubt.'

'You continue to surprise me, Miss Brown.'

No more was said on the subject and I plunged into the enjoyable task of decorating the tree. The various ornaments were beautiful and very fragile and had to be handled with care. The wax candles were the last to be added and we stood back to admire our handiwork.

'I think your side of the tree is better,' the Count observed with a half-smile. 'I hope you will feel at home here with us. I know you must be missing your family.'

I nodded, holding back the prick of tears that came to my eyes. Seeing the room decorated so beautifully had reminded me painfully of home.

The Count took my hand in his and lightly caressed its palm. 'Do not be anxious over them. They are well cared for in your absence.'

'Thank you,' I whispered, not daring to look into his eyes, 'for sending my wages in advance.'

He released my hand. 'It is I who should thank you for coming here.'

I thought it was an odd comment considering he had paid me to do so, but I refused to dwell too much upon it. The Count interested me more than any other man had and the fact alarmed me.

I left the room feeling strangely elated.

Perhaps I mistook his kindness for partiality but it felt wonderful to be noticed.

*     *     *

That night I noticed someone else treasured the Count's attention.

After dinner, in the music-room, Dara begged a seat beside me. 'I wanted to thank you for visiting me,' she said. 'Please come again.'

'I will,' I promised.

'You and I, we are of the same stock. We have had to make our way in the world whereas everyone else here inherited the comforts of privilege and position.' Her gaze rose to where Sibylla played the pianoforte and the Count turned the pages. 'I believe our little princess,' she whispered, 'intends not to mourn long for her husband.'

I didn't want to appear interested but I was. 'Oh?'

'We cannot talk here,' she said. 'You should visit me again.'

I found an opportunity the next day. There was no sign of the boy and the cottage appeared empty. Heidi answered the door and let me in.

Dara greeted me from her leisurely position on the settee. 'Today is significant,' she began, 'today is the anniversary of the Countess's death.'

I sat down. 'Did you know the Countess Malena?'

'Know?' Dara smiled. 'I saw her once or twice. When she was alive, I was not permitted at the castle.'

Did this confirm her position as the Count's mistress?

'The Countess was very beautiful and proud. As a princess of the Hapsburg line, I didn't expect anything else when I came to live here.'

'How long have you been here?'

'A year. The Count has been most kind . . .'

*I am sure he has.*

'I used to be sure . . . but now I am not so sure. You noticed last night how he paid Sibylla more than the usual attention.'

'But the princess is his cousin and she is grieving. It is only natural to comfort one's grieving relative.'

'Comfort.' The word rested on her slightly parted lips. 'There are many kinds of comforts. I say our little Princess Sibylla wants a special type of comfort. She wants Max. I have seen her little ploys. She uses her grief as a weapon.'

'I thought she loved her husband?'

'Yes, but my friends from Vienna tell me our little princess did not benefit from his death. Had she produced a child, matters would have been different. As it is, she has only an annuity and the annuity is not large.

She will have to marry to secure her future.'

I remembered what Lady Gisela had said. 'Are you quite sure of the princess's financial situation?'

Dara laughed. 'My information is always correct. Lady Gisela is often misinformed.'

I could sense her agitation over the matter. Should the Count take a new bride, she might insist Dara give up her little cottage and move away. Everybody knew Dara was attached to her cottage and the threat of losing it obviously distressed her. 'Have you approached the Count with your concerns?'

'How can I? In our society, we must behave very discreetly. I will have to wait and watch what happens. I should be surprised if that mug-faced Sibylla actually captures him. Now if she looked like Malena, I would understand.'

'Then you can have confidence in the fact,' I murmured, aware that what she had told me was a very great confidence.

'Yes, you will not tell anyone of our private little chat, will you, Cristabel? May I call you Cristabel?'

'Of course you may,' I heard myself saying. Her 'little chat' had put a dampener on my hopes, foolish hopes perhaps, but hopes I refused to surrender. Until the Count took a new wife, he was fair game.

And I wouldn't allow Dara Quinn, or any woman for that matter, to take my chance from me.

*    *    *

We gathered in the drawing-room on Christmas Eve. Everybody seemed silent and pensive and I supposed they could display little else considering what had occurred on this day last year. Liesel surprised me. I thought she might have worn black this evening as a tribute to her mother, but she came down in a red satin skirt and white blouse.

I had chosen to wear a blue and white striped gown for the occasion, the gown in which Granny had hidden the bracelet. For this reason, I felt special tonight, though sadly lacking in the jewellery sported by Sibylla and Dara.

'Where is Max?' Sibylla chorused. 'He's not usually late.'

I exchanged a look with Dara and noted the tiny curl on her lips. The reason for the curl came in through the door: the Count carried in a jubilant little boy.

I recognized him immediately as Dara's son from the cottage.

'Paul, darling!' Dara rushed over to her son.

The boy's natural excitement at the festivity removed any resentment I may have felt. That this was a once-a-year occurrence was obvious and for the child's sake, everyone was prepared to dismiss the shadow of his

84

parentage.

All except Liesel. I caught her almost violent gaze upon the boy when the Count deposited him in the great armchair by the fire. Perhaps there was another reason why Paul didn't attend Friday evenings with his mother: Liesel. Her insecurity since her mother's death, her irrational moods, her sulky tantrums might intensify if the Count lavished attention upon Paul every week.

'Poor little mite,' Lady Gisela whispered to me. 'They have to put hot irons on his legs in the hope he'll walk one day.'

'Who is he?' I dared to ask.

'Ah,' Lady Gisela grinned, 'who is anyone?'

I gathered I would learn no more from her about the mysterious Paul. Despite my irritation with Dara, whose self-satisfied smile threw significance on her son's presence, my heart went out to the boy. He couldn't walk and that wasn't pleasant for his lively disposition.

Dinner proved a grand affair. On this special occasion, Frau Vetsera joined us at the scrumptious feast prepared in the great hall.

'Carinthian tradition,' the Count invited, making sure Paul was settled close to his mother. 'Our best known dish is *Känudeln*,' he said, I thought, for my benefit.

I followed his gesture to the fist-sized pockets of pasta dough filled, Frau Vetsera informed, with meat, spinach, potatoes, mushrooms and a special sweet one using mountain berries and prunes.

Special wine had been brought up from the cellar and tempted by its smooth, spicy flavour, I tried the local fare. To my surprise, the food was delicious and I soon found myself on my third glass of wine.

I should have stopped there. My hot cheeks should have warned me, but the food, the wine, the merry company. 'A recipe for disaster', my mother would say.

The dancing started after coffee and cakes were served. Redeeming my dizzy head with a little coffee, I nodded when Karl asked for my hand.

A group of townsfolk musicians had been invited to the castle to perform the music.

'Folk dancing.' Karl's blue eyes burned into mine. 'Don't worry. I'll lead you.'

And lead me he did. Around the room so many times my head began to swim and when it settled, I found myself standing beside him out in the cool on the balcony.

'Beautiful night, isn't it?' His low murmur tickled my ears. 'Look at the stars. Have you ever seen stars so bright?'

'No,' I said, my voice throaty.

Karl chuckled. 'Want some more wine? I must admit, Miss Brown, I'd never expected to see you so . . . unguarded.'

I turned sharply, my senses not as dull as I thought. 'What do you mean?'

'Oh, nothing.'

His hand closed over mine, soon followed by his arms around me. 'How about a seasonal kiss, eh?'

Caught in his playful embrace, I tried to think. I didn't want to give him the wrong impression but nor did I want to appear prudish. As he said, it was a festive occasion and there could be no harm in a small, brotherly peck on the cheek, could there?

'If you release me, I will,' I promised.

He dropped his arms. I leaned forward on my tiptoes and planted a perfunctory kiss on his cheek. 'There? Now will you let me return?'

Karl seized my hand. 'What if I want you for myself?'

'I can't dance with you *all* night,' I replied, in the flirtatious spirit we had contrived around us. 'Herr Mendel is waiting.'

'Herr Mendell.' He shuddered in disgust. 'Then I am profoundly sorry for you. Just one more dance then I vow to relinquish the goods to my fellow comrade.'

He performed such a good pleading sulk, I could do little but agree. 'All right. Just one more dance.'

Led into the room by Karl, I saw that our sojourn on the balcony had been noted. The Count's thunderous gaze followed us around the room, accompanied by Herr Mendel's polite disappointment and Dara's delight.

It was bound to happen. Karl and I collided into a dancing Sibylla and Liesel. We ended up in a giggling mess on the floor, the Count striding over to raise his daughter to her feet while Karl attended to me.

His dark mood surrounded us. Earlier on, Liesel had tried to get her father to join us but he was very adamant. I wondered if he declined to partake in the festivities because of the aura of suspicion surrounding his wife's death. He sat at the table and continued to drink like a lone depressed soul.

But he wasn't alone. Lady Gisela, Dara and Paul remained at the table with him as eager spectators. Dara didn't look so eager now. Her rouged lips compressed, she hastily reached for her glass of wine.

The tinkling bell summoning us to the 'gift room' came as a welcome relief. Liesel led the rush and it was amusing to see such highly polished society behave like children. The Count carried Paul and I followed last with Lady Gisela.

The Christmas room was not as we left it. Everybody had begun raiding the tree, searching for gifts with their names upon it.

'You go on,' Lady Gisela nudged me, 'I have eyes to watch the kerfuffle and Ingrid will bring me my gifts.'

We entered the mêlée and I enjoyed seeing the delight on Liesel's face as she examined her newly opened presents. Everywhere, there were exclamations of 'Oh, it's beautiful', 'You didn't', 'How perfect', 'I simply *adore* it'.

Paul beamed at his toy soldiers fashioned into a chess set and I observed a special fondness in Dara's eyes as she bade her son to thank the Count.

My own presents were very modest in comparison. I shouldn't have expected any different. Sibylla bought me a box of ribbons, Liesel chose a pretty pair of gloves, Lady Gisela a box of chocolates and a book, another pair of gloves from Frau Vetsera and Herr Mendel, a hand-knitted woollen scarf from Ingrid, a silver-backed grooming set from Karl and a small box from the Count.

I didn't want to open his gift here in front of everyone. It was a foolish notion, but I considered his gift a personal one and wanted to keep its contents a secret.

'Oh, you are so *slow*,' Liesel complained. 'Do you plan to sit there and look at it all night?'

Suddenly under scrutiny, I unwrapped the box. Therein lay an exquisite miniature, certainly too valuable to have been intended for me.

'There must be some mistake—' I began.

'There is no mistake,' the Count assured me. 'I'm afraid it is a poor copy of the original, but I thought you would like it. You recognize him?'

It was Conrad, in all his warrior glory. The

miniature had been expertly painted and encased with seed pearls and gilding work. 'It's beautiful . . . thank you.'

I noticed he had been overly generous with his gifts. He had given Ingrid some lovely new material and Dara couldn't stop smirking over her new diamond ear-rings. She made a point of sitting beside me and showing them off.

'What do you think of them, Cristabel? Do they not capture the light?'

I glanced at the Count and was surprised to see him watching me rather than his mistress. There was a faint curl on his lips too. I flushed in anger. How dare he monitor my reaction?

Liesel was jubilant with her gift from her father. She dangled the ruby pendant before all of us. 'Oh, I love it, Papa! Thank you so much!'

I fussed with my gift for the Count under my woollen wrap. I didn't want everyone to see it, so I'd brought it into the room myself, waiting for an opportunity to give it to the Count alone.

An opportunity arrived when he slipped out of the room for a cigar. I waited a few minutes then made some pretext to Lady Gisela and followed him.

He did not go to his study but back to the balcony where Karl and I had engaged in our flirtation. The winter air surrounded him, his expression cold and passionless as he stared out into the night.

Using cautious steps, I approached. 'My lord.' I laid my modest gift on the stone battlement for his perusal.

When he said nothing, I turned to go, pausing at the slight sound of ruffling paper. *So he was going to open it.*

I couldn't resist gauging his reaction.

Putting his cigar to one side, he took the book in his hands, slight flickers of amazement teasing the bones in his face. 'Is this . . . ?'

'Yes,' I grinned. 'It was a difficult task choosing something for the man who has everything.'

'Everything.' A bitter laugh rumbled from his mouth. 'You think I have everything?'

'A beautiful castle, a coffer full of history—what more does one want?'

A sad smile touched his lips. Still flicking through the pages of the book, he said, 'You grossly misread me, but thank you for the book. It is indeed a coffer full of history and will be treasured in my collection.'

He was still smiling.

'What is it?' I asked.

'It is odd,' he murmured, 'that we have both chosen Conrad as the subject for our gifts. Now I realize I should have had Elaina painted again.'

Elated by the intense pleasure emanating from his face, I moved closer to him. 'I couldn't believe my luck when I found it. If one had to buy something for the man who had everything, I thought this would be it.'

'You chose well,' he laughed. 'I can't remember the last time I received such a perfect gift.'

'Oh, you needn't be *that* kind, my lord. Now, this is a very interesting part . . .'

In my quest to show him the passage, my hand brushed against his. I struggled to resume the search but it was hopeless. The beautiful evening, the stars glittering in the sky, the wine . . .

He felt it too. I knew he'd been drinking heavily. The anniversary of his wife's death commanded his sombre mood.

'What is between you and Karl?'

The question lashed out at me.

'Are you in love with him?'

'In love,' I echoed, 'with Karl?' I knew I'd been drinking, but not as much as him, obviously.

'If you're aiming there, forget it.'

'May I remind you, my lord, you are my employer, not my father.' I gasped after I'd said it. 'I'm sorry. I didn't mean to—'

'Yes, you did.' A low laugh left his lips. 'I confess I don't like you leading him on. How much do you know of men, Miss Brown? A lot? A little?'

Before my hand could strike his face, he captured it and pulled me close. The fusion between us rose to a feverish heat. Mesmerized, excited and intrepid all at once, my lips parted in tingling anticipation.

His mouth came down hard on mine, hot, demanding and relentless. Lost in the wonder of it, I didn't care about what was right and what was wrong or who should see us. I had never been kissed so thoroughly before.

My inexperience must have been evident for when we drew apart, he chuckled. 'My sweet, innocent Cristabel, how little you know of the world and men. Dare I warn you? You should go, leave us wretched souls be. For that is what we are.'

A cynical laughter ensued and he turned back to the battlements and his private thoughts.

I rushed back to the company. A quick 'toilette' was the general assumption for my absence and I said nothing to correct it. The Count returned within the hour and when he did, we made our way to the family chapel for *Mitter-nachtsmesse*, the traditional midnight mass.

It was a beautiful night and the snow fluttered down like tiny feathers, tickling our noses and revitalizing us with its cool purity.

'I hope you are not too homesick tonight, Miss Brown.'

The Count stood behind me. I had not been aware of his approach. 'No,' I said honestly. 'I do not feel homesick.' *Homesick!* There couldn't have been anything further from my mind. I sped up my walk to avoid the others pressing in on us.

'I wanted to apologize,' he murmured, once out of earshot. 'My behaviour on the balcony was unforgivable.'

'It's a festive occasion,' I replied, 'and I've had more than my share of wine.'

He scuffed the ground with his boot. 'Are you happy here, Miss Brown?'

The abrupt change of mood startled me.

'You can leave at any time, you know.'

'I shall leave at the end of the assignment, my lord, and no time sooner.'

He touched the back of my coat. 'You are angry with me.'

'Yes, I am. Why do you try and force me to go when all I want is to stay?'

'To stay,' he echoed with a sad smile. 'Are you prepared for what you might discover if you stay?'

The chapel loomed ahead of us. 'I am prepared for any eventuality.' I lowered my voice, raising my eyes to meet his face. 'That includes you, my lord.'

'Then you put yourself at great risk.'

'Oh?'

His dark eyes glittered in the darkness. 'I am a known libertine.'

'I'm not afraid of libertines,' I smiled. 'In fact, they say a reformed rake makes the best husband.'

I cringed, realizing I had spoken out in error. Why did I have to mention husband? It was the biggest mistake for any woman.

The others had caught up. I followed the Count inside the chapel ablaze with lighted candles. Its cheerful occupants rendered the service a little less sombre. As Ingrid and I sat at the back with Lady Gisela, we were the first to see the arrival of the newcomer. In a city, the arrival of a newcomer wouldn't have been an extraordinary thing, but as we were in the remote mountains, one did not expect visitors at this late hour. I noticed her immediately, standing there in her austere black cloak, her face crimson with rage.

We followed her gaze to Karl, watching the young woman move down the aisle in slow, stilted footsteps. She removed her hood and stopped before the Count. 'Good evening, Count von Holstein.'

She held out her hand and the Count stepped forward to receive it.

'You will be wondering who I am,' she said, her voice shaking with emotion as she went to stand beside the Baron. 'Hello, Karl. Did you miss your wife?'


# CHAPTER SEVEN

A week after her dramatic arrival, I had my first conversation alone with the young Baroness von Lichtenburg. She was the

Baron's secret and judging from his expression that night in the chapel, their marriage did not seem to be a happy one. A dark flush of anger had crossed his face before he resumed his usual devil-may-care attitude.

I liked Baroness Rachel. She was English and how could I fail to like one of my own countrywomen? She appeared to be frightened of her husband and in awe of him at the same time. Obviously, Baron Karl did not expect his little wife to defy him in this manner and he treated her attempts for peace with thinly disguised contempt. Perhaps his brutish and unfair treatment led me to befriend the young baroness. I liked to think so though it would be fairer to say I had a vulgar fascination with the troubled couple.

Rachel welcomed the idea when I suggested we go down to the village one day. Liesel was settled with her cousins and I had a desire to leave the castle for a day, to clear my mind. The Countess had died at this time last year and I, along with everyone else, found myself drawn to the mystery.

What had happened last year? I felt a burning need to uncover the truth behind the secrecy, to acquit the Count. But he too had changed on the night of Christmas Eve. After the chapel mass, he rarely spoke and preferred to spend his time in his study alone. The only time I saw him make some perfunctory effort was to publicly acknowledge and welcome

Rachel to the family and chastize Karl for keeping his marriage a secret.

I discovered a little of the story from Rachel as we set out for our day to the village.

'I met him in Paris. I was staying there with my godmother. My parents had died the previous year and my godmother wanted to see me properly settled.' She lowered her doe-shaped brown eyes. 'Papa had left me a rather large sum and my godmother was always shooing away the fortune-hunters. "Undesirables", she would call them. "He's not for you, my girl." She wanted me to marry a young man with a face full of spots. "Now *he* is a decent young man", she said to me every night, unwilling to forget the idea. "I can't marry someone I don't love", I had responded to which my godmother laughed. "What has love got to do with marriage?" and now I see that she was right.'

I imagined her two years ago: innocent, yearning for love, and believing in the purity and honour of true love.

Her face paled considerably as she spoke and I concluded the last two years had wrenched many of these former beliefs from her.

'I should have known.' She tossed a brown curl over her shoulder. 'I should have realized he was only after my dowry. My godmother tried to warn me but I refused to listen . . . and now I have to pay for my mistake.'

I touched her hand. 'Are you truly so alone?'

'Yes,' she whispered. 'I gave up all my friends to live in Austria with Karl. His estate is in the country, near Salzburg. A very quiet place where nobody visits. When our honeymoon was over, he left me there while he went off to Vienna. I didn't hear from him for three months.'

'Three months!'

'He said he had some important business to attend to and foolishly, I believed him. It was only after the next eight letters, I began to suspect the truth. I imagined him living a dissolute life in Vienna, spending *my dowry* doing it. He is a city person and soon all the pieces began to fit together. I felt betrayed, shocked, embarrassed. I couldn't turn to my godmother for advice for she had warned me about him. And to my friends, what could I say? I had left them boasting of my "grand match". I was to be a baroness and married to one of the most handsome men in the empire. They all envied me and I couldn't allow myself to destroy the only thing I felt I had left— pride. Pride kept me from speaking out, but now, I feel I can no longer sit at that estate, growing old and ugly, while *he* enjoys himself and pretends he doesn't have a wife!'

Yes, I thought. He did indeed act like a town bachelor. I recalled his behaviour in the coffee house in Vienna. I never would have believed him married.

'You, too, have been a victim of his charm, haven't you?' Rachel peered into my face, looking for the answer.

I had to smile. 'No. However, I will say that given the opportunity, I wouldn't have returned his attentions.'

'Are you quite sure?'

I nodded, leaning over to whisper, 'My affections are engaged elsewhere.' I glanced meaningfully at the crest on the carriage.

Her eyes widened. 'Oh, that gives me comfort. I am glad to have a friend here and I shan't betray your confidence.'

I returned the assurance. 'Rachel, have you ever tried to befriend your sister-in-law?'

'They are twins, you know, inseparable. Sibylla came to visit once or twice but she lived in Vienna and saw her brother often enough there. I don't think I made such a great impression upon her for she did not return to the country house again.'

'I suppose she must have been busy preparing for her wedding.'

'Oh, *the royal wedding.* She only married him to get the title. She chased him for two years before he yielded—somewhat reluctantly, I might add.'

I lifted a questioning brow.

'I shouldn't be saying this,' Rachel murmured, keeping her voice low in the presence of our driver, 'but in one of his drunken rages, Karl laughed and boasted about the whole thing. His sister had landed a "great catch" as he had "caught" me and they both considered themselves terribly clever.'

I recalled what Dara had said about Sibylla and her financial situation. Because Rachel had confided so much in me, I wanted to return the confidence.

The news did not surprise her. She began to laugh. 'It's so funny . . . and it's set down Sibylla a notch or two. She didn't love the prince, but I know she cared for him and to be left with almost next to nothing can be harsh. What good is a title without the wealth behind it? Her freedom is as limited as those who have nothing else to trade but their beauty.'

And now Sibylla was after another crown, a crown formally worn by the late Countess Malena. I asked Rachel if she knew anything about Malena.

'No,' she said, 'I know nothing about her.'

We spent a lovely morning touring the various little villages in the valley of the great *schloss*. A sense of peace overcame us both until on the ride home when Rachel suddenly clutched my hand, her eyes urgent.

'You won't tell anyone what I've said, will you?'

I assured her I wouldn't, wondering why she was so afraid.

\*       \*       \*

100

On our return, Liesel stopped us in the parlour.

'Oh, there you two are! Guess what? Baroness Outten has invited us to skate tomorrow. Their lake is frozen.'

Rachel seemed even more terrified. 'I don't like skating,' she mumbled.

I saw the mocking contempt in Liesel's face. 'Why? You needn't worry. I don't think Karl will let you fall.'

She could be very insensitive at times and I felt our relationship had taken a backward step. I fervently wished Karl and Sibylla hadn't come but for Rachel. Since their arrival, Liesel treated me like the paid tutor, the annoying woman who pestered her to keep up her lessons.

I told myself to be patient. When the festive season ended and Karl and Sibylla returned to Vienna, we would return to normal. I couldn't see Karl and Sibylla staying any longer than another month in the mountains. Their eagerness to return to Vienna was apparent in everything they said and did.

I wasn't alone in being ignored and dismissed. Liesel's nurse, Frau Bruns, suffered the same fate.

She came to me once, shaking her head.

'Liesel won't listen. She won't do her lessons and she was quite rude to me this morning.'

'Yes, I know,' I sighed.

I realized I would have to do something

about Liesel's behaviour if her attitude didn't improve, once the cousins left, I thought, and took their influence with them.

But the cousins were not leaving as quickly as I expected.

I learned this from Sibylla's own lips. 'I adore the mountains,' she beamed, as we travelled down to Baroness Outten's *schloss*. 'They are so mystical and silent. If only they could speak, imagine what secrets would be surrendered. I must climb the *Grossglockner* before next year is out.'

'Oh, yes!' Liesel cried. 'I want to go too.'

'I shouldn't like to go,' Rachel murmured. 'It is too high and too cold.'

Sibylla smiled, but without condescension. To her credit, the princess endeavoured to show kindness to her sister-in-law and on occasion championed her cause against her brother.

The marriage was a bizarre one. Every time I looked at Karl, I could feel the anger rising within me. How could he treat Rachel like forgotten baggage? Had he forgotten what a large dowry she had brought to him? Rachel remained in awe of him and I wanted to protect her from any further unpleasantness.

Therefore, it came as no surprise when Karl paused beside me as we stood on the courtyard balcony of Baroness Outten's *schloss*. The day, clear, still and beautiful, shone radiantly down upon the frozen lake on which we would be skating after luncheon.

I saw the hand rest on the balcony first and my heart hammered because I thought the hand belonged to the Count.

Karl grinned. 'Were you hoping for someone else?'

'I don't know what you mean,' I said coolly.

'I can see you have become my wife's champion.'

'Have I?' I challenged him. 'Anyone can see you ignore her and, as I happen to like her, it grieves me when she is so obviously unhappy.'

'Unhappy with me? Rachel is young—'

'She may be young, Baron, but she deserves to be treated like a wife and not as a child.'

'You are very pert with your opinions.'

I shrugged. 'You decided to stand next to me.'

'I will endeavour to win your good opinion then,' he smiled. 'What do you advise me to do?'

I turned around and glanced at Rachel, relieved to see the Count had come to sit beside her and had diverted her attention from the Baron and I. 'There is no point my advising you if you are not serious about the matter.'

'I am serious about the matter,' he insisted. 'It stands to reason if Rachel is unhappy then so am I. You can be our private counsellor . . . the English governess who is pert with her opinions, but is liked by everyone in the

103

household. You think I have not noticed your influence with certain members . . . including my cousin—'

I thought he meant the Count and held my breath.

'—Liesel. She has never tolerated any influence from a governess but with you, she has. Dare I hope you can use some of your magic on Rachel and I?'

'I am no expert on the subject,' I said.

Those dazzling blue eyes examined me with an air of worldly knowledge. 'I think you have scarred more than one man's heart, Fräulein Cristabel. It is not difficult to see why my cousin and every other man here is interested in you. You are beautiful and spirited and exhibit an intelligence unusual in one so young and inexperienced in the ways of the world.'

I smiled. 'Here is your first lesson, Baron. Reserve your compliments for your wife. I am certain if you pay her some attention, things can be mended between you.'

'I confess I have neglected her.'

'Cruelly,' I added.

'You are harsh on me, undeservedly so.'

'Then you intend to prove me wrong?'

'Yes,' he murmured, 'how could I fail Fräulein Cristabel?'

To my astonishment, for I did not believe it had been a serious conversation, he went to Rachel and asked if she would like to try skating on the lake. I knew she didn't want to

104

and when she accepted immediately, I began to see the first fruits of my success.

'You are congratulating yourself on something?'

I turned around. The Count stood behind me with a pair of skates in his hands. 'Do you care to join us on the lake?'

He could have been speaking to one of his own class. 'Are you going too?'

A faint smile touched his lips. 'It is an annual tradition.'

'Then I must accept,' I said, aware I might never have another opportunity. 'Is it very hard? I don't care to fall over.'

'If you will permit me, I will escort you until you are confident.'

I glanced over to where Karl and Rachel twirled around the lake, he confident, she reluctant but jubilant because he assisted her. The intimacy excited me and I could not refuse.

I took my first timid steps with the Count's arm steadying me.

'I thought the English hid their timidity,' he joked. 'It does not have to be such a painful experience. Do you trust me?'

Did I trust him? I glanced up into his handsome, smiling face and wanted to tell him how much I trusted him. He was so close I could smell his cologne, an alluring scent that intoxicated the senses and left me speechless.

'I take your silence for the affirmative,' he

105

smiled, placing an iron arm around me.

I will never forget the experience. His expertise guided us around the lake in long, languid strokes where the fear of falling lessened by the minute. If I closed my eyes, I could almost believe anything possible on such a magical day.

'Are you ready to try it by yourself?'

We came to a stop and I nodded. I had to prove my English courage, not cower to my English timidity. I saw Liesel skate past; she turned backwards and smiled, luring me to come out to her.

'Come on, miss! It's easy.'

I saw Rachel watching me. I knew if I tried, she would too, I started out slowly and managed to complete a circuit. Rachel did the same but as soon as she finished, we nodded at each other and left the frozen lake to the expert skaters. It was much more enjoyable watching them parade around while we sipped hot coffee.

Rachel couldn't stop grinning. 'Oh, Cristy! May I call you Cristy? I've never been so happy! What did you say to him?'

'I merely reminded the Baron of his duty.'

'Duty,' she echoed. 'Do you think all can be well between us?'

I knew I had to appear positive for her sake. 'Why, of course. He wouldn't have married you if he didn't like you.' I hated to say the lie because he would have married her regardless of his tastes. But many other men married for material purposes rather than love. Did that make the Baron any worse a man?

Poor Rachel! She couldn't handle him and the brief display of courage she had shown in coming here only deserved his contempt. I hoped, I *prayed* he would make a sincere effort to mend his ailing marriage.

But I feared the outcome for Rachel.

\*       \*       \*

News arrived from home.

I had been scanning the empty bureau top where the maids placed my letters for so long now, I'd given up hope. Used to an empty platter, I blinked twice before I realized the white envelope was indeed no figment of my imagination.

> *Dearest Cristabel*
> *By now, you will have discovered the trinket I concealed in your clothes. Do not be alarmed by its presence or your possession of it. It is ours, my dear girl, yours and mine and I trust whatever you do with the bracelet will be right.*
>
> *I have exciting news to relate. A man came to see us a month ago—an estate attorney by the name of Mr Fairchild. He said he represented a European gentleman who needed urgent tenants for the newly*

*acquired Lowen Lodge. The terms were generous indeed. Lowen Lodge, my dear! Your mother, as you can imagine, is elated at the prospect and the village somewhat bamboozled by our sudden elevation in society. I am not so easily persuaded. I suspect this has something to do with your Count.*

*My dearest child, I do urge prudence. Perhaps this letter will arrive too late but the comfort of your family is not worth the sacrifice of your virtue. Forgive me if I speak plainly, but I have your best interests at heart. Your mother still expects you to marry Lord Hugo and he has been here once or twice to enquire after you with Miss Emily. Miss Emily, poor child, adores Hugo, and is desperate for his attention. I had a moment alone with your ardent suitor. He also expressed concern over your relationship with the Count.*

*Dearest Cristy, what is happening? You can be assured of my discretion in this matter.*

*Your loving grandmother,*
*Frieda*

I didn't need to glance in the mirror to see my face had turned scarlet. I could feel it. What did it mean? Why would the Count concern himself over the affairs of my family? Why would Granny assume I would accept a carte *blanche* from the Count when I had refused Hugo?

I would never, never sell myself so short. Well, at least I liked to think I wouldn't. I hoped I possessed the strength to overcome temptation.

I reread the letter again and tried to picture Granny's face. Perhaps she had conjured up this assessment to soothe a troubled mind? Perhaps the Count needed a trustworthy tenant and thought my family would serve the purpose? An act of kindness, nothing more.

No matter how I persuaded myself it meant nothing, I felt its significance.

\*       \*       \*

The Baron continues to surprise me. Three weeks have passed and I cannot fault his treatment of Rachel. He has behaved like an adoring husband to her in public and, judging by Rachel's ever-present smile, I suspected this conduct followed in private.

Rachel thanked me effusively. 'Whatever you said made a difference. How can I ever repay you?'

'By allowing me to be your friend,' I replied, with a smile.

She clasped my hand. 'Karl has asked me to return to Vienna with him . . . he wants a child . . . he says we must have an heir.'

'That is wonderful news,' I said. 'We are

leaving for Vienna in a week or so. Perhaps we can meet there?'

'Oh, yes! You're my dearest friend. I never had a *true* friend before and I will never forget your kindness. You've saved me from a life of misery.'

I laughed. 'I do believe you exaggerate my talents.'

'No,' she murmured, her eyes pensive, 'you have a way with people. They gravitate toward you.'

'I should warn you: I'm not a saint, Rachel.'

'But you are. You just don't know your powers yet.'

I allowed her to think that way.

Though I spent a great deal of my time with Rachel, I still kept to my routine of reading to Lady Gisela in the afternoons. Sometimes Rachel would sit and listen, other times she would join Sibylla and Liesel.

'I like the girl,' Lady Gisela said to me, 'You have given her independence.'

'It was always there,' I said. 'One just had to recover it.'

She chuckled. 'Looking forward to Vienna? I daresay Karl had designs on you before our little Rachel popped up. No point in denying it. I know my nephew very well. He has a penchant for a pretty face.'

'Rachel is—'

'Tolerably handsome,' Lady Gisela conceded. 'Now you have lost Karl, whom

110

shall we go for? Ernst, perhaps? I know he's only a steward, or are you after bigger game?'

To divert her attention away from the subject, I asked her about Vienna.

'Oh, I'm not going. I detest city life, always have. And Max will need someone to preside at the *schloss* while he is away.'

'Won't Frau Vetsera be staying behind?'

She shook her head. 'Max likes to take the household with him, even Liesel's silly old nurse Frau Bruns will go. It is tradition.'

'Tradition,' I echoed.

\*     \*     \*

The next morning, Rachel rushed up to my room to say they were going to visit Baroness Outten and did I want to come? I had spent a restless night, wondering why my family's fortunes had suddenly changed. I possessed our only piece of fortune: the bracelet. Dare I imagine the Count pictured me in the role of his mistress or wife? 'I think I'll stay behind and rest.'

Rachel nodded. 'We are going skating again, so you won't be missing much.'

I hugged her. 'Enjoy yourself.'

She grinned. 'I will.'

Once alone and feeling revived after a hearty breakfast, I decided I would go and visit Dara. She had not come to dinner last Friday evening and I had heard she was ill.

111

I put on my new fur-lined cloak and headed down to the parlour and out to the courtyard. I groaned when I saw Herr Mendel approaching me from the gatehouse.

He gazed down at the flowers in my basket. 'Are you planning to visit Miss Quinn?'

'No,' I lied, for I did not want him accompanying me. 'I promised Liesel I would put these on her mother's grave.'

He nodded solemnly. 'Then I shall accompany you to the gate. Fräulein Cristabel. I have been wanting to talk to you for some time—to congratulate you on your successes.'

'Successes?'

'With the Von Lichtenburgs. Your influence is rather remarkable.'

'I fear you exaggerate my talents.'

'You don't like me, do you?' His statement startled me.

'Herr Mendel—'

He laughed. 'Oh, do me the courtesy of being honest. I detest liars.'

His behaviour alarmed me.

'I can see I have offended you. Please forgive me. We shall be moving to the villa in Vienna soon and I should like us to start anew as friends. Will you do me the honour and please call me Ernst?'

I agreed, if only to get rid of him. He left me at the gate and I knew I'd been harsh with him. In an effort to inspire jealousy in the Count, I had encouraged Herr Mendel. I had danced with him, I had sent him smiles, I had poured his coffee . . .

Poor Ernst. Why could I not consider a young man like him? Was I so ruthless and ambitious to want wealth and a title?

Perhaps. A part of me wanted to succeed, to show those in the village back home that I could do it. To return to London in triumph, sporting a new fabulous husband. And part of me didn't care about any of those shallow considerations. Almost to the point where I'd consent to become the Count's mistress if that is what he wished.

I couldn't understand his hold over me. Was I so infatuated with the man? I measured every other man against him. I wanted only him: Maximus, Count von Holstein, not for his title but for his soul.

The knowledge terrified and amused me. I was going to visit his mistress and here I was confessing my love for him.

My love for him! I barely knew the man . . . or did I? Somewhere in my heart, I felt I had known him for an eternity. It was a disturbing belief and one I hoped would leave me when we left the mystical mountains for the reality of Vienna.

When I reached the Countess's grave, I discovered Frau Bruns there, kneeling beside the tombstone.

I must have startled her for she jumped up in fright. I made my apologies and she nodded, eyeing my basket of flowers.

Without saying a word, I laid the flowers Frau Vetsera had grown inside the *schloss* on the Countess's grave. It seemed only fitting I should do so in light of the excuse I'd given Ernst Mendel.

'She died so very young,' Frau Bruns murmured. 'She was frightened.'

'Frightened? Of whom?'

'*Him.*' Her eyes squinted at me. 'You should be careful, *fräulein*. Very careful.'

I walked away, shrugging away the sound of Frau Brun's voice. An old nurse with little else to employ her mind than dark suspicions.

Heidi answered the door to Dara's cottage.

'I know Fräulein Quinn is not expecting me,' I began, and I heard Dara's voice in the background, demanding to know who was at the door.

Heidi replied, 'It's the English miss, m'lady,' and after a brief silence, the door opened.

To my surprise, Dara was sitting on the floor with her son Paul. A look of fright crossed his little face at my approach.

'This is Cristabel,' Dara assured him with a smile. 'She's come from England to teach Fräulein Liesel at the castle. Do you remember her? You saw her at the party.'

The boy eyed me in awe. 'You live at the castle?'

'Why, yes, but I don't own it.'

His dark blue eyes, so like the Count's,

widened. 'So it's not your home?'

'My home is in England, in a cottage like this one.'

He nodded and resumed his play.

'I've been teaching him whist,' Dara laughed, 'haven't I, Paul?'

'Paul?'

'Yes, it's a family name and it suits him, don't you think?'

*Whose family? Yours or the Count's?*

'Poor little darling. It's a terrible thing for a child to go through with the hot irons and the sleepless nights, but my Paul suffers it all with *such* nobility.'

Her pride in him was evident. 'Is he the Count's son?' The question blurted out before I could stop it.

Dara went to sit on the settee facing me, a queer smile on her lips. 'My Paul should be heir, you know, except he is born—what is the expression?—' "on the wrong side of the blanket." '

I nodded, trying to control my emotions. 'Does the Count know about him?'

Dara laughed. 'How else do you think we came to be here?'

'He doesn't seem to be a man who would set up a mistress on the same estate as his wife.'

'The von Holstein men have always been passionate,' she sighed. 'Not one of them has remained faithful to one woman, not since the time of Conrad and Elaina. Had they lived, perhaps Conrad would have forsaken his love in time.'

'I don't believe it,' I said, a little more zealously than I intended.

She grimaced. 'You like to believe in fairy-tales.'

'Why not? They still do happen.'

Her lips pursed. 'Let us be frank with one another. Do you endeavour to be the Count's mistress or his wife?'

Silence enshrouded us. Blood gushed to my face for, despite my brazen attitude, I knew nothing about the life of a mistress. 'What would you say if I said both?'

'Then I'd consider you a formidable rival,' Dara answered, with a smile. 'Let us not quarrel. I did not mean to offend you. In fact, I believe you are the only woman worth knowing at the *schloss*.'

I stared at her and she laughed.

'I like to shock people and I see I have offended your English sensibilities, but I won't retract the statement. I detest all of them up there, except the Count, of course. He is the only reason I stay here.'

I gazed down at Paul, playing happily on the floor. 'Was the Countess aware of the existence of your son?'

'Yes, but not at first. She came to visit me once, bearing all that haughty arrogance that comes with being a royal princess. She resented the fact the Count had set me up in

Vienna and plainly offered to set me up in the country—somewhere obscure, no doubt. I refused and she called me a "fool" and said I would pay for humiliating her. I never saw her again until I heard they'd found her body up in the mountains. I didn't believe it. I had to go and see for myself.'

'You went to the chapel?'

She nodded. 'They displayed her beauty for Liesel's sake, I think.'

'Not for the Count?' I dared to ask.

A smile touched her lips. 'It had been a *marriage de convenance* for some years. You must understand it is this way in the noble houses. They marry; produce an heir—in this case, Liesel is a poor heir. The estate is entailed on the male line so she cannot inherit. My Paul should inherit. This is why I must keep him safe.'

'Has the Count made arrangements for him?'

Her face softened. 'Oh, yes, he never fails me.'

'You never once suspected him of killing his wife?'

'Max,' she laughed, 'is a man of secrets. Who can read his mind?'

'Then the event hasn't clouded your judgement of him?'

'Why should it? I expect no more of him than he expects of me. And I am hardly in a position to judge him.'

The visit disturbed me more than I wanted to admit. She neither confirmed nor denied her relationship with the Count. What had become apparent was that she openly confessed my potential as a rival. Could I snatch the Count out of her hands?

Yes. She knew it and feared it.

I returned to the *schloss*. I had to reply to Granny's letter and I had been mulling over what to write and what not to write.

I chose a safe medium and described the present occupants of the *schloss* and supplied the family's villa address in Vienna. I wrote of the legend of Conrad and Elaina and how the Count had given me a miniature of Conrad for Christmas. I sealed the letter before lying on my bed to study the miniature. It was a very good likeness of Conrad, but the gift was more precious to me because it had come from the Count.

I remembered the original miniature of Elaina had gone missing in Vienna while in the Countess's care. How had she misplaced it so carelessly? Who now had possession of it?

I was content with my version of Conrad. I would treasure it forever, no matter what ensued in the coming months.

I must have fallen asleep for I did not stir until someone knocked rather urgently at my door.

It was Frau Vetsera.

'They are asking for you downstairs,

Fräulein.'

I had never seen her face so pale. 'What has happened?'

'There's been an accident . . . involving the young Baroness.'

# PART 3

# The Villa

# CHAPTER EIGHT

Fear for Rachel sped me down to the drawing-room where I found them all grimly assembled. I only had to look at Karl's face to learn the truth.

They had laid her by the fire, uselessly wrapped in a dozen fur rugs. Her face was still and pale and her lips were blue.

'She fell in the lake . . .' Liesel began.

I knelt down before Rachel and buried my face in her lifeless, frozen hands.

Around me, I was aware the physician had arrived and the Count guided me to a chair. A glass of sherry had been thrust into my hands and I was persuaded to drink it, the liquid burning down my throat.

'A terrible tragedy,' Sibylla whispered. 'Karl found her first, but they had to wait to fish her out. The ice is treacherous.'

I gazed at Karl. He sat in the armchair by his wife and I couldn't fault the look of shock on his face. Was it put there for my benefit? A few weeks ago, he had resented Rachel's intrusion into his mock bachelor life. Did he now feel liberated, or was his grief genuine?

'I feel responsible,' Baroness Outten's anguished cry echoed throughout the room. 'I should have had the ice checked. It was safe this time last year. The poor child must have noticed the cracks, but by then perhaps it was too late to turn back.'

There would be no turning back for Rachel. She had died alone in the icy water beneath the frozen lake, abandoned by the merry skaters whose skill and expertise far surpassed hers. How she'd wanted to impress Karl. She believed in their chance of reconciliation and she had died to achieve it.

'She will be buried here, in the family chapel,' the Count murmured, when the physician, after making his examinations, sadly shook his head. There was nothing else to be done but to arrange her funeral.

'Her relatives will have to be informed,' I said.

Karl nodded. He stood by the fire, his face pale with shock. I felt guilty for suspecting his involvement in Rachel's death. The doubts had arisen the moment I realized she was dead and he was free.

'This is a sad state of affairs.' Baroness Outten pressed the Count's hand. 'I will go home and change. Please send word when you have news.'

Sibylla and Liesel soon followed suit, leaving the Count, Karl and I.

Karl paced the room. 'I shouldn't have allowed her on the ice. I shouldn't have persuaded her to come. Perhaps I am guilty of her death. It is what you think, isn't it?'

He had directed the question to me.

'You are not in your right mind, cousin,' the Count said, 'and you are trembling with the cold. Why not go and change? There is little you can do here.'

'Aye, little,' he echoed gloomily. 'I should never have married her . . . she was only a child.'

The Count helped him to the door. 'There is not much one can say in the situation,' he said on his return. 'I have never seen my cousin so shaken.'

'He wanted to be rid of her a few weeks ago,' I reminded him, trying to keep the bitter tone from my voice.

'You are angry, as a true friend would be.'

'Her last words were so full of hope and happiness. She confided in me, you know. I was an English face in a foreign land and she attached herself to me. She said she admired my strength and courage. What strength and courage? I wasn't even there to save her.'

The deluge I had been holding back now sprang forth with uncontrollable weeping. I despised weeping of any kind and so tried to hide my face in my hands. 'I should have been there . . .'

Warm hands touched my hair, so fleetingly I might have imagined it. 'My dear Cristabel, don't torture yourself. Even if you were there, you would not have been able to save her. Do you trust me on this?'

I nodded, miserably.

125

'There now,' he smiled, handing me a handkerchief from his pocket. 'Wipe your face and I'll carry you to your room.'

I began to protest, but it was too late. There was I, imprisoned in his great arms, a fortress of strength and compassion. I shut my eyes and allowed my head to rest against his chest.

It was over too quickly. I was placed on my bed, Frau Vetsera and one or two maids hovering about me. I didn't want the Count to go, but how could I ask him to stay? The staid face of Frau Vetsera soon reminded me of my duty and I banished these feelings from my mind. It would not do to provide those below stairs with fresh gossip. I already had enough to contend with: the Baron's previous pursuit of me and my camaraderie with the Count. Not to mention Herr Mendel and his recent declaration.

A hot bath and the sherry sent me into a deep slumber, from which I didn't awake until eight o'clock that evening. I dressed and went downstairs. The house was deathly quiet and the rain lashed against the windows.

I paused to stare out at the sleet encasing the mountains. As I stood there, I was certain I heard a voice calling to me out of the mist. *Beware*, the voice said in a strange, high-pitched whisper. I peered further into the mist and fancied I saw the makings of a face . . . a face of such quiet solemnity I could never forget.

126

*Elaina*, I thought. She is warning me, warning me to leave.

The mist dispersed, leaving me to wonder at my own sanity. I prided myself on my English common sense. One did not see faces out of the mist, nor hear voices from the past.

But even as I walked away from the window, I felt the creeping certainty overwhelm me.

The legend could be true.

*　　　*　　　*

No one spoke in the chapel.

I noticed Liesel was very pale. She had teased and laughed at Rachel and now felt guilty for doing so. She sat beside Sibylla and stared up at the displayed body, a queer kind of fear in her eyes. The death had come as a shock to her, a month after the anniversary of her mother's death. Her face matched everyone else's: gloomy, sombre, reflective. Could the accident have been prevented? This question reigned in the silence as each person tried to answer it.

We met back at the *schloss* where I overheard the Count asking his cousin if 'word had been sent' to Rachel's relatives.

'No, not yet,' came his odd reply. 'I hardly know what to say.'

Yes, I thought darkly. If *you* hadn't neglected her, she never would have *died* trying to win your favour.

To my astonishment, Karl smiled. 'What does a man do in this situation, but move on?'

He glanced in my direction and I turned away in horror. His low murmur had also reached the ears of Frau Vetsera, who stood by the door, directing the staff with their trays of tea, coffee and other refreshments. I felt, rather than saw, her heated, enquiring gaze upon me.

I was not surprised when she asked to see me later.

Summoned to what the servants called her 'office', I sat in the chair opposite her desk and raised my brows in expectation.

She shuffled a few papers on her desk. 'Fräulein Brown, thank you for coming so promptly. This is indeed a grievous time.'

'It is,' I echoed.

'One would think you have been affected quite personally by this tragic affair.'

I remained silent.

'Your friendship with the Baroness . . . and the Baron . . . is the favourite talk among the staff. Shall I tell you what they are saying?'

'If you like.'

'They are saying *you* are the reason for the marriage upset. They talk of you meeting the Baron in Vienna in the coffee house.'

I shrugged. 'And?'

Her eyes narrowed. 'We are a small community here, *fräulein*. Nothing escapes our notice. Just what exactly is your plan?'

'My plan,' I murmured, 'is to teach Miss von Holstein English. My plan is not to become the Baron's mistress or indeed, entertainment for any man.' I said it with force, though my hands shook in my lap. I had suspected the cause for the whisperings behind my back. I had almost expected them, especially when the Baron appeared to be pursuing me before his wife arrived. And now the young Baroness was dead: it was all so simple in their minds. I was the mistress. *I* was the reason why the Baron wanted his wife out of the way. *I* was to blame.

I hated the censure and the injustice. I could not grieve for Rachel as I should like because I was suspected of being . . . of being an accomplice in her death!

The absurdity suddenly hit me and I laughed.

Frau Vetsera was not impressed. 'You laugh, *fräulein*?'

'Yes!' I replied. 'For that is how ludicrous these accusations are to me. The Baroness was my friend and I have not betrayed her trust in any way or form. I simply tried to assist her with her problems.'

'But the Baron—' she persisted.

'The *Baron*,' I said firmly, 'should answer your concerns, not I.' I said this knowing she would never dare approach the Baron with her suspicions.

She might, however, approach the Count. It grieved me for I believed she would choose to do so. I could imagine her saying: *that woman should never have been permitted in the house. She doesn't even look like a respectable governess. She looks like a play actress . . . an adventuress. And did not your cousin the Baron supposedly meet her in a coffee house in Vienna? Perhaps she is his mistress and has deceived us. Perhaps they planned to murder the young Baroness and made it look like an accident. Don't you think this Miss Brown should be removed at once?*

The very idea of her meeting with the Count tortured me. I did not want him thinking badly of me, especially when I was innocent in the matter. But he had seen me with his cousin and could have misinterpreted those encounters like everyone else. And when Karl had murmured those words after his wife's funeral: *what does a man do in this situation, but move on?*

I hid my face in my hands.

'You should be embarrassed,' Frau Vetsera snapped in my ear, 'you have caused enough trouble in this household. I suggest you return to your room at once.'

*At once.* I almost smiled on my way up. I had been right about something and wrong about everything else. Why did I believe I was special to the Count in some way; why did I assume Frau Vetsera's accusation could not hurt me?

I studied my face grimly in the mirror. I

130

looked a little older, wiser. I suppose I could pass for a play-actress or an adventuress. One was always judged by one's looks. It was a fact I did not particularly like, especially now.

If I had been plain, the Baron never would have pursued me and I would not be the centre of suspicion in his wife's sudden death.

Oh, Rachel! *How had it happened?* I wish I'd been there. If I had gone, she might not have ventured out on to the ice. And if I had gone, she certainly would not have been alone at that moment.

Yes, I was guilty of her death. I could have prevented it by going along instead of choosing to stay behind. A purely selfish decision I now bitterly regretted. But how could I have known she would have died that day, drowned in a prison of icy water?

I shuddered at the thought. Why had no one tried to rescue her? They said it was dangerous; they said there was nothing they could do. Did I believe them? In part, I did, but in part, I did not. A month ago, the Baron had wanted to be rid of his wife. The fact couldn't be ignored. Nor could the fear I had glimpsed in Rachel's face from time to time. She had been afraid of her husband. Perhaps she believed he might try to kill her.

I alone knew more about Rachel and her feelings than anyone suspected. Oh, they had seen us together, chatting amiably but wouldn't it seem natural for Rachel to

131

gravitate toward one of her own nationality? She was a young Englishwoman in a foreign land and so was I. She did not care for status and nor did I. She did not have any friends and she saw a friend in me.

I made an oath then never to break her trust. A bright star had faded and I felt her loss acutely.

Somehow, I would avenge her death.

*     *     *

I saw Dara the next day.

She hadn't come to the funeral because her Paul was ill.

'He caught a chill and the fever came to him in the night. I couldn't dare leave him. I won't trust him with anyone but myself.'

I asked her if she sent for the physician.

'No, physicians are useless in my opinion. My mother was a herbalist, you see, and I learned some of the art.' She smiled fondly at the boy who was sleeping. 'He's fine now, just a little weak. We'll leave him and go downstairs. I want to know everything.'

I explained the events of the last few days, omitting my 'chat' with Frau Vetsera, though I wondered if Dara had heard something through Heidi for she looked at me enquiringly.

'A very unusual death, isn't it? They often pull them out before they freeze to death. I've heard it is a delicate process which certainly has its own dangers. One false step and the whole block of ice can crack.'

She offered her sympathies. 'You were very close to the Baroness and yet you say nothing of the affair. Don't you think it odd that her husband refused to take the risk?'

'They said it was too late to save her. She was dead when they arrived.'

Dara raised a brow. 'Did they? I suspect *someone* must have seen her fall. Even if you are skating in front, you get a sensation if something happens behind you. Tell me, how is Liesel coping in all this?'

I glanced at her sharply. Surely, she did not suspect Liesel had anything to do with Rachel's accident? 'She is shocked.'

'Shocked?' Dara echoed. 'Yes, I suppose she might very well be shocked.'

'What do you mean?'

She lifted her shoulders in an elegant, dismissive fashion. 'Oh, nothing.'

'You did mean something,' I persisted.

'Very well. Since you insist, I will tell you. It has to do with Liesel's mother.'

'Liesel's mother?'

She nodded. 'Malena, the Countess. You are aware she was a princess of the Hapsburg line?'

I remembered Frau Bruns' story of how she became nurse to the infant princess. 'Yes, I have heard a little of her background.'

133

'Were you ever aware Malena's father, the prince, died from madness?'

'Madness?'

She smiled as one does when one is in possession of knowledge. 'It is a very interesting affair and one the family endeavours to hide. A friend of mine from court happened to overhear a conversation relating to Malena's father. He had shown signs of deterioration from his early manhood—erratic moods, uncontrollable tempers, odd laughing fits, but it didn't really become evident until his later years. When he became too much of an embarrassment to his family and the court, they separated him from his daughter and exiled him to one of the family manors. It was to be his prison.'

'How old was the Countess at the time?'

'Twelve. She was disconsolate for months and refused to believe his tender affection toward her had been diagnosed as madness. On her sixteenth birthday, she decided to rescue him. The rescue proved fatal. When she unlocked her father's door, he set out like a crazed man, kicked his two guards to death and then went roaming the streets with a broken bottle in his hand. He started to attack the soldiers on the street until one of them shot him in the head. Of course, the soldier didn't know who he had shot and his identity was never revealed. They thought some drunken madman, never suspecting a royal

134

prince.'

'It must have been terrible for—' I couldn't seem to say her name.

'Malena?' Dara supplied with a smile. 'Yes, I believe it was. She too had shown some inconsistencies in her behaviour. They hushed it up and were more than happy to marry her off to the second son of a count. Wouldn't you think a royal princess deserved more than the second son of a count? That proves the madness must have been somewhere in Malena too, and Liesel has the same blood.'

I gazed into the fire, watching the logs crackle down into the hot coals. Hereditary madness. Liesel—mad? I had thought her spoilt, unmanageable, rude, but mad? I had to ask the question. 'Do you believe madness drove the Countess to her death?'

Dara didn't answer immediately and when she did, her words seemed carefully chosen. 'What else would drive her up to the mountains in such weather? She liked to go up there when she was angry, you know. It was her escape. Sometimes she took friends with her, sometimes she went alone.'

'Isn't it dangerous?'

'Malena laughed at danger, she *mocked* it. She had grown careless in the last two years before her death. She scoffed at convention and became indiscreet, an *embarrassment* like her father. Some considered it a blessing she failed to return from the mountains, and you cannot blame them for thinking so. You only have to think of Liesel. Seeing a mother behave so erratically cannot be healthy for a child, especially one with Liesel's *blood.*'

As she spoke, it became more obvious to me that Malena had not deliberately taken her own life. Anger had driven her up to the mountains on the night of Christmas Eve. Frau Bruns' words came back to haunt me: *There was a big fight. He didn't want her anymore.*

Dara seemed to follow my thoughts. 'I wanted you to know the story, so you can help your pupil.'

I stared at her. 'Surely you don't suspect Liesel had something to do with Rachel's accident?'

She shrugged. 'All I know is that you can manage Liesel where others have clearly failed.'

'I don't know about that,' I replied, 'we have scarcely had a lesson this past month.'

'Schedules are always interrupted when visitors arrive. It has always been so.'

She wanted to say it but I held up my hand. I did not want to hear what private 'schedules' she had with the Count.

She pouted instead. 'I won't be accompanying the family to Vienna: it wouldn't be *seemly*, now, would it?'

'I imagine you will come later,' I said, somewhat mechanically.

'Yes, one must be discreet in these

circumstances. The family has a tiny villa attached to their villa. You might see me there before long.'

I stood up and nodded. 'I hope your son recovers swiftly from his illness.'

'Oh, he will,' Dara beamed. 'He has the stamina of his father.'

*　　*　　*

*Stamina of his father.*

Her sweet, honeyed voice consumed me with rage. Why couldn't she act with more discretion? Why did she always have to mention *him* when I came?

Because she had to secure her position. Even my emotional state would not prevent her from carrying out her plan to win.

I did not go straight back to the house. I had to collect my senses and remove the anger in my step. I couldn't afford to have any more gossip construed against me and there certainly would be gossip if I returned red-faced and angry.

I was walking in the copse near Malena's grave when I heard a twig snap behind me. Fear imprisoned me. I wanted to call out and demand who was there but my throat constricted and I could not speak.

Cautious footsteps approached.

I considered running, but my legs refused to obey me.

'*Fräulein?*'

Relief overcame me. No aggressive voice matched the footsteps. An uncertain voice, deep, commonplace. Had I heard this voice before?

He walked around me and I gasped. It was one-armed, one-eyed Old Josef from the gatehouse.

'I didn't mean to scare ye,' he said. 'Josef's got to speak to the English *fräulein* at the castle.' His eyes squinted. 'Are ye she? The little Baroness's friend?'

I relaxed. 'Yes, I am.'

He nodded, staring down at the cap in his hand. 'I've seen something. Old Josef sees all with one eye. They think I'm dumb up at the *schloss* but I'm not dumb.'

'I never thought you dumb, Josef.'

'Ye seem to 'ave a good heart, miss. I hear what they say about ye and it I tell 'em it's not true. It's the Baron who is the bad one.'

'The Baron?'

He looked around him, obviously afraid of being overheard. 'The Baron. I seen him talkin' to his sister and he says he wants to be "free". She says, "why? For the little English miss?" (that's ye, miss) and the Baron just smiles. His wife, the Baroness, was comin' and Josef hears him say to his sister, "It won't be long before I'm free".'

I stared at him, shocked, numbed by his disclosure. 'Was anything else said?'

'No, miss. That's all.'

'Thank you, Josef, for coming to me. Does the Count know what you saw?'

The man paled.

'What is it, Josef? Are you afraid of the Count?'

'Ye must promise me ye won't go to the Count.'

'Why? This could be *murder.*'

His one eye focused on me, intense and urgent. 'Ye must keep it to yourself, miss. Others 'ave gone missin' when they weren't wanted anymore.' He gestured over to right. 'That's one of 'em.'

He pointed to the Countess's grave. I suddenly felt very weak.

'You mentioned "others". Who are the others, Josef? You can trust me. I shan't repeat it.'

'Lord Rudolf.'

'Lord Rudolf? You mean the Count's brother? The one who died in a shooting accident?'

Josef gazed at me. 'I won't say no more, but it don't seem like an accident to me. I liked Lord Rudolf. He always used to stop and say hello to Old Josef.'

'Surely you don't believe the Count had anything to do with his brother's accident?'

Josef shrugged. 'Ye need to be careful too, miss. Ye don't know the past. Evil is here; Old Josef can feel it.'

139

Part of me wanted to say, 'Don't be ridiculous,' but I could not. I too had experienced similar fancies. They could no longer be brushed aside as nonsense. Rachel was dead and, as the hours passed, the growing certainty overcame me.

Murder.

*     *     *

I met the would-be murderer in Lady Gisela's apartment the next day. I heard voices on entering and naturally assumed them to belong to Ingrid and Lady Gisela. Therefore, I was shocked to see Karl sitting there, sipping his coffee in a contented, almost leisurely fashion.

'Oh, there you are.' Lady Gisela winked at me. 'We have just been discussing you. Do come in. Ingrid, pour Miss Brown some coffee. She looks as if she needs it.'

I tried to smile, choosing a seat beside Ingrid.

'My poor nephew has only this morning completed a most disagreeable task. He has written to Rachel's relatives, informing them of the accident. We thought, as you were a friend of the poor child, you might want to add your own condolences in the express?'

It had crossed my mind to write my own letter to Rachel's relatives. 'When does the express leave?'

'After luncheon,' the Baron replied. 'They would like to hear from you. My wife didn't have many friends.'

*No, because you kept her prisoner in the country and she was embarrassed by the fact.* I smiled. 'I shall go and write one now. May I have their names?'

Karl produced a list from his pocket and handed it to me. 'If you give me yours at luncheon, I would be happy to include it with my own.'

'Thank you, my lord, but I prefer to give mine to the courier directly.'

Lady Gisela frowned. 'You don't have to leave yet, Miss Brown. I haven't seen anything of you for a week. What have you been doing? Dreaming up murder suspects?'

I flushed and said I had spent my time visiting Dara and writing my own correspondence.

'Oh, your *own* correspondence.' Lady Gisela chuckled. 'How secretive. I hope you didn't name my nephew as suspect there. He is quite innocent, you know, and deserves your consolation.'

Ingrid glanced at me in surprise. She, too, must have heard the rumours circulating about me, and so had the Baron. He was studying my reaction, faintly amused, I suspected, however, he hid his emotions well.

At the first opportunity, I made my excuses to examine the names on the list. What Lady

141

Gisela thought I would do, I did. I wrote the condolence letters, carefully omitting names, (in case they should be read), but highlighting the sudden and unexpected nature of Rachel's death. A parent would immediately be suspicious. As Rachel's parents were dead, I could only hope her godmother or her aunts, uncles and cousins would pick up my meaning between the lines.

I did not feel particularly comfortable with the idea of this letter being handed to Karl's courier. I went downstairs, deliberately avoiding the invitation to lunch with the family, and waited outside the Count's study. Before Frau Vetsera had approached me with her suspicions, I would have asked her to arrange the delivery of it. However, anything I gave her now would be regarded with mistrust.

Old Josef's warnings sifted through my mind as I waited. Perhaps I shouldn't ask the Count. He had been there that day with his cousin. They had arrived too late. They were unable to save Rachel. Or had they been there early to lay a trap and watch her demise?

I hid in the shadows when I heard voices. His and Karl's. I did not want to see Karl and experienced acute relief when his footsteps faded down the stairs.

I stepped out into the light when the Count approached.

'Crista— Miss Browne.

'Sorry for startling you, my lord, but I must

see you.'

He nodded solemnly and opened the door to his study. I went inside, chilled by the lack of a fire.

'You are cold,' he said, removing his own coat and placing it around my shoulders. 'Do put it on. I won't need it for the moment.'

Once he began to stoke the dying embers, I did so. The faint scent of his cologne rested lingeringly on the collar of his coat. I wanted to close my eyes to absorb it and fought the inclination. Old Josef's words haunted me: *you must be careful.*

'You came to see me.' The Count smiled in reminder.

'Y—yes.'

'I assume some disturbing rumours have reached your ears in relation to my cousin?'

*How much did he know?*

'I believe Frau Vetsera has spoken to you?'

A whimsical smile touched my lips. 'In a manner of speaking. Did you ask her to speak to me?'

'No! I suspect her reason for advising me of the household gossip was to see you dismissed. I told her the rumours were unfounded and preposterous. My cousin has just lost his wife and my staff have you married off as baroness number two.' He laughed. 'It is just as well we are leaving for Vienna in a few days. A seasonal change is always beneficial for one's mental health, wouldn't you agree?'

143

'Yes,' I grinned, dismissing all doubts from my mind. I refused to believe ill of the Count. He didn't appear a man who would murder his own brother for a title. As for Malena . . . perhaps her insanity was to blame for her mysterious death. The marriage may not have been a happy one but unhappiness could be managed. One didn't murder for unhappiness or embarrassment: one murdered for greed, hate, jealousy, or so I believed.

'Is there another matter on your mind?'

I glanced up at his concerned, handsome face and wished I could confide in him. But to do so, I would surely betray the feelings of my own heart. How foolish! To be enamoured of a man who already had a mistress! Perhaps he intended to marry Dara in the near future, once Liesel had grown accustomed to the idea. Why else would Dara be invited to dine with the family once a week? Why else would Dara be following us to Vienna if she didn't have a special place in the Count's affections?

'Er—no,' I lied. 'It's nothing.'

'Nothing.' He echoed, a smile appearing on his lips. 'You seem very perturbed over a "nothing". There must be "something" bothering you.'

Why did he have to persist? Exhaling a sigh, I joined him at the window. 'It's just . . .'

'Just?'

'You, I suppose. You perturb me.'

'Do I?'

I nodded.

'Why do I perturb you?'

I dared not face him. An uncomfortable lump formed in my throat. Why could he read me so easily? Was I so transparent?

'I think I understand,' he murmured. 'It's my shocking behaviour on Christmas Eve, isn't it? It was completely unprofessional and I can only seek to blame my inebriated state for the crime of kissing you.'

Startled by his confession, I started to shake my head when he lifted a hand.

'Will you forgive the crime, Miss Brown?'

There was a faint amusement in his voice. 'You needn't ask it, my lord,' I replied, establishing space between us. 'I was a willing participant.'

'Even so, do you grant it?'

'If you wish it.'

'I *do* wish it.'

'Then you have my forgiveness.'

He nodded and resumed his seat at his desk.

Amused by his deep sense of honour (or was it pride?), I invited myself to sit down opposite him. 'My lord, I received a letter from my grandmother this week and there is something which disturbs me.'

He lifted a brow. 'Yes?'

'It is very odd,' I went on. 'They have been given a new home I fear they cannot afford. I don't know what to do about it.'

He met my gaze. 'Surely your family has

sufficient wit to judge their means of living?'

I cut him short. 'I suspect *you* had something to do with it.'

'Me?'

'Yes. Before you begin to deny it, I wanted to thank you but really, you shouldn't have.'

'There is no need to thank me. I do more for my own boot polisher.'

'*Boot* polisher?' I stared at him. 'You have your own boot polisher?'

'I'm teasing you, Miss Brown. Let me set your mind at rest. Yes, I am behind the mysterious new home. No, you don't have to thank me and no, your family is under no obligation and nor, I should add, are you.'

'But—'

'And no buts. It is purely a business arrangement. I wanted to invest in a little English greenery and *voilà!* this house became available in your neighbourhood.'

I sent him a woebegone look.

He sighed. 'I wanted tenants whom I could trust and if one can't trust his own daughter's governess, who can one trust?'

'I could have come from a disreputable family.'

He shook his head. 'Not you, Miss Brown. You cling to values, all evidence of a good upbringing.' At my reproachful groan, he added, 'What is the point of a man having everything if he cannot help those who are less fortunate?'

I couldn't argue with him there. 'Very well, I retreat.'

He smiled at me pensively from his armchair. A moment more and I might have thrown myself into his arms and kissed him shamefully. Thankfully, a curt knock at the door prevented me from doing so. I blessed the intruder, for if I had behaved so foolishly, I knew I would have to return to England.

Liesel was at the door, peering into the room. 'Who's in there with you, Papa? I heard voices.'

'It is Miss Brown. I am glad you have come for I have noticed you have been negligent of your lessons this past month.'

Liesel looked at me sullenly.

'Miss Brown has voiced no complaint about you,' her father insisted. 'She has come to see me on another matter.'

'Another matter? What matter?'

'A private one.'

'Is it about Karl?'

'It is a matter that does not concern you,' her father replied firmly. 'However, what does concern you is your new schedule when we reach Vienna. Every morning during the week, you will attend your lessons with Miss Brown. If I hear you err once in this regard, you will be sent back here to Aunt Gisela.'

The threat was very real. I could see her mind going over the possibilities. Sitting at lessons during the mornings or spending the summer in the mountains with Lady Gisela. The lively crowd would be in Vienna and Liesel would not want to miss out.

'I accept your terms, Papa,' she said, and coolly nodded to me before racing away, no doubt to air her wrath with Sibylla.

I monitored the Count watching her and glimpsed the brief uncertainty in his eyes. Would Liesel inherit the madness?

*     *     *

I did not approach the Count with my doubts about Karl.

The opportunity had passed and I handed my letter to the courier, hoping it would reach the intended recipient.

*     *     *

I could not avoid going down for dinner on Friday evening. I had promised Dara I would come and, as it would be the last family gathering, as Sibylla and Karl planned to leave in the morning, my absence would be noted.

I selected my modest black velvet gown. It suited the occasion and my mood. I thought of pinning Granny's brooch there and decided against it. I wanted to appear black and morbid, especially to Karl.

The Count, Ernst Mendel, Lady Gisela and Ingrid occupied the room when I entered. I

148

arrived early on purpose for I did not wish to make a spectacle by arriving late.

The others soon joined us. Sibylla, in her fashionable black, created competition for Dara who managed to look equally entrancing with her red hair dressed high. Karl wore his usual evening attire and pretended to be solemn. And Liesel . . . Liesel arrived in a pink dress, bedecked in frills and elaborate embroidery. Even Lady Gisela, who refused to wear black, had chosen a reticent blue to mark the occasion.

As I expected, Lady Gisela questioned her about it. 'Did Frau Bruns not light your dressing-room, Liesel darling? Have you not a black dress to wear?'

'I don't like black,' Liesel retorted. 'The colour reminds me of Mama's funeral.'

Reference to the Countess immediately squashed conversation and we moved to the dining-table to conceal the uneasy silence.

If I thought Liesel's selection of clothes inappropriate, her behaviour during dinner was worse. She interrupted six or seven times and made no apology for it and when Sibylla gently reminded her to behave, she laughed.

'Behave? I am not a child, Sibylla.'

'I know you are not a child, my dear. When we are in Vienna, nobody shall dare treat you like one.'

It would have ended there if Dara hadn't smiled and said, 'Vienna does not countenance

149

ill-behaved young ladies.'

Liesel jumped out of her chair. 'What would you know? You're just a cheap whore who used to sing at the Opera. *Used to.* You don't anymore, do you?'

'Liesel, that is enough—' began the Count.

A wildness had come into her eyes. 'No, Papa, I will not be silent. Since Mama died, you pretend she never existed. All of you do! How she used to *laugh* at you all . . . "insipid, vile creatures", she called you, and that is exactly what you are—'

Her father had left his seat.

Sibylla quickly rose. 'No, please, allow me.' She whispered into Liesel's ear and whisked her away before the Count reached them.

A disturbing, uncomfortable silence followed. Lady Gisela tried to break the silence by talking of the weather and Karl soon joined her. The Count remained silent and pensive.

Ernst and I discussed Liesel's outburst after dinner.

To my relief, he had not renewed his addresses to me since Rachel's death.

'An unusual dinner,' I remarked casually. 'What do you make of it?'

He accepted my offer of coffee with a smile. 'It certainly wasn't dull, was it?'

'I have noticed Liesel's moods are rather erratic. At first, I believed her to be a difficult child, but now I am not so sure. There might

150

be another reason for her behaviour.'

He raised a brow. 'Oh?'

I lowered my voice to a whisper. 'Do you know of any madness in the family?'

'Madness?' he murmured.

'Yes, madness. In my village back home, there was a boy I knew whose erratic behaviour often attracted attention. One day, he killed a dog and a special doctor came down from London to investigate. He declared the boy insane and took him away.'

'Madness in the family . . .'

'You have been here a long time,' I persisted. 'You would know, or you would have heard.'

'There was talk once, around the time of the Countess' death. The investigator believed madness had driven her up to the mountains in that weather.'

I nodded. 'Did the Countess behave unusually at times?'

He shrugged. 'She was a bored, spoilt princess who behaved like many royals who throw tantrums when they don't get what they want.'

'In public?'

'Yes, in public. It rather embarrassed the Count, I believe.'

Lady Gisela had spotted us. 'What are you two chattering about over there?'

Ernst looked embarrassed.

'We were speaking of the weather, my lady.'

'The weather,' Lady Gisela winked, 'is the best known disguise in the book.'

'Stop gaping at her, Mendel,' the lady admonished. 'But I don't blame you. Our Cristabel is such a pretty thing. *Any* man would consider himself fortunate to have her.'

Dara looked at me with a raised eyebrow and questioned me about it as she prepared to leave for her cottage.

'The Count always walks me home,' she smiled, 'he is so kind and attentive. Speaking of attentive, Ernst seems rather taken with you.' She sounded surprised and delighted. 'Do you return his feelings?'

'No,' I answered too quickly.

'Oh? But I saw *you* approach *him* this eve, did I not? I suppose we women must employ these devices to bring a male to heel.' She glanced at the approaching Count. 'It is so difficult to keep them interested sometimes. I do hope I shall be truly settled this year. My finger has been positively itching to wear a ring.'

The Count arrived.

I bad her good night.

She tilted my chin. 'Try and look a little happy about your success, won't you?'

'You are mistaken,' I said.

'I don't think so.' She smiled with quiet authority.

\* \* \*

I undressed and slipped into bed, thinking of the extraordinary events of one night. I tried to read in an effort to calm my mind, however, each member of the household rose up to haunt me.

It was an odd household, unlike any I had ever encountered, and yet why did I feel as though I belonged here?

The answer could not be explained. These walls seemed so familiar, yet I had never dreamed of them. I had never even imagined such a place.

It must have been about midnight when I heard the cry. Startled, I left my bed and looked out of the window. I could see a light in Liesel's tower. I hastily put on my slippers and grabbed a woollen wrap before leaving my room.

Liesel.

I hoped she had done nothing foolish. I hoped, for her sake, the madness in her blood could be controlled.

Now I understood why all the other governesses had left in a hurry and why the wage had been so generous. Liesel was not an ordinary girl. I should have noticed it sooner.

The castle held many secrets and my investigation could dislodge more than one unhappy skeleton. Were the answers worth the risk?

153

# CHAPTER NINE

The light from the tower glowed ominously in the darkness.

The cry had not been repeated and the household still slept. I knew I should return to my room but the light compelled me forward. I had a suspicion I would discover a secret tonight and my curiosity refused to yield.

Creeping along the silent corridors, the wind lashing the windows, I climbed up the winding steps to Liesel's room. The silence was unendurable. When I reached the top, I paused in the darkness, listening. I could hear a faint rustle of a skirt and a sigh. The rustle came closer. I drew further into the shadows but I had been seen.

Frau Bruns peered into the corridor. 'Who hides there?'

I stepped out slowly, feeling like a child who had been caught.

Her sharp eyes dissected me. 'You!'

'Yes, I heard the cry. Was it Liesel?'

She turned around. 'Come with me.'

I followed her inside the room that interested me most and yet repelled me at the same time. I knew this fascination had something to do with the Countess's portrait above the fireplace and the serpents engraved on the wall.

Frau Bruns pointed to the bed. 'She's sleeping now. I've sedated her.' I studied the sleeping, peaceful face on the pillow. There was no sign of the girl I had seen earlier tonight. 'Is she—'

'Mad?' Frau Bruns finished for me, guiding me away from the bed. 'The poor little thing has bad bloods, just like her mother.'

'The Countess was mad too?'

She glanced up at the beautiful woman in the portrait and nodded reluctantly. 'I knew there was something different about the little princess. She didn't cry and her moods were erratic. Her daughter, unfortunately, has inherited the same weakness.'

'What are you giving her?'

'Laudanum.' Her little brown eyes studied me. 'Now you know all of our secrets. Why have you come?'

'To teach Liesel, of course.'

'No, I think you are here for a very different reason.'

'I have to work,' I sighed. 'My family is dependent on me.'

'Ah, yes, your family. They are poor, aren't they?'

'I suppose they could be called poor.'

'But if you should marry well . . .'

I could see where this was leading and wished to put a stop to it. 'I have to go. You can be assured of my discretion, Frau Bruns.'

Weary with the evening's discoveries, I

walked back down the chilly passages in silence. I thought of Fräulein Suski and hoped Liesel wasn't responsible for her demise. And Rachel? No! She couldn't be.

But was she?

*      *      *

I began to treat Liesel differently after that night. She had to be handled with care and her tantrums carefully examined. The slightest provocation could send her into a fit of anger or of laughter.

We gathered outside in the courtyard to say farewell to Karl and Sibylla. I watched Sibylla with Liesel and marvelled at her influence over the child. She must know about Liesel's illness and yet she regarded her as a dear friend. Perhaps sensing the Count's negligence as a parent had driven her to fill the void the child needed so desperately.

I shouldn't really think of her as a child. She had changed dramatically since I had arrived and, dressed in the appropriate clothes with her hair pinned up, she might well pass for eighteen.

To my relief, the Baron did not attempt to talk to me. He merely smiled and waved as he climbed into their waiting conveyance. He would return to Vienna a rich widower, free of a wife whom he had once considered a hindrance. I hated to see him there, smug in his new security. Rachel's death had been proclaimed an accident. There would be no investigation and, in time, everyone would forget the pale, frightened girl who had so bravely confronted her negligent husband.

Except me. I would never forget Rachel or the manner of her death.

The day passed uneventfully. Frau Vetsera advised the family would be leaving the day after tomorrow and seemed surprised to learn I would be part of the travelling party. She expected me to be dismissed and because the Count had ignored her feelings on the subject, I had gone down further in her estimation. I registered the scorn in her eyes. She believed me to be some kind of adventuress who had come here to ensnare a rich lover or a husband.

I supposed Lady Gisela's open assessment of my love life didn't assist my cause.

She gazed at me pointedly when Karl and Sibylla had left. 'I hope you don't think dearest Karl had anything to do with the girl's death. He didn't. He's very distraught over the matter.'

I said nothing.

'Your silence condemns you, but let me assure you, accidents do happen and more frequently in the mountains.'

'Yes, this place seems to attract fatality.'

'That bitter tone doesn't suit one so young and pretty. Let me put your mind at rest, dear girl.' She removed a letter from inside one of her books. 'Karl gave me this to show to you. It wounded him to see you regard him as a suspect.'

The letter was thrust into my hands. Ingrid's timid shrug behind Lady Gisela confirmed she knew nothing about this letter.

'Read it aloud,' Lady Gisela commanded. 'I am interested to hear what it has to say again.'

*My dearest Karl, you made me the happiest woman in the world last night. I always knew we could be happy—given the chance. We owe a great deal to Cristabel. What a friend she has been to both of us! Thank you, darling. Your loving wife, Rachel.*

'There!' Lady Gisela chuckled. 'He's acquitted by his own wife.'

I did not want to raise the fact that probably none of us knew Rachel's handwriting to verify the authenticity of the note. Nor did I want to raise the possibility of his acting ability. What better way to ensure his innocence than by being the loving, devoted husband in the eyes of his own wife? He could have written the note himself!

I handed it back to Lady Gisela. She continued to press me for my opinion and to keep her quiet, I assured her of my new 'belief' in the Baron's innocence. She smiled her

158

satisfaction and offered me some of her sweets. I politely declined.

'I admire the English self-control. I suppose I should stop gorging one day, but I am too fond of my food. I shall envy you all in Vienna. Oh, the pastries! I grow faint just thinking of them.'

'Why don't you join us, Lady Gisela?'

'Oh, no. We are too comfortable here, aren't we, Ingrid?' Ingrid nodded hurriedly.

'And what do I care for all that noise in the city? Now, if I were young, pretty and *slim* like you, I might enjoy it,' she sighed. 'All those handsome soldiers . . . I shall be very disappointed if you are not snapped up there.'

'Lady Gisela, I am not searching for a husband.'

'Of course you are! What else is a girl to do but to hunt for a husband? Now if you were an old, plain maid like Ingrid, I shouldn't think your chances very high, but as you are, I wager you can make an advantageous match. And this year will be the most crowded of seasons. Have you heard of the exhibition?'

I said that I had not.

'It's to be in Vienna this May and since these legs render me somewhat infirm, I should like you to go and report back to me. I am interested in new findings.'

I promised I would write.

She studied me with those shrewd, merry eyes. 'Yes, I believe you will. A word of

159

warning, my dear, be wary of new and old acquaintances in our city of music. The season breeds the unscrupulous as well as the deserving.'

'I'll remember that.'

I moved forward to curtsy and she nodded abruptly, eager to dismiss emotional farewells. She had grown as fond of me as I had of her and I couldn't say whether I would see her again. It depended on how long the family planned to stay in Vienna.

Vienna. The magical city with its lively colours and beautiful music beckoned. I couldn't wait to get there, to start afresh. A change is what we needed and with the optimism of youth, I returned to my room.

*       *       *

We left the *schloss* at eight o'clock on a chilly, February morning. I awoke early and made one last tour of the castle, consigning each part to memory in case I should never return.

The portrait gallery filled me with a sense of loss. I couldn't describe the uncanny, almost haunting feeling when I paused at Conrad's painting. I had my own miniature of him yet it could not compare with the original. Those blue eyes wanted to convey something of importance to me. Perhaps it was a trick of the light or the way the artist had skilfully painted his eyes, but I certainly felt a connection.

I dismissed the fanciful notion the moment I heard Frau Vetsera's voice booming downstairs. She was conducting her own orchestra by organizing the household for the villa in Vienna. The staff had been selected for the annual event and I noticed more than one glum maid on my way down. They had not been chosen this year, evidently, and would have to spend the summer months confined to the mountains.

Our party seemed quite large to me. A line of carriages filled the courtyard and I saw Old Josef watching from the window in the gatehouse. His grave look unsettled me as much as his suspicions. I almost wished he hadn't confided in me. How could I possibly change matters? Why had he come to me with his doubts?

To my relief, Dara was not present at our departure. I didn't want to see her or her son, for I knew the sight of them standing there would haunt me during the journey.

Liesel was excited. 'Oh, miss, you'll love the villa and our gardens there even rival the palace!'

'A slight exaggeration,' her father advised with a smile. 'Would you favour us with your company, Miss Brown?'

I looked at Liesel for confirmation.

'Yes, you must come with us, miss. If you are with us, Papa won't lecture me as much.'

Frau Vetsera didn't approve of this

161

arrangement. She frowned at me.

Liesel laughed and leaned over to whisper, 'She's a horrid old woman. I don't know why Papa keeps her on.'

'She is very efficient, I daresay.'

'I suppose efficiency could be a reason,' she murmured. 'Are you efficient, miss? Is that why Papa keeps you on?'

She liked to tease and because I had recently learned of her illness, I allowed her to continue.

'Oma has to travel with Vetsera the vulture. I would have her here, but Papa says she's only a nurse and nurses travel with housekeepers and stewards. I wonder why he makes an exception for you, miss?'

I did not respond and she smiled slyly. I thought with panic, she knows! But how could she, unless my face betrayed my feelings? I tried to appear disinterested.

'I like you, miss. You are not like the others.'

'No? Why am I not like the others?'

'Because you just aren't. The others were never pretty. They never attracted men like you do. You must have some special power.'

'That is nonsense, Liesel.'

'Is it?' She pondered thoughtfully. 'I've never seen Ernst so enslaved before. The poor man thinks he has a hope of succeeding. He is very conceited.'

I smiled in spite of myself.

'He doesn't look it but he is. And I know why.'

She smiled secretly and refused to say any more on the subject. Ernst Mendel? What did she know about him? It was childish of her to leave me in suspense but since it amused her, I let it pass.

The Count returned. I waved to Lady Gisela and Ingrid on the landing and watched the castle fade from view as we rumbled down the drive. Old Josef still sat at the window of the gatehouse, silent, watchful. I remembered the same watchful look on the day I arrived and recalled his suspicions with a chill. He wouldn't believe the Count responsible for the mysterious deaths of his brother and wife unless . . . it was true?

I dismissed the ugly thoughts from my mind. How could I ponder them when the Count sat across from me inside the carriage, an attentive and charming companion? Liesel's silence evoked his loquaciousness and I found his knowledge and perception of the world so entertaining I scarcely noticed how quickly time escaped us.

The carriage was remarkably comfortable with its scarlet-coloured velvet seats. Liesel leaned in one corner, pretending to snooze or read her book, while the Count and I talked.

'We shall be going into your ancestors' country,' he said when we arrived to board the train at Zell.

Liesel scowled. 'What do you mean, Papa? I thought we were going straight to Vienna.'

'No, I have business in Innsbruck. It will delay our arrival a day or two.'

Liesel didn't look happy. 'It mustn't be very important business or you would have mentioned it. Must we go to Innsbruck now? Sibylla expects us to be in Vienna today.'

'Sibylla will have to wait.'

Liesel crossed her arms and remained petulant for the remainder of the journey. She refused to eat her lunch and merely stared out of the window.

I felt a minor discomfort knowing I should not be sitting with the family but with Frau Vetsera, Frau Bruns and Herr Mendel in the second cabin. When I mentioned this to the Count, he frowned.

'I'm afraid we are rather poor company, aren't we?'

'No, I did not mean to infer—'

He grinned. 'You are perfectly correct. Our Miss Brown is always correct, isn't she, Liesel?'

Liesel shrugged indifferently.

'No one can be always correct,' I said. 'It's an impossibility.'

'An impossibility? I thought the English didn't admit to impossibilities.'

'One must be sensible, my lord.'

He laughed. 'The practical Englishwoman speaks. Where is the impetuous German in your blood?'

164

'It's there,' I assured him with a smile.

'Is it? Perhaps tomorrow you will find it.'

'Tomorrow?'

He nodded. 'We are staying overnight in Innsbruck. There will be time for a visit to Mittenwald.'

'Mittenwald!' I couldn't conceal my excitement. To see Granny's home town, to meet my family there . . . oh, what could be more perfect?

'I trust,' the Count smiled, 'you will return more German than when you arrived.'

*      *      *

Liesel's mood improved with the promise of a trip to Mittenwald.

'I'm glad,' she sighed. 'I hate Innsbruck and it will amuse me to see where your grandmother grew up. Who are her family?'

She was not asking for names but for situations. 'They are merchants.'

'Merchants of what?'

'They make violins.'

'Violins!'

The awed look came into her eyes and I smirked. 'Yes, violins, but as you know, I failed to inherit the family talent.'

Liesel gave me a pitying look. 'You don't play the pianoforte *that* ill.'

'Perhaps not, but I am not musically gifted like you. I should think my family will be

165

delighted to meet you, a true musician.'

'Oh, do you think so? Really?'

'Yes, I do. *Really.*'

And for the first time in many days, I believe I saw a genuine smile on her face.

We made an early start and Frau Vetsera elected to come along with us.

'Why does that vulture have to come with us?' Liesel demanded. 'I don't want her to come.'

'Nor do I,' I admitted.

Liesel nodded. 'She doesn't like you. She tried to get rid of you. She thought you were Karl's lover.'

'Liesel—'

'Don't lecture me. I'm not a child and I know more about the world than you do.'

She refused to say any more and once again, I was left to wonder at her words.

Frau Vetsera made the arrangements for our excursion. She went over them at breakfast, Liesel pulling faces as she read the details out to us. By her austere look of displeasure, I understood she didn't consider me a fit chaperon for Fräulein von Holstein. She also knew I planned to locate my family there and, as they belonged to a lower class and therefore were unfit associates for the daughter of a Count, she decided to supervise the affair. Her unwanted presence put a damper on what promised to be a perfect day.

The weather was perfect, at least, and the

166

clear sunny day warmed our spirits as we travelled. The scenery compensated for the lack of conversation and by the time we reached Mittenwald, Frau Vetsera had learned of her unwanted presence. She made the error of trying to control our day and Liesel wouldn't have it.

'Don't dictate to us, Vetsera. We never asked you to come along.'

Frau Vetsera looked furious.

'You only came to snoop,' Liesel continued, 'and there's no point you trying to hide it. I suggest you leave us be or otherwise I will tell Papa you ruined Fräulein Brown's day.'

The threat worked and Frau Vetsera, somewhat reluctantly I might add, agreed to meet us in a couple of hours.

'That was very rude,' I said to Liesel, as we walked into the little town filled with charming houses, their painted façades and ubiquitous flower boxes setting the district ablaze with colour.

Liesel giggled. 'Admit you're relieved.'

I failed to suppress a smile and she seemed pleased with her efforts on my behalf. 'Now where is your family? I should like to meet them.'

I couldn't have felt happier to hear her say it and I knew instinctively this was going to be a special day. I had an opportunity to regain her friendship and I so much wanted to help this lonely and distressed girl. I believed her hereditary tendency might be halted in the right circumstances and loneliness and grief had driven her to it. One must act now to prevent a calamity.

We went into a pastry shop where Liesel enquired after the names of my relatives. The large, cheery woman behind the counter nodded enthusiastically. 'Everyone in town knows the Klotz family. You might try with the shop first. Hannah Klotz is never missing from the shop.'

We thanked her and followed her directions.

Liesel peered at a swinging sign in the distance. '*Klotz Family Violins* . . . that's it!'

I allowed her to seize my hand and we raced down the lane toward the sign.

Liesel peered inside the glass. 'There's people in there. I can see them working in the back room.'

'Liesel, step away from the window at once.'

'Well, are we going in or do we just intend to stand here all day?'

We had attracted attention. I saw a young man in a black suit coming toward us and my heart started to pound. Could he belong to Hannah Klotz?

Liesel went inside and opened the door for me. 'Oh, miss! Look at all the beautiful violins. What a pity I didn't get more money from Papa. We might have bought one today.'

The sales assistant looked disappointed.

I smiled in apology. 'I'm afraid we have not come to look at violins, sir. We are searching for a Hannah Klotz.'

He looked stunned. 'Hannah Klotz?'

'Yes. Do you know her?'

'Know her? She's my grandmother.'

'Your grandmother?' I repeated weakly.

'Then you're cousins or something,' Liesel interrupted excitedly, 'for this is Miss Brown and her grandmother was Frieda Klotz before she married. *Frieda Klotz*,' she emphasized, '*from England?*'

The shadow lifted and the man grinned, shaking my hand rather roughly. 'Forgive my slowness. I'm Hans Klotz and my grandmother is upstairs. Wait a moment and I'll call you up. She'll like the surprise. We've heard all about you and your brother Tommy.'

'Your brother Tommy,' Liesel mused, when he darted up the stairs, 'is he as good-looking as you?'

'Half the village girls are in love with him and he's only sixteen.'

'He sounds interesting.'

'He is but he's not—'

'—for me. I know how it works. The rich must marry the rich and the poor marry the poor. Do you think it will ever change?'

I didn't have time to answer for a triumphant Hans waved us up.

'My sister Elfie is with her. We've asked her to close her eyes for we've a surprise for her.'

I lifted my brows to Liesel. This had been extremely easy. I thought he might have asked more questions first.

Liesel revelled in the excitement and tiptoed behind me. Hans called for someone to watch the shop before guiding us into a smallish sunroom, decorated with white lace curtains and delicate furniture. A young, dark-haired girl sat reading to an old lady with a rug over her knees. When our party interrupted, the young girl who must be Elfie dropped her book and gasped. Before I could ask what was wrong, Hans prompted me forward.

'Oma, someone special is here to see you.'

The old hooded eyes peered at my person and a slow smile developed on those thin, grey lips. She opened her arms to me and I embraced her. She held me for quite some time before releasing me. Her green eyes, so like Granny's, were filled with tears of joy.

'You're Frieda's girl,' she murmured, placing her cool, thin hands to explore either side of my face. 'I always knew you'd be a beauty.'

Elfie grinned. 'Cousin Cristabel! How I've longed to meet you. You're quite a celebrity in our house.'

Hans frowned and Elfie immediately lowered her head in remorse. 'I'm afraid I talk too much. I always get in trouble about it. Won't you introduce your friend?'

The hands released me to beckon forward

Liesel. 'Come forward, young girl. I will hazard a guess at your identity.'

Liesel curtsied, a little overawed by the reception as I was.

Those shrewd green eyes squinted. 'You're a von Holstein, are you not?'

'Yes, ma'am. Liesel von Holstein.'

'The Count's daughter,' I quickly interrupted. 'Did Granny write to tell you of my assignment here in the mountains?'

Hannah smiled coyly. 'We were inseparable as children and now we've grown old, nothing much has changed. But now you're here . . . my prayers have been answered at last. If these old legs had permitted, I would have come to England to see you earlier. Tell me, how fares your grandmother? We never write each other of our ills. They make for tepid correspondence, hardly worth our effort.'

'Granny is well,' I assured her. 'She suffers with her legs, though.'

She nodded. 'A sign of old age but we shan't talk about that, shall we, Elfie, Hans? Not when we have such distinguished visitors.'

Liesel blushed and asked about the violins.

'Ah, perhaps Hans will give you a tour of the workshop while we catch up on family affairs. Elfie, please go down to the kitchens and inform cook. We have much to celebrate.'

Once alone, Hannah asked me news from home. I suspected she might have known the answers, but I replied to all of her questions and she nodded in satisfaction.

'Now I want to hear all about your assignment with the von Holsteins. 'What do you think of the castle in the clouds?'

'Enchanting . . . like a dream.'

'Well worthy of its title?'

'Well worthy.'

'And your employer? *Count Maximus Alexi Nikolaus von Holstein*, if I recall correctly?'

'Yes, that is he.'

'I can hear the warmth in your voice. Is he a handsome widower?'

I should have shown more care with my reply. 'I suppose one might call him handsome.'

'Is he handsome to you?'

When I didn't answer, she laughed. 'You must forgive me . . . the von Holsteins are interesting fodder. They seem to attract comment and scandal as a lamp attracts moths. Don't believe all you hear, my dear. There are many exaggerations in this world. Is the Count cruel to you?'

'No!' I said, maybe a little too vehemently.

'He is thought to have murdered his wife.'

'That's not true.'

'No? I am glad to hear it. Now, there's the bell for luncheon. I wager your companion will be as hungry as you are.'

Hans came to carry Granny Hannah into a room along the corridor. She smiled at me. 'Go on. I have a chair downstairs but they

172

don't fit in these tiny corridors so poor Hans has to carry me from room to room.'

'Yes, *poor me*,' Hans joked, 'I think you grow heavier each week, Granny.'

Liesel waited with Elfie outside and I followed them to the dining-room. Hans and Elfie tried hard to make Liesel feel welcome and she responded better than I expected. In fact, when luncheon was over, she did not want to leave. I smiled to myself, for yesterday, she had been in a hurry to get to Vienna. How quickly the youth changed their minds!

I found it difficult to say goodbye.

'You will come back,' Elfie made me promise.

'Of course I will. How can I ever forget this day?'

I hugged Hans before crouching beside Granny Hannah. She lifted my chin up to face her. 'Don't you stain that pretty face with tears now. Today has been a happy day, a day to remember, not a day to mourn.'

Liesel was thinking. 'If only Papa had come, we could have spent the night in Mittenwald.'

'There'll be another time,' Granny Hannah said in her wisdom. 'What a fine young woman you are, Liesel von Holstein. I am glad to have made your acquaintance.'

Liesel beamed and spontaneously kissed her on both cheeks. 'I shall never forget your kindness!'

We had stepped out onto the street when

Elfie came running after us. 'What is it?'

'Grandmother needs to see you again. She said it wouldn't take long.' I went inside while Elfie stayed with Liesel.

Hans shook his head apologetically. 'She is often forgetful.'

I assured him it didn't matter, though I had a vision of a very put out Frau Vetsera tapping her fob watch outside the inn.

Granny Hannah looked relieved to see me. 'I thought they wouldn't catch you in time.'

'Elfie is quick,' I laughed, and sat down beside her.

She studied my face intently, a slow smile on her lips. It was a smile of recognition and I wondered at it for she had never seen me before. Mother had thought of having a photograph done once but the thought had never materialized. Did I resemble Granny Frieda in her youth perhaps?

'My child.' She pressed my hand urgently. 'Do you have the bracelet?'

'The bracelet?'

'The one your grandmother gave you. The one she found.'

'Yes, I have it. It's at the hotel in Innsbruck.'

She nodded. 'Have you worn it yet?'

I said I thought wearing it might be a mistake.

'Why do you think that?'

'I know I am being overly sensitive, but the serpent forms part of the von Holstein coat of

174

arms and I didn't want to presume—'

A low chuckle erupted. 'Do you think it might have belonged to them once?'

'It's certainly possible. It must have belonged to some noble family.'

'And you don't want to wear it because you don't want to be called a thief?'

'Y-yes and . . .'

'And?' she prompted.

I shook my head with a smile. 'It's silly, really.'

Those green eyes peered into mine. 'What is silly?'

'The feeling . . .'

'What feeling?'

'The feeling I get when I look at the bracelet.'

'You shiver,' she smiled. 'So you should. It is worth a great deal more than anyone will ever know. You must keep it safe.'

'I have it hidden amongst my clothes. Why did Granny keep it a secret all those years?'

Granny Hannah smiled. 'You must ask your grandmother that. I will let you in on a secret. The bracelet,' she whispered, 'has special powers.'

'Where does it come from? Do you know?'

She leaned back in her chair, a faint light in her eyes. 'Oh yes, I know where it comes from.'

'You won't tell me?'

'I cannot. You must discover its origin for

yourself.'

'Is it so important that I do so?'

I had asked the question before I remembered Granny gently persuading me to do the very same.

'The bracelet has a history . . . a dark history. You sense it too.'

'Perhaps I should sell it?'

'But you won't. The bracelet is safe with you. While it remains with you, you are also safe.'

'Safe from what?'

She smiled mysteriously. 'Soon, the bracelet must make an appearance into the world.'

'An appearance?'

'It will look charming on your arm.'

'But I cannot—people would think—'

'There will be comment, but I promise you will not be called a thief.'

'You know the owner, don't you?'

'The owner,' she chuckled, 'is you. While the bracelet is in your possession, it belongs to you.'

'But if Granny Frieda found it, it must have been someone else's. Someone who lost it and now seeks it.'

She shook her head. 'No. Those who seek it are not entitled to ownership.'

'How can I be entitled to it?'

'Because your grandmother bequeathed it to you. She would have impressed its importance to you then, but she felt it was too

I disappeared into the background, overawed by the family's summer residence. I thought the villa would be a quarter of the size and imagined a cosy, friendly atmosphere. This atmosphere boasted the rigid ideals of convention and class distinction in a dimension the castle never had.

The Castle of Dreams; I smiled whimsically.

Yes, indeed it had been a castle of dreams to me.

\*         \*         \*

I did not feel so gloomy the next day.

How could I, surrounded by such beauty? After breakfast in my room, Liesel insisted on showing me the villa. She spoke in English and through her laborious effort, I recognized the promising young woman I had glimpsed in Mittenwald. I only prayed the season here would not spoil her development.

'Does the villa have a name?' I asked, as we began the tour from the parlour downstairs.

'Yes,' she giggled. 'We call it "big villa" because there is another "little villa" hidden in the gardens. The "little villa" was built first and my great-great-grandfather Rollo-Josef completed the "big villa" a few years before Louis XVI of France lost his head. He had been to the glorious Versailles, you see, and wanted his villa to rival its magnificence.'

I nodded as Liesel pointed out the

181

similarities in the black and white tiled flooring, the gilt work present in each of the elaborate gold and white salons and in the paintings.

'When the revolution began, many *chateaux* were looted in France and the priceless furniture and paintings disappeared. Some were destroyed but many of them found a new home in the finer houses of Europe. Rollo-Josef made it his private mission to collect many of these missing treasures to furnish his new villa. Come . . . look at this writing table. It was said to have belonged to Louis XIV himself.'

At Liesel's invitation, I touched the ebony top. It felt cool and smooth beneath my fingers. 'It's not used now?'

'This one is just for show. We use the other pieces around the house, though.'

Those 'other' pieces she dismissively referred to would be the pride of Munroe Manor.

'You look pale, miss. Do I boring you?'

'*Bore*,' I corrected with a smile. 'No, you do not bore me, Liesel. I just never expected you would—err—'

'Be so rich?' she suggested triumphantly. 'Was that right, miss?'

'Yes. Your English is coming along nicely.'

'I'm glad,' she nodded, 'I want to please Papa. Sometimes . . .' She shook her head. 'No, it is too—how do you say?—*difficult* to say in

182

English.'

'Then say it in German,' I prompted, interested to hear what she wanted to say.

She considered before shaking her head again. 'No, better left unsaid, I think. Let's go, now, miss. I want you to see the ballroom and the gardens.'

The servants were removing the sheets off the chandeliers in the ballroom. They all paused and stared when we entered.

I had never seen such a beautiful room. The entire eastern wall was a fretwork of mirrors, designed so the sun would stream through the western glass doors, bounce on the mirrors and set the entire room ablaze with light.

'It's a poor copy of the Hall of Mirrors in Versailles,' Liesel murmured, 'but it's the pride of Vienna. An invitation to a ball here is much sought after.'

'When do you hold the ball?'

'We have many where we have dinner with dancing. The first will be—say—in a *fretnight* to let people know the von Holsteins are in town. You smile, miss. Did I do wrong?'

'It's *fortnight*.'

She nodded in concentration. '*The first will be in a fortnight.* Is that right, miss? I am good at English, no?'

'Yes, but we shall have to work on your grammar,' I said, in my strict governess voice, conscious of the servants watching us. 'The gardens look beautiful. Shall we go out there?'

183

I never imagined any garden could be so beautiful. The design, rather than being the symmetrical and orchestrated perfection of so many palaces, instead favoured a new style. Or perhaps it belonged to an old exotic custom where a garden intended to convey the beauty and freedom of the outdoors. I was certain in such a place one could find the solution to any problem.

The garden boasted several arbours and rusting gates, overgrown hedges and weathered stone benches, all surrounded by a glorious array of flora and fauna.

'The summer blooms are coming.' Liesel snapped a rosebud from a nearby plant. 'We have a greenhouse too by the "little villa". It makes certain the villas have flowers all year round, even in winter.'

'I thought you spent your winters in the mountains?'

She shrugged. 'Sometimes we change. Sometimes we spend summer there and winter here. I wanted to spend winter here . . . not at the castle.' She shivered. 'There are too many unpleasant memories at the castle. You do call it a castle in English, no?'

'There you two are,' said a voice, which caused my heart to flutter.

'Papa! I have showing the gardens to Miss Brown as you said I should.'

'I am showing or I have *shown*,' he smiled. 'Your English is *show*ing a rapid improvement,

184

Liesel.'

She beamed.

And what does Miss Brown think of our villa?'

'Magnificent,' I breathed in answer.

'There's a word for you, Liesel. *Magnificent.* Our English tutor is rather magnificent, isn't she?'

Liesel looked confused and her father advised her she had a visitor in the parlour.

'A visitor!'

She raced off and I watched her go.

'You seem very pleased, Fräulein Cristabel, as you should be. You've made a remarkable change in my daughter.'

I stared up at his handsome, smiling face, wishing I didn't feel so gauche in his company. 'I hardly think I have made the difference, my lord. Liesel has always been that girl underneath. She only needed encouraging.'

He nodded. 'I followed you out here for two reasons: one to inform Liesel of her visitor and the other to talk to you.'

'Talk to me?' I echoed weakly.

'Yes. Things need not change between us. I value your friendship, Fräulein Cristabel.'

I couldn't look at him. 'As I value yours, but—'

'No buts.'

'There has to be buts. It wouldn't be wise for you to pursue friendship with me.'

'Why? If I wish it, it will be so.'

185

I smiled. 'It is easy for you to do as you please without fear of consequences.'

He studied my face, a faint smile on his lips. 'What consequences do you fear?'

'It wouldn't be polite to say.'

'You fear I will ask you to be my mistress.'

'No!' I denied it, though I imagined the rising colour in my face gave me away. 'Why should you? You already have a—'

'I already have a . . . ?'

'Nothing, my lord.'

He turned away. I thought he had left until he said, 'Fräulein Cristabel, will you promise me something?'

'It depends what the promise entails, my lord.'

A brief smile showed on his lips. 'I want you to promise me you will always tell me the truth. I want you to promise me you will never lie to me.'

'I think I can safely promise that.'

'Safely,' he grinned, 'the English are always very safe.'

'It is in our nature to be so.'

'But you are not all English. Tell me, did you find your other self in Mittenwald?'

'I don't know what you mean.'

'I think you do.'

'There is your Austrian arrogance professing I know what I know I don't know.'

He laughed. 'That was an ambiguous sentence for an English tutor.'

186

'I suppose it was,' I laughed back, our old camaraderie returning.

'There should be no restraints on friendship,' he said, after a silence. 'If I command it, it shall be so.'

'You can't command everything as lord of the castle.'

'Can't I?' His lips twisted. 'We von Holsteins don't recognize the word "can't". It doesn't belong in our vocabulary.'

'Then it must be put in because convention must be obeyed.'

'You are determined to thwart me.'

'No, I am determined to remind you of your duty.'

'My duty to convention?'

'Yes. There's not many counts I know who would pursue friendship with a paid employee in their house.'

'Unless they had ulterior motives?' he suggested, and I blushed. 'How many counts do you know, Fräulein Cristabel? I am aware of only one.'

'You are being ridiculous. I said it in a manner of speaking.'

' "In a manner of speaking . . ." ' He grinned. 'Convention is meant to be broken. I promise, if you agree to be my friend, I won't ask you to be my mistress. But if you won't agree to be my friend, then who knows what I might be inclined to do.'

I gazed at the man and instead of the

polished count, I saw the wild warrior of old
. . . Conrad, seated on his medieval destrier
with his medieval arrogance.

To confirm my thought, he said, 'I could
carry you off and who would be able to rescue
you?'

'We don't live in the dark ages,' I reminded
him.

'But they are never very far from us,' he
warned. 'History is prone to repeat itself.'

'Not in this case.'

'Especially so in this case.'

'Will you never give up?'

'No. I have never had an English governess
as friend before and the idea amuses me.'

'And counts always get what they want?'

He lifted his shoulders in a helpless fashion.
'I suppose I have no choice but to agree.
But Frau Vetsera—'

'Don't concern yourself with Frau Vetsera.
If I am not mistaken, I am still the lord of the
castle.'

'You will always be lord of the castle even if
you didn't have one,' I smiled.

'You see,' he said, 'the idea amuses you too.'

I watched him go, elated, excited, hopeful
. . . until I saw the faces at the window. It was
Liesel and Sibylla. They must have seen us
talking together and I registered the look on
Liesel's face as one of betrayal.

Suddenly feeling like Judas in the Garden of
Gethsemane, I quickly returned to my room,

wondering how I could mend the damage I had been so careful to avoid.

*      *      *

I soon learned life at the villa did not resemble life in the mountains. At the *schloss*, where the family rarely received visitors, convention could be ignored: in Vienna, it could not.

The day after Sibylla arrived, the villa received caller after caller. Liesel was inattentive at her lessons and still regarded me with suspicion. I wanted to ease her mind over what I believed had been insinuated to her by Sibylla. I had been seen 'laughing' with the Count in the gardens, scarcely the behaviour of a respectable female servant in his house. Again, I felt the sting of my appearance. Now if I looked like Frau Vetsera, there would be no fuss.

Sibylla came to the villa every day. I suppose it was her duty, since the Count did not have many female relatives and his daughter was too young to act as hostess. She smiled graciously whenever I encountered her, however, I felt she had cooled towards me.

I almost expected her reserve because when we first arrived, Frau Vetsera followed me up to my room to specially inform me 'things were done differently at the villa'. By this, she inferred meals would now be sent to my room and I would not be invited to dine with the family unless asked to do so.

Liesel's withdrawal hurt me the most. She diligently attended her lessons each morning, as her father had dictated, but treated my attempts at friendliness with cool civility. I wondered whether she had been instructed by Sibylla to do so.

Frau Bruns also suffered. She would shake her head and say 'no good, no good,' and I would calm her and say, 'Miss Liesel will return to her old self. We only have to wait.'

As time went by, I doubted my own words. Instead of putting her energies into developing a friendship with me, she transferred them to her lessons and began to make rapid progress.

I understood her reasoning: the sooner she developed her English, the sooner I would be gone.

To make matters worse, the Count developed a habit of dropping by on our lessons on one pretence or another. Liesel behaved warmly to me on these occasions and resumed her cool civility when he left. Nothing was ever said of these visits, but I believe they added to her dislike of me. She wanted to please her father and regarded any friendship of his beyond the confines of their family jealously.

When it became evident these visits distressed her, I decided to speak to the Count.

It was difficult to speak to the Count these

days as Frau Vetsera informed me he was too busy to be disturbed by trivialities.

'Leave your concern with me, Fräulein Brown,' she said to me on my fifth attempt. 'I will see that he gets it.'

'No, thank you, Frau Vetsera.'

She lifted a brow. 'Is it a private concern?'

I refused to answer and she studied me in her favourite condescending manner. She must be aware of the Count's frequent visits to the schoolroom and considered it to be my fault. I envisaged her saying, 'How dare you behave in this *vulgar* manner?'

My suspicion was close to the reality. Those cool eyes studied me, as one would an insect on one's arm. 'May I remind you of your position here? A governess should not seek private audiences with their male employer. Whatever your concern is, I am sure I can help you. I have served this family for twenty years.'

I forced a smile. 'It doesn't matter, Frau Vetsera. I will see the Count another time.'

'Who wants to see me?' said a faintly amused voice.

Frau Vetsera flushed crimson. 'The English governess, my lord.'

'Why was I not informed?'

I could have laughed at the arrogance in his voice; however, Frau Vetsera's pathetic attempt to explain proved even more diverting.

'I-I thought you said you disliked interruptions this time of the day.'

He cocked a brow. 'Do I? I don't remember discussing my preferred interruptions with you and Miss Cristabel is definitely a *preferred interruption.*'

Frau Vetsera's eyes bulged open in shock.

'Thank you, Helga, that will be all.'

'Y-yes, my lord.'

When the door to his study closed, I said, 'That wasn't wise.'

He drifted to the chair at his desk, completely unperturbed by the incident. 'I don't believe you would have taken on the dragon unless you especially wanted to see me.'

I read the humour in his eyes. 'It might be funny to you, but I shall suffer afterwards.'

'Cristabel slays the dragon in order to see the lord of the castle . . .'

'*Please* be serious.'

'I am deadly serious,' he replied earnestly, 'and flattered my friend deigns to visit me in my lair.'

'Unlike you, I have to answer for my actions.'

'Unlike you, I am loyal to my friends.'

I sat down in the hope of recovering some formality.

He continued to lean against the back of his chair, a strange smile on his face. 'You look severe.'

'I am merely trying to work you out.'

'And am I proving to be such a difficult

subject?'

'Well, yes. One minute, you *demand* me to think of you as a humble friend and in the same breath betray the arrogance of your breed.'

'My *breed*,' he laughed. 'I am honoured to feature so frequently in your thoughts. Do you have a name for my *breed* yet or do you require further study to perform an accurate diagnosis?'

'Conundrums need no further study unless I have more information.'

'Then I shall give you what you require. *The wicked lord of the castle has his brother killed in a shooting accident so he can claim the title and fortune for himself.*'

I tried not to laugh. It sounded so absurd.

'*Then the lord of the castle, unhappy with his then present wife, decides to remove her in the most complex way imaginable. He is acquitted of the murder but the truth remains hidden in a grave never to be disturbed.* There. I have raised two accounts, transmitted as faithfully to the popular version as possible.'

He turned away, the smile disappearing from his face. The change occurred suddenly and, as I gazed up at him, there was no sign of the flippant man who had raised such a dire subject. Yes, he knew of the rumours circulating about him all too well. And the reminder of them had changed him. Why?

'My lord, I came to talk to you about Liesel.'

193

'Liesel,' he echoed, as though the reminder of her was painful to him.

'She so desperately wants your approval.'

'Does she?'

I stood up, furious at his indifference. 'She tries hard to win your favour and is crushed every time you ignore her. If you would only show a little more interest in her—'

'Do I not visit the schoolroom each morning?'

'That is true,' I agreed reluctantly.

'But you do not believe it is Liesel who attracts me there?'

'I can hardly answer that.'

'You could try.'

He was toying with me, like a cat does with a mouse, and received the cat-like satisfaction of knowing I was trapped.

We stared at each other in silence, he amused and I helplessly irate. Why had I begun this conversation? I should have recognized the futility of doing so.

He met my gaze steadily. And how does my relationship with my daughter affect *you*, Fräulein Cristabel?'

The heat rushed to my face. 'It affects me because I care about her and her future.'

He frowned, as though he expected a different answer and did not like the one he received.

'I know in a matter of weeks I shall leave and—'

194

'Leave?'

'Your daughter is making such rapid progress, I believe you will have no need of me beyond the season.'

'Your contract was for a year.'

'Yes, but Liesel—'

'Your contract was for a year,' he repeated. 'The von Holsteins fulfil their obligations.'

'Even when there is no need to do so?' I didn't wait for his nod to continue. 'Then I release you of your obligation. When Liesel is proficient in her new language, I shall have to leave because there will be no more use for me.'

'I think there will always be a use for you,' he murmured, with a faint smile. 'In a matter of months, you have made a distinct impression in true English fashion. Aunt Gisela cannot stop informing me of your special qualities; Liesel has never shown more promise than she does now; Ingrid has a champion and a model to look up to, Herr Mendel, my imminent secretary, is quite in love with you . . . as is cousin Karl, I wager. Did you ever expect to make such a grand conquest?'

'You grossly exaggerate my talents, my lord.'

'I never exaggerate.'

'In this case, I fear you do. The impressions you refer to are all temporary and will be forgotten the moment I leave.'

'Then we shall make another bargain, shall

we? I may release you when the time arrives if *you* honour your promise.'

'Promise?'

'Did you not promise to consider me as a friend?'

'I suppose I did.'

'And do friends call each other by titles?'

'Not generally, but—'

'Friends also do not hide secrets from one another. What else did you wish to discuss with me? The shadow behind your eyes alludes to it.'

I was startled he could read me so well.

A brow lifted. 'Well? I assure you, I can keep a secret.'

'There *is* a matter on my mind,' I began tentatively, 'but I should hardly voice it.'

He waved a regal hand. 'You have my permission to do so.'

'It concerns Rachel.'

He returned to his desk. 'Ah . . . a grievous concern.'

'I believe she was murdered.'

He studied me closely. 'And what gives you that impression?'

'She confided in me her fear of her husband. Do you remember the night she arrived at the chapel?'

'The chapel is a place I can never forget.'

'I was sitting at the back with Ingrid. I don't know if you saw your cousin's face, but I did: he looked murderous.'

196

'And you believe his murderous look turned into a murderous action?'

I shrugged. 'I don't know, but the manner of her death does seem strange when one considers she was an unwanted wife.'

I sensed his eagerness to dispense with the subject; however, because of our recent declaration of friendship, he could not dismiss me as easily as before.

'Do you have any other information?'

'Only what I feel. I knew Rachel was afraid. She feared she would be put aside and once believed I could be a reason.'

He reached inside a drawer to produce an ebony box. 'Do you mind if I smoke?'

I said no, watching him light his cigar.

'These matters always require a cigar. Where were we? Ah . . . my cousin, the Baron. Cousin Karl has a certain reputation where women are concerned. He pursues them wherever he goes. I cannot agree with his tactics to keep his young wife hidden for these unscrupulous pleasures—'

I stared at him. 'You *knew* about Rachel?'

He smiled. 'Nothing escapes my attention, and nor should it as I am the head of the family.'

'But you acted so . . .'

'Shocked? I thank you for your commendation of my acting abilities. Yes, I knew of Karl's little secret. He took particular care to keep the matter hidden from me, for

197

what reason, I cannot say. He had always boasted about making a grand match. ' "A princess of Hapsburg for me, no less", he used to joke but the princesses of Hapsburg would not consider a penniless baron and Karl knew this. He had to marry, for financial reasons, and his choice fell, unfortunately, on this young English girl. Had I learned of the elopement earlier, I would have interfered.'

'You considered her unfit to be his wife?'

'The disapproval in your voice does your friend credit; however, I am appalled you would rate my judgement so poorly.'

'You said *unfortunately*. What else was I supposed to think?'

'Like a friend, I would hope.'

'Even friends have their differences.'

'Your wisdom astounds me.'

'*Please* go on.'

'Since the matter is close to your heart, I will. I would have interfered in the match for Rachel's benefit, not Karl's.'

'Then you know your cousin is unscrupulous?'

'Unscrupulous, yes: a murderer, no. I was with him that day on the lake. He wanted a loan of money so he never left my side, not even for a moment. Together we found Rachel, and by then, it was too late to save her.'

I couldn't tell him of my vision of Rachel trapped beneath that frozen lake, her face bewildered as she stared up at her death.

'I dare say Karl was the reason why you neglected to join our tea party?'

'He was one of the reasons.'

'And the other?'

'The general complaint.'

He frowned. 'Such a complaint should not raise itself between friends. Since you believe your time will be shortened with us, I want you to promise to accept any invitation I give you. And that includes our fête on Saturday. You did receive your invitation?'

I nodded.

'Do you have something suitable to wear?'

I nodded again. 'My former charge was very generous.'

'You consider yourself fortunate to be the recipient of discarded clothes?'

'One must be in my position.'

'How old was your former charge?'

'Miss Emily Munroe is three years younger than I.'

'And you are still friends?'

'Yes. I have had one letter from her.'

He smiled. 'And yet, I don't believe her clothes matched what you have now.'

I blushed at the compliment. 'I should have explained. My grandmother reworked everything Emily gave me.'

'Your grandmother sounds like a remarkable woman.'

'She is. I miss her sorely.'

199

'Is that why you're eager to leave us?'

'I am not eager to leave you.'

He smiled at the *you.*

'I didn't mean—'

Tilting my chin up to face him, he murmured, 'Of course you didn't.'

I swallowed at his proximity. He was so close I could smell his cologne and its scent swept me away into a world of my own fantasy. The best I could do was to focus on his cravat. 'You should give your valet a bonus, my lord, that design is a work of art.'

Instead of looking down, he took my hands in his, smiling at my obvious discomfort.

'Cristabel . . .'

'Oh, Max!' I flung my arms around his neck and hid in the paradise of his warm neck. I knew the moment couldn't last; perhaps that's why I held on so tightly, shutting my eyes, unwilling to return to reality.

His hand began to stroke my hair. A sweet burning sensation overcame me. It was such a gentle move, hardly passionate, but it meant so much to me.

I wanted him and I didn't care how.

'I'm sorry.' I drew away, terrified by my own thoughts. 'I—I shouldn't have done that.'

'Done what?' he asked softly.

I headed for the safety of the door, lingering a moment longer. I wanted to go and yet, I wanted to stay. I betrayed my uncertainty by stealing another glance at him.

His dark-blue eyes seemed to penetrate my soul.

I fled, lest I betrayed myself again.

*           *           *

A feverish excitement pervaded the villa.

The first ball of the season. The winter chill had left the air as the beauty of spring began to bloom around us. The warmer weather seemed to affect everyone's mood and I revelled in this fact.

Frau Vetsera, though she still disapproved of me, could be seen smiling at her post as she directed the arrangements for the ball. Sibylla came each day to supervise and, in the furore, forgot I was only the tutor and assigned various tasks to me. Liesel, the one who mattered to me, behaved like any girl before her first formal ball.

'Miss!' She rushed up to me, completely oblivious of her treatment of me these last few weeks. 'Papa says I am to be at his side to welcome the guests. Isn't that wonderful? And my ball gown has just arrived. Do you want to see it?'

I said I would be delighted to and followed her as she skipped gaily up the stairs to her room.

'Sibylla helped me choose it. It's my first real ball gown and it's all mine.'

I remembered she had often worn

something from her mother's wardrobe.

She led me to her bed. 'Here it is. What do you think?'

Beside the opened box lay an elaborate ball gown of cream and pink, the delicate shade of cream a perfect choice for Liesel's magnolia complexion. The gown was simple in design and suited a young girl of fifteen. I touched a row of tiny pink embroidered roses. 'I think it's beautiful, and you will look beautiful in it.'

'Do you think I'll look like Mama in it?'

She was staring into nothing, hugging herself with the vision.

'I think you look very much like your mother, in the dress or out of it.'

Her face softened. 'Do you really? I've been—what's the English word—*unkind* to you, miss. I thought you . . .'

I knew what she thought. 'No, Liesel. I am not an adventuress and I did not come here to seek your father's favour.'

'I thought so.' She tapped her lips. 'What are you wearing, miss? Do you have a dress?'

I told her about the red ball gown I had last worn in London. 'It sounds lovely. Can I see it?'

We went into my room and I took it out of its box.

'You smile, miss. You are remembering the last time you wore it, no? A young man, perhaps?'

I almost mentioned Hugo, then thought

better of it.

She giggled. 'Do say, miss Does Herr Mendel have a rival?'

'Liesel—'

'Oh, I know you don't like him but he still likes you. I see it in his eyes when you pass. *Please* tell me about your English lover.'

'Gentleman,' I corrected. 'A respectable woman has no lover but her husband.'

'*Gentleman*,' she tried. 'Who is he? Handsome, no? Rich, no?'

'Rich and handsome,' I conceded.

'And this is not good, no?'

'No. He was a cousin of my former charge Emily—and Emily was in love with him.'

'This man . . . this . . .'

'Hugo,' I offered.

'Hugo, he were in love with you?'

'*Was* and I don't think it was love but infatuation. I would say he has forgotten me by now.'

'And this bothers you not?'

'Not really. I don't think we should have dealt well together.'

'But you miss the idea of him, no?'

'Maybe the "idea of him",' I smiled.

She touched the dress. 'When you wear this, maybe you find another handsome man here in Vienna. There many, some bad, some good. And all the men, they not take their eyes off young pretty Englishwoman in red dress.'

I laughed. 'Liesel, I do believe you are

203

fantasizing matters. In any case, I shall only stay an hour or two. Governesses should not socialize with their employer's guests.'

She frowned. 'I suppose you are right, miss. You are always right.'

'Governesses,' I grinned, 'are known to be right. It is their fortune as well as their misfortune.'

'Do governesses go to balls in England?'

'Not many of them.'

'But you went and now you come to this one.'

'I was fortunate.'

She smiled thoughtfully. 'You are pretty, that is why, miss. Do you have other ball gowns beside the red one?'

'No. This is my only ball gown.'

'Then you must have the maids press it for you.'

'I will,' I promised.

*         *         *

It happened the following day, on the morning before the ball.

I went downstairs early, helping wherever I could. When the ladies retired to their bedchambers for an afternoon nap, I followed their example. We would all need to be fresh when the guests started to arrive.

I walked up the grand staircase and along the corridors to my room. From the morning's

204

boisterous activity, the house seemed very quiet, uncannily quiet. I smiled, knowing the silence should help me to sleep.

As I turned into the last corridor, I began to suspect.

My door was open: someone had been in my room. I thought the maids must have done so, to deliver the newly pressed dress, and had forgotten to shut the door.

The hope died the moment I entered the room.

For there, on a pile on the floor, was the shredded remains of my red gown.


# CHAPTER ELEVEN

I sat down in horror.

Who could have done it? Why?

My immediate suspicions fell on Liesel. I had only shown the dress to her. She had asked about it. But why would she do such a terrible thing?

She didn't want me to go. She didn't want me to attract the attention of her father . . . or any man. It was obvious in her remarks to me.

I heard a noise in the corridor. I rushed outside and my ashen face must have startled the housemaids for they all followed into my room, equally horrified by the ruin of my only ball gown.

This commotion soon alerted the head maid who came expressly to my room. She looked at the dress on the floor and began to question the maids. Each of them attested to their innocence. The maid who had delivered my newly pressed dress *swore* she had closed my door on her way out.

The matter deeply distressed the head maid. She sent one of the maids running down to Frau Vetsera's room.

Frau Vetsera was as puzzled at the rest of us. For a brief moment, I thought she could have done it. But such a method didn't suit her disposition. She would employ other tactics; shredding a gown would never have occurred to her. It was a hateful, selfish thing to do—it was the behaviour of a moody adolescent.

Liesel.

I refused to believe it, not after our talk yesterday. Yet, someone had done it and all the evidence pointed to Liesel.

This occurred to Frau Vetsera when one of the maids said she had seen Miss von Holstein in the corridor earlier. We established the time, and were satisfied as to the identity of the culprit, Frau Vetsera left the room, the troubling facts of Liesel's involvement overshadowing her delight at my inability to attend the ball. How could one go to a ball without a ball gown?

I glanced at my dressing table where Liesel had left a red silken flower to weave into my hair. I was completely duped by her performance. She resented me; she resented the attention her father bestowed upon me: she slashed the dress.

I bent down to retrieve the pieces, recalling the one and only time I had worn it. I thought of Hugo and the events of that night. It seemed so long ago, a lifetime away.

Frau Vetsera returned as I bagged the last piece. She shook her head and said it was a 'terrible' business and that the Count wished to see me.

'The Count?'

She nodded gruffly. 'He is with Miss von Holstein in the library.'

'You informed him of the affair?' I thought she would have done so *after* the ball and not before.

She didn't answer and I wondered about it as I went down to the library. Liesel's hysterical voice floated into the corridor.

'I didn't do it, Papa! How many times do I have to tell you?'

'You're a consummate liar, like your mother. I will ask you one more time . . .'

I listened to the angry voices inside. Two volatile von Holsteins together. Dare I interrupt?

Taking a deep breath, I knocked and entered the room.

Liesel turned her stricken face to me. 'I *didn't* do it! You believe me, don't you, miss?'

'Don't allow that penitent face to distort your judgement,' the Count warned me. 'It's in her blood to lie, a hereditary trait from her mother.'

I looked from one to the other, unsure of the truth. What mattered most was my answer. Whether Liesel had committed the crime or not, (which I believed she had), it would serve none of our interests to pursue the matter at this time.

Liesel's violet eyes pleaded, *begged* for mercy.

I turned back to the Count. 'I believe in her innocence, and even if she is not innocent, I don't think she *intended* to do it. It is not the Liesel I know.'

If the Count was surprised with my answer, Liesel was even more so. She grasped my hand, fervently assuring me of her innocence. When her father dismissed her from the room, she let go of my hand and I registered the gratitude in her eyes.

'You are too kind to her,' her father murmured. 'I know my daughter, Miss Brown. I know what she is capable of and how she tries to hide it.'

'I . . . er . . . did hear a rumour of madness in the family.'

A faint smirk appeared on his lips. 'Did you? You are quite a sleuth, I'll warrant.'

'Nosy is what my mother calls it.'

He nodded. 'Then there is no need for me

to repeat myself. Liesel has the same blood as her grandfather. We are not yet sure how it will affect her but the madness is there, just as it was there in her mother, Malena. I had hoped Liesel would remain unscathed but the tainted blood flowing through her veins is strong.'

'It might be strong,' I said, 'but surely, there are ways to combat it?'

'There is no medication for this strain of madness. We tried a dozen on Malena and in the end, the only thing that managed to sedate her was laudanum.'

'Laudanum . . . Frau Bruns—'

'Yes. Frau Bruns looks after Liesel like she did Malena. She has witnessed three strains of the madness and assures me Liesel's case is only minor. Minor is defined by sudden bursts of anger, severe mood swings and memory loss. What you witnessed just now was one of those memory losses. She cut your dress and in her insanity, the incident is removed from her mind as though it never happened.'

I mentioned the conversation I had with Liesel in the morning.

He nodded. 'Her madness does not render her maliciously evil, at least, I hope not. I have been monitoring her behaviour closely and recording the results. There is a doctor here in Vienna who is an expert on these matters. Liesel is one of his patients through my notes. It is imperative everything concerning Liesel is recorded and that is why Frau Vetsera informed me of your dress.'

I saw the pain wash over his face, thinly concealed by a smile. 'Now you know our struggles with the family madness, we shall proceed to the matter of your ball gown. You will be compensated for the loss of it—no, I insist—and Sibylla has kindly offered to lend you one of hers. She heard of the incident at the same time I did and rushed off to her room to select a few choices for you. Those choices will be waiting in your room when you return.'

I didn't know what to expect as I made my way up the grand staircase. I certainly didn't expect my room to be full of dresses and a note waiting on my dresser.

*Dear Miss Brown*
*Sorry to hear of your dilemma. I trust one*
*of these will appeal to you.*
    *Sibylla*

'Oh, dear me,' sighed one of the maids, 'what will you choose? This is like a dream!'

'I don't know . . .'

A dream it was. I examined one gown at a time and finally narrowed the choices down to two. Surprisingly, they both fitted. I considered the first one, in a delicate shade of mauve, to be a safe gown and one which would not offend my betters in its simplicity. I should have made my choice then, but the other kept reminding me of its presence, *tempting* me to wear it.

The unusual royal-blue material, a combination of gauze and another I couldn't identify, shimmered in the light, its many layers artfully arranged in a procession of wave-like splendour. Tiny beads followed the embroidery across the daring neckline to create an enchanting ball gown, worthy of a princess.

I put it on again, to the delight of the maid who refused to leave my room.

'That one,' she nodded excitedly.

My better judgement warned me against it. It was too daring, too elaborate and certainly a dress a simple tutor should not wear even if she could afford it.

But the temptation seized me.

I *had* to wear it . . . for I would never have another chance to do so.

I could see Granny smiling at my decision and the image overruled any further doubts I might have entertained.

\*　　　\*　　　\*

The villa glowed with light.

As I stepped out into the corridor, a little afraid of who might see me, the music beckoned. Like out of a dream, I glided toward it, completely entranced. Elegant ladies with sparkling jewels had started to

211

arrive on the arms of their escorts. I counted many arrogant noses; however, it wouldn't have mattered for the night was destined to be a memorable one. I knew it instinctively, like one can predict the response of a dear friend, and the magic drew me closer, past the point where I could not return.

I experienced no desire to turn back. I felt empowered by the bracelet on my wrist.

Oh, I shouldn't have worn it, but it went so perfectly with the dress. And once it slipped onto my arm, it stayed there as though it belonged there.

The uncanny sensation sent me into the fray, where curious eyes strayed in my direction. The first face I expected and wanted to see was not at his post by the door. In his place arrived the very unwanted face of an elaborately dressed Ernst Mendel, who lifted my hand to his lips.

'Miss Brown, I have never seen you look more beautiful.' His gaze fell casually upon the bracelet.

He stepped back, startled.

'What is it, Herr Mendel?'

'Your bracelet . . .'

I studied his alarmed face. 'Yes. What about it?'

'Forgive me, but it resembles a piece that was lost a long time ago.'

'A piece belonging to the von Holsteins?'

He pulled me under the light. '*Where* did

you get it?'

'My grandmother gave it to me. It's not a fake, is it?'

A peculiar smile appeared on his lips. 'No, it's not a fake.'

'Then what is it?'

'A legend. A *lost* legend.' He touched the face of the serpent as though hypnotized. 'Max will pay handsomely to have it back. You could blackmail him for it.'

I withdrew my hand. 'Blackmail, sir?'

He shrugged. 'One must make a living in this world.'

'By fair means, not foul.'

'I have offended you, for which I am deeply grieved. What will you do?'

'What I'll do, sir, is no concern of yours.'

I sped away, disturbed by the exchange. He behaved strangely for a mere steward. He said he had inherited the position through his father and thus felt licensed to address the Count by his given name. What impudence! Or perhaps the Count had *given* him licence to address him so freely?

So lost in my thoughts, I failed to notice Baroness Outten until we nearly collided.

'My dear,' she gushed, 'how charming you look. I would have hardly recognized you.'

She stood on the outskirts of a group of people I didn't know, nor wished to know. They all seemed very pleased with themselves—the usual bored, indulgent aristocrats who treated expensive parties with casual indifference.

'How well Sibylla's gown suits you.' She leaned over to whisper, 'I *heard* of the unfortunate affair.'

'I'm sure it was an accident,' I said.

'With dear Liesel,' she smiled, 'how can one be certain? She's a headstrong child. She has her mother's spirit and her mother's . . .'

'And her mother's?' I prompted.

The Baroness lowered her eyes. 'I really *shouldn't* say, especially since Liesel is doing so beautifully this evening. Look how proud she looks beside her father!'

Yes, she did look proud, proud and happy. I felt my gaze drawn to the Count, to his fine black evening attire. He stood out amongst the other men, tall and distinguished, compassionate and charming.

'I suspect it won't be long before he takes another wife,' Baroness Outten murmured, 'and there are many who are hopefuls. See them all lined up there, hoping to dance with the Count? They are Vienna's finest daughters and their fathers would pay handsomely to have a connection with the house of von Holstein.'

I glanced at Liesel, understanding why she acted the way she did. She regarded any female in her father's path as a hostile invader. She couldn't allow them entry, not when she fought so hard to retain her position in his

214

affections. With her resemblance to her mother and her madness against her, I imagined she would go to extraordinary lengths to hold her place, even shred the dress of her governess.

Once the guests arrived, the music stopped to allow the Count to open the ball. I imagined he would select Sibylla as his partner and this he did. I saw the hope and the disappointment shadow Liesel's face and went to stand beside her. Her gaze never left the couple waltzing in the middle of the room.

'I thought he would pick me. He still thinks I ruined your dress, but I didn't do it, miss.'

'I believe you.'

'Do you?' She lifted a brow. 'If I am mad, I might have done it and forgotten it.'

'That is true.'

She nodded. 'Perhaps I *am* mad because I can't remember doing it. I thought your red dress was nice. I never would have cut it up, but now I'm glad it happened because you look better in Sibylla's gown. Quite beautiful, in fact. I've been watching you and I've watched the men watching you, too. Herr Mendel, in particular, can't keep his eyes off you.'

'Herr Mendel,' I grumbled.

'You don't like him, do you? You're still thinking of your Hugo.' She turned away from the dance floor before I could advise her to the contrary. 'Oh, *there* is Cousin Karl. I

215

couldn't find him before.'

The sight of the Baron dancing with a ravishing brunette on his arm didn't surprise me. He must be searching for a replacement for Rachel. I wondered if his current partner was as well endowed in her pocket as she was in her bosom.

The waltz ended and a new waltz began, one by Johann Strauss. The couples dispersed and new couples emerged. To my horror, the Baron, having deposited his lovely brunette to her group of friends, now stood before us, asking for my hand.

'My hand?' I stammered. 'Don't you mean Miss von Holstein's?'

Those dazzling blue eyes tried to appear penitent. 'No, I believe her hand is taken.'

I glanced to where Liesel had disappeared on the arm of her father. Her radiant smile met my uncertain one and, as I couldn't think of an adequate refusal quick enough, I accepted the Baron's offer mechanically.

I was thankful Emily had taught me the basics of a waltz because dancing was not my forte. Fortunately, my partner seemed to be an expert and led me around the room. Within moments, the rhythm and the sweetness of the music relaxed me.

'Don't smile,' my partner warned, 'you might enjoy yourself.'

'Why did you ask me to dance, Baron?'

'So, it's *Baron*, is it? I am deeply grieved you

feel so set against me and here I was *trying* to be charming.'

I tried not to smile and failed.

'You don't look like a governess when you smile. In fact, you are the most exquisite woman in the room. A temptress. A goddess.'

'You exaggerate, Baron.'

'So, it's *still* Baron, is it? The truth is, I had to talk to you. You run the other way whenever I'm about so now is my only opportunity to defend myself.'

'Defend yourself?'

'I didn't murder my wife, Cristabel. I want you to know that.'

'I don't remember giving you licence to use my name.'

Again, he looked penitent. 'Rachel and I were *reconciled*. Why would I have wanted to kill her?'

I thought of Old Josef and what he had heard. 'I don't know. Perhaps because you kept her hidden on your little estate and were ashamed of her is one reason why one might consider you responsible.'

'Rachel's death was an *accident*. An *accident*,' he repeated. 'You must believe me.'

'Why does my opinion matter so much to you?'

His blue eyes searched mine as the waltz dwindled down to a close. 'Can't you guess?'

I was acutely relieved when the music stopped. The participants of the waltz clapped, but I stood there like stone, horrified by his impudence. How dare he imply his regard for me—his wife's friend—so soon after her death! His very callousness fired my resolve to find him guilty. *He* must be guilty, for who else stood to gain by her death?

'Come, I will return you to your place.'

He attempted to take my hand and I withdrew it from him. 'No, thank you. I am quite capable of walking there myself.'

His blue eyes seemed to sear mine. 'No, I *insist.* You look troubled; you need assistance and I need to explain.'

'What do you need to explain, Cousin?' The Count moved to us. 'There can be no excuse for bad dancing with Strauss and a pretty partner.'

The Baron smiled at his gibe. 'No, of course not,' and left at once.

'Thank you,' I whispered.

'He appeared to be causing you certain discomfort.'

I lowered my eyes. 'I'm sorry if I made a scene.' I lifted my head when the music began. 'I think I should retire now.'

'I think not.' He collected my hand. 'You would not deny me the privilege of dancing with you—'

His face whitened.

I followed his gaze to the bracelet. 'Is something wrong?'

He quickly recovered his equilibrium,

218

smiling as he led me around the dance floor. No more mention was made of the bracelet. In fact, neither of us spoke for the duration of the waltz. The enchanting music breathed magic into the air and the room soon became a swirl of colourful dresses, of glittering diamonds and lovers' smiles—a place where dreams become realities.

Perhaps the endless turning and the wonderment of being in his arms could be blamed for what happened next. I recall the faces merging, the women whispering before complete darkness.

And somewhere in the darkness, trapped in a moment of unconsciousness, lay the irrefutable truth. I was in love with my employer, a man whom I should not love and a man who could not love me.

The hopelessness of my situation dawned when a faint smell alerted me to my senses.

I opened my eyes. I was lying on my bed in my room with Sibylla and Liesel peering down at me. They both looked concerned.

'She's awake now,' I heard Liesel say. 'I'll go and tell Papa.'

'Is he still waiting outside?' Sibylla asked, but Liesel had gone.

I closed my eyes, the horrible realization descending on me like a pack of vultures. I had fainted! I, Cristabel Brown, who thought herself able to control all situations. The Cristabel Brown who detested such inconsequential displays of feminine fragility, usually contrived to captivate an audience.

Sibylla pressed a hot cup of tea into my hands, her diamond earrings dangling as she turned away. 'You gave us quite a shock.'

I sipped the tea, amazed at how quickly it revived me. 'I only fainted. You needn't worry, my lady.'

Her lips twisted at the title. '*My lady*,' she echoed, 'yes, I'd forgotten our different stations for a moment. I have come to regard you as something of a rival, Mademoiselle Brown.'

'A rival?'

My voice sounded very small.

'You danced with the Count this evening, you fainted in his arms.'

'I could have fainted into any man's arms. He just happened to be my partner at the time.'

Her pale-blue eyes connected with mine. 'Are you in love with him?'

'No,' I denied hotly, astounded she could ask such a private question.

'Is he in love with you?'

I almost spilt my tea as I drew up my knees. 'I should hardly imagine he would be.'

'But you would like it if he was?'

I set down my tea. 'My lady—'

'Ah,' she laughed, 'I'm only teasing. Max is my cousin. I am allowed to look after his interests.'

The door opened and Liesel flooded into the room, her father behind her.

'She is well, you see.'

I felt the colour rising to my face. 'I apologize for causing this disruption, my lord.'

'Disruption?' He grinned. 'We should thank *you*, Miss Brown, for managing to entertain our guests this last half an hour. Wagers are being laid at the outcome.'

'Yes,' Liesel piped in, 'whether you'll return or stay in your room, miss. They gamble over any silly thing.'

'I hope you didn't make one,' I said.

Liesel grinned. 'Not me, miss, but Papa did. He wagers you'll return to the ball.'

'Then you shall lose your wager, Cousin,' Sibylla smiled, 'for *mademoiselle* has decided to retire.'

'Before I learned of the wager.' I left my bed to arrange my skirts. 'I cannot allow the Count to lose a wager on my behalf.'

Liesel clasped her hands excitedly, Sibylla shrugged, and the Count grimaced as he offered his arm to me.

His grimace accompanied us downstairs. 'I thought I engineered your return remarkably well.'

'How much did you wager?'

'The money was not my motivation.'

'Then what was your motivation?'

'Merely the selfish pleasure of your company. Did you think you could escape me

221

so easily?'

'Escape you?' I whispered incredulously, aware of Sibylla and Liesel directly behind us.

We had reached the ballroom. A dozen or so faces eagerly watched our return and pocket books drawn and wagers promptly settled. Baroness Outten's husband had wagered with the Count and he came to congratulate the Count on his success. His little black eyes strayed toward me and I did not like the implication I saw there.

'I should retire,' I said to the Count at the first opportunity.

'Not yet.' He took my hand and drew me into the gardens. 'You cannot leave the ball without first viewing the lights from the summerhouse.'

'The summerhouse? I don't remember Liesel showing me the summerhouse.'

A faint smile touched his lips. 'It's a secret and kept under lock and key. Come . . . I will give you a private tour.'

The gardens at night! How lovely they looked against the spectacular lighting of the villa. I breathed in the fragrant air, praying the coolness would diminish the high colour in my face.

My heart began to rush. Why he brought me out here? Was it the usual reason a man drew a woman into the gardens? I was ashamed to admit I hoped it would be. The virility and the arrogance of this man captivated me. He tried to disassociate himself with the arrogance of his breed but it was there in every line of his body. He could not escape his destiny as much as I could not escape mine.

We had paused inside one of the arbours and my hand remained enclosed in his.

'Cristabel . . .'

My heart leapt in answer. Losing myself in those liquid eyes, glimmering faintly in the darkness, I mouthed 'Yes?'

He captured my face in his hands. 'This must be insanity,' he laughed.

A deadly insanity.'

'Insanity . . .' I breathed.

I closed my eyes the instant his lips met mine. Somewhere far away I could hear the music of Mozart playing and it seemed like magic. I was living a dream, a sweet, forbidden dream.

We clung to each other awhile there, both unwilling to interrupt the moment. The music enchanted us, led us into a world of our own, a world apart from this one.

'I have never seen such a beautiful sight,' I whispered.

'The summerhouse is better,' he promised, drawing me away.

In silence, we walked through the gardens, the cool night air adding to the perfection of the evening. The fragrance of the roses almost made me feel dizzy.

He smiled. 'Too much wine?'

'Or not enough,' I laughed back, stopping to pluck one pink rose which caught my attention.

'Pink isn't the colour for you.'

Before I could respond, he disappeared through the bushes to bring me one huge yellow rose.

Gently tickling my nose with the flower, I raised a brow. 'Yellow, my lord?'

He looked hurt that I'd called him by his title.

'Max,' I amended quickly, inspecting his offering with a grin. 'It's beautiful . . . and exotic. Thank you.'

'No, *you* are beautiful and exotic. Yellow, because you throw sunshine into our dark world—unstintingly, I might add—and yellow because it conveys goodness and purity, wit and intelligence. There was a reason why our great empress chose the colour to furnish her imperial city.'

'You make me sound like a saint! And whatever I am, I know I'm not a saint.'

'No?' he teased.

'No.' I shook my head in merry reflection. 'I'm not a saint because, like every one else, I call down evil upon my fellow man and like every one else, I possess a degree of selfish interest. I know I should not keep the host away from his guests for too long, but I'm not prepared to release you yet. You promised me a tour.'

'So I did.' He laughed, looping my arm under his. 'It is this way.'

'Tell me about the summerhouse, does it have a name?'

'We call it the Alexandra.'

The Alexandra, a grand three-storey whitish building cloaked in ivy, stood ghostly silent beyond its neglected path.

'The summerhouse has not been opened for years,' the Count said when we arrived at the massive wooden carved doors.

'Why?'

The heavy door opened with a low creak. 'I shall tell you the story from the morning-room.'

'The morning-room?'

'It has the best view of the villa at night.'

I couldn't conceal my excitement. It was like stepping through time. Once inside the marble-floored mansion, impressive with its red-carpeted grand staircase and gilded furniture, I just had to touch something. Anything. I settled on the ebony hall table where a gilded frame stood by the small, chiming French clock. I picked up the gilded frame and peered at the portrait of a lady painted there. Dressed in a velvet blue gown, her dark hair swept up, long diamond ear-rings dangling at her ears, her beauty captured me.

'Who is she?'

'My great-grandmother Alexandra. She was

a Russian princess.'

I put the frame down in elation. 'And this was her house? Why is it shut up? It's beautiful!'

He smiled, lighting the small lantern resting on the ebony table. 'I confess I agree with you, that's why you see half the furniture uncovered. I am having the place restored.'

Eager to hear the rest of the story, I followed him through a narrow corridor to the morning-room. The old boards creaked under my feet.

I didn't have much experience with grand houses but I expected a morning-room to be somewhat smaller. The massive chamber completely restored with its antique medieval furniture, tapestry-covered walls and a great Ottoman rug warming the cool, wooden floors held me spellbound.

Gasping in delight, I rushed to the glazed windows draped in their original gold brocade curtains where one had an enchanting view of the villa at night. 'Gorgeous!'

'I've wanted to show you this place for a long time.' He joined me at the window, pleasure shining in his voice.

'Then why didn't you?' I scolded. 'How dare you keep all of this to yourself.'

'Dare I admit to a selfish interest to have it perfect before a lady inspects my work?'

'Your work?' I joked. 'Don't you mean your army of servants?'

I had turned around to face him and the smile gradually faded from my lips. He wore an expression I'd never seen before and I was curious about it. A gentleness had come into his eyes, those eyes that I loved. And for the first time, I glimpsed beneath the mystery to the bare soul of the man.

I don't know how long we stood there staring at each other. It didn't matter. Time didn't matter. The world didn't matter. Only we mattered.

'Max!' I cried and ran into his arms.

He laughed as he caught me, his mouth hunting down mine. His mouth tasted warm and spicy, tender and strong. Locked against him, my innocence and naivety suddenly twisted into a greater need, a need primeval, raw, natural and, as yet, unfulfilled.

My fingers slipped up to caress the back of his neck. I loved that part of him. In fact, I loved every part of him and intended to indulge what I'd only dared to dream about.

'Cristy,' he breathed, his lips nibbling on my ear. 'My sweet Cristy . . .'

The longing I heard in his voice inflamed my desire for so much more. Pressing wantonly to him, I traced his lips with my own, nudging and sampling, inhaling and exploring. I felt his response grow and form below. My heart expanded within me. 'Oh, Max,' I cried. 'I want you so much!'

'Not as much as I want you.'

His low groan confirmed the fact. Placing my mouth on his again, I kissed him with all the passion I felt for him, to assure him of my intention to go further, I didn't want him to speak. I just wanted him as much as he wanted me.

'Oh, my darling . . .' He groaned again. Are you sure?'

I put my finger on his lips. 'Don't talk.'

'We should—'

I answered him with my mouth, eager to continue my discovery of him. Hugo's kisses seemed so weak in comparison; there had been no fire, no deep yearning, no tingling magical sensation. But with Max . . . oh with Max, sheer joy.

A light laugh escaped my lips when he suddenly picked me up and carried me over to the sofa. There, enshrouded by the shadows, we gazed lovingly into each other's eyes. Max's hand reached out to touch my cheek, to draw a feathery line down the column of my neck. I closed my eyes, swallowing, immersing myself in the wonder of a simple touch.

'My beautiful Cristy.' His lips gently grazed my forehead before depositing tiny kisses all over my face, neck and shoulders.

My stomach stirred like a fluttering butterfly. I think I murmured this to him and his faint laugh seduced my ear. He moved closer to me on the sofa, slowly inspecting each part of me with his lips as his fingers worked to undo the lacing at my back.

He stopped abruptly to remove his evening jacket.

'Damned obstruction. There shall be no obstructions between us tonight.'

'No. No obstructions,' I whispered back, snaking my hand up to pull away his half undone cravat. The snowy white creation slithered to fall in a neat pile.

If only my dress were as easy!'

'Ball gowns are entirely too modest,' he agreed.

I frowned at him. 'I suspect you've done this before.'

He grinned. 'Experience can be useful. Do you trust me?'

Yes, I trusted him. Yes, I wanted him. Now, not in an hour's time. Whipping a hand up inside his shirt, I strived to undo his buttons.

'Not so fast,' he laughed.

I bit my lip. 'But we don't know how much time we have.'

'We have enough.'

As it happened, we had plenty of time. Plenty of time to remove each item of clothing with a painful slowness. Following his lead, I submitted humbly to his ministrations and shortly, he had me stepping out of my monstrous ball gown.

'Now for the hoop.'

Encircling me like a predatory animal, his hand at my waist, he loosened the string and it too fell to the ground.

Anticipation bubbled inside my mouth when he drew near to shed my petticoats. Now standing in my chemise, stays and garters, I felt suddenly shy and naked.

Making a slight adjustment to the top of my chemise, he stood back to appraise me with his eyes.

I read his approval there, his glowing need.

Ever so slowly, he entered the circle of my privacy and wrapped his powerful arms around me. My hands stroked his buttocks before moving up to rid the distraction of his breeches. Whilst engaged there, I had no control over his magic hands roving archly down the shape of me, plucking at the laces of my shift.

'How perfect you are,' he murmured, drawing my mouth to his. I watched his breeches fall to the ground, freeing the mystery at his groin. 'Oh . . . I've always wondered.'

He pulled me closer. 'No, you don't have to wonder.'

Standing in our underclothes, he engaged me in a slow dance. So alive and curious, I could only follow, marvelling in the intimacy of our freedom.

All too much like a dream, we danced, serenaded by the moonlight and celebrated our need for each other. I don't know when my shift landed on the floor or when his shirt lifted to expose the strength of his male beauty. I did, however, register his teeth drawing at my silken garters and I did forget to breathe at the first touch of his hands on my bare skin, stroking my private place, caressing my hips, thighs and breasts. What little embarrassment remained vanished at the fusion of his skin on mine.

My heart hammering inside, I surrendered to the music of our bodies mingling as one. The pain of his entry soon dissipated with a series of tender kisses, caresses and loving movements and soon I embarked upon a new course of discovery. The end, the beautiful release, freed a cry deep within me. Max let out a cry of his own and together, we lay on the Turkish rug, two entwined lovers bathed in the moonlight.

Curled up against Max, the sensation of our touching skin still new and exciting, I ran my fingers across his chest.

'Did I hurt you?' he asked.

I was not going to lie. 'A little . . . but only for a moment.' To reassure him, I put my lips to his and deepened my kiss.

He responded as I hoped he would and soon, we were one again.

'I don't want this night to end,' I whispered in his ear.

His hands held my face. 'Nor do I.'

We were very reluctant to leave the summerhouse. Even afterwards, dressed, we stood in each other's arms by the window, watching the night lights, both of us unwilling to speak.

'I should go back.' I drew away slowly. 'And you should too. You're the host. You have guests to bid goodnight.'

His eyes answered me.

'It's the responsibility of being lord of the castle,' I smiled. 'I do believe at this moment I have the upper hand—I can slip in undetected back to my room. Will our absence have been noted, do you think?'

He swept me up in his arms again. 'I don't know and let's not spoil the night by thinking of others.'

Giggling, I allowed him to carry me across the threshold of the front door. As soon as my feet touched the ground and the night air swirled around me, I knew our time had come to an end.

He attempted to speak then but I silenced him with a chaste kiss. 'Goodnight, my love.'

I hurried away before he could stop me, weaving through the maze of gardens until I reached the villa. Pausing at the entrance, I drew in a deep breath and smoothed my dress and hair. Had anyone seen me return?

The last of the guests were leaving. Hugging the walls, I inched further down the hall, steering away from the lights.

Horror stuck in my throat. Less than three feet away swished the glittering skirts of

Sibylla. She was on the arm of some young gentleman, laughing and twitching her fan, looking as if she might turn.

Instinct propelled me to the centre of the corridor, a theatrical yawn hopefully disguising my fear.

Sibylla saw me. 'Cristabel! We thought you were abed.'

'I was,' I lied. 'But I couldn't sleep so I thought I'd go for a walk.'

She nodded. 'The gardens are always lovely at night.' Her eyes narrowed. 'I hope you weren't alone. There are some desperate fellows about.'

Her companion laughed. 'Oh, *very* desperate.'

I realized they were both drunk and relief hit me like fluttering snow. My frazzled nerves soothed, I walked as calmly as I could through the main corridor toward the staircase leading up to my room.

I should have lingered awhile longer for Max entered in through the glass doors, saw me, smiled and turned, only to face the accusing tone of his daughter.

I hadn't seen Liesel approach. She must have interpreted the smile between us for her hostile gaze flickered from her father to me and back to her father.

'How *could* you?' she cried, spinning around to me. 'Everything you said about your Hugo was a lie, wasn't it? You wanted me to believe

233

it to conceal your *real* motive.'

'Liesel, it is not her fault but mine—'

'No. Don't try to explain. You *both* sicken me.'

She ran off and I rushed after her. So intent in my chase of her, I did not see the other face in the darkness.

The face that was smiling.

*     *     *

The events of the von Holstein ball would not be repeated.

I knew it the instant I awoke the following morning. The music had vanished and the magic had gone with it. Therefore, it did not come as a surprise when the Count asked for me after breakfast. I went to his study, grieved to find him sombre and reflective. Could this be the same man in the summerhouse last evening? Did he even recall the incident?

Yes, he did.

'Miss Brown, I must apologize for my behaviour last night. It was unforgivable of me to take advantage of you—someone in my employ.'

I would have intervened but for the words *someone in my employ.*

Now I understood. I had been but a brief dalliance last night and he was eager to establish the fact. I believe I hated him in that moment, the coldness of his eyes, the taut line of his mouth. What had happened to the man I loved? Or perhaps he never existed. Perhaps he had only been a figment of my imagination.

'I understand, my lord,' I said coolly. 'Is there anything else?'

'Cristabel, I—'

'Don't trouble yourself, my lord. What happened between us will remain a secret, that I can promise you.'

'It is my fault,' he sighed. 'I shouldn't have allowed it.'

A mixture of anger and hurt flared within me. Fighting off useless tears, I flexed my hands in a nonchalant manner. 'We don't need a post-mortem. You are afraid I shall make unrealistic demands of you. Don't be. I have more than my share of pride. I expect nothing from you.'

His eyes searched mine. 'Is that the truth? I fear you will want more than I can give.' He looked away. 'You deserve so much better than me, Cristabel. You deserve someone young, untouched by the bitterness of life.'

'Untouched?' I queried. 'You paint a picture of a saint. I don't like saints and I never wanted one.'

'What do you want?'

*You!* I wanted to cry. *To be your wife.* Instead, I said, 'To continue on as we have. Why can we not continue our friendship?' He stared at me in astonishment.

I shrugged. 'One must be adult about these

235

things. Did you speak to Liesel?'

'Yes,' he murmured. 'She caught us kissing, nothing more.'

'Does she suspect more?'

'If she does, she didn't say.'

I nodded and left the room, my hands shaking with rage. I couldn't have stayed a moment longer. I couldn't bear to have my dreams shredded before me.

Hot tears blinding my eyes, I hurried back to my room. I felt as low as a chambermaid and he had dismissed me as such. What did I expect? A proposal of marriage in the morning?

Yes, I was ashamed to admit. I wanted everything.

Instead, I had nothing.

Reaching the safety of my room, I washed my streaky face with cold water and repinned my hair in a savage style. I breathed, staring at the image of the new Cristabel Brown.

*You've nobody to blame but yourself.*

Refusing to think any more about my problems, I went up to Liesel's room and found her sitting on a chair by the window. Her face still looked pale, pale and mysterious. I noticed her bed had not been slept in and wondered where she had spent the night.

Her maid left the room as soon as I entered.

'Liesel—'

'The subject is closed, *fräulein*,' she said in German. 'We shall resume our lessons tomorrow. Today, I am ill.'

'Perhaps you would prefer me to leave?'

'Leave?'

By her mystified tone, I realized she'd never considered I might leave.

'Yes, leave,' I persisted. 'Perhaps I never should have come.'

'Then I wouldn't know English as well as I do know, would I?'

I hid a smile. 'There are many tutors. I am certain I can be easily replaced.'

My remark distressed her. 'You don't need to leave, miss.'

'I think I do.'

'Why should you leave now? You are settled with us and we are used to you. And a good tutor does not leave a pupil halfway through her assignment.'

'Has it really been six months?'

'Yes,' Liesel smiled faintly. 'I remember our first morning on that cold October morning . . . and it is April today. April fool's day.'

She stared out of the window.

'Are you still there, miss?'

'Yes, I'm still here.'

'Your bracelet, the one you wore last night, where did you get it?'

'My grandmother gave it to me.'

'Your grandmother? The sister of the old lady we met in Mittenwald?'

I nodded.

'Can you go and get it? Baroness Outten

237

says it's a serpent bracelet and the *serpent* is part of our family insignia.'

'It is part of many European families' insignias,' I replied.

She lifted her shoulders. 'Maybe you are right, but I still want to see it.'

I retrieved it and brought it to her.

Her eyes glowed as she slipped it on to her wrist. 'Look how it glitters, even in the daylight! It's a beautiful piece . . . I wonder if it once belonged to us? I remember something about Elaina and a bracelet.'

'It looks more Egyptian,' I said, eager to divert where her comments were leading.

She was not going to be dissuaded so easily. 'No . . . I'm certain. There's a legend attached to the bracelet about reuniting lovers. I remember now. It's in the book at home.'

I swallowed at the *reuniting lovers* part. 'Back at the *schloss*?' Liesel nodded, twisting the bracelet for further inspection. A tiny smile lurked at the corners of her mouth. 'The legend is a secret. The book is secret. You haven't seen it, but I have.'

What was she saying? 'Do you mean the legend is not in the manuscript your father read for us?'

She gave me a weary look. 'The legend book went missing years ago. I'd forgotten about it.'

Her words unsettled me. Feeling suddenly ill, I sat down to dissect it. Did Granny know

238

of this legend? Had they lied to me, telling me some tale about the power of the bracelet when it was only a charm once worn by a woman in love?

'Have you had it valued?' Liesel's voice drifted before me. 'You could sell it and your family would be rich?'

I managed a wan smile. 'I hardly think the sum would last us a lifetime.'

'Oh, you never know . . . Your bracelet caused a sensation last night. I could find a buyer for you. Name your price and I'll get it.'

'I'm sorry but I can't sell it. It's my grandmother's.'

'But she gave it to you.'

'Yes, but—'

'Then you can sell it! Aren't you even curious as to what it might fetch?'

I thought about it for a while. It might be a good idea, especially if I had to leave in a hurry. I did not want to be dependent on a man who had rejected me so brutally. If I sold the bracelet for a handsome sum, I could return to England.

Granny. I recalled the words in her letter: *I trust whatever you do with the bracelet will be right.*

How could I sell it when she did not? She had kept it all those years, *cherished* it in secrecy and bestowed it on me to use at my discretion. No, I could never sell it, not without her consent.

239

'Well?' Liesel prompted. 'A price wouldn't hurt, would it?'

'It isn't my decision to make, Liesel.'

'But if you get an offer, you can write to your grandmother about it and *she* can make the decision.'

I considered it. 'Very well, since it amuses you.'

'It *does* amuse me,' she replied with a small smile.

\*     \*     \*

I decided to walk into town that afternoon. The villa had suddenly become oppressive and I needed to refresh my mind.

Vienna buzzed with activity. All kinds of carriages and cabs ruled the streets and I passed several new arrivals on my way in. These travellers must have come for the exhibition: families, businessmen, merchants, foreigners . . . and no, could it be?

It was.

And I could not avoid them for they had spotted me.

I groaned as the hired cab approached and stopped on the side of the street where I stood. Hugo leapt out, in a smart black coat, and held out his hand to help Emily out of the coach.

She immediately embraced me in a flutter of pink frills. 'We just called at the villa. We wanted to surprise you. You see'—she showed me the diamond on her finger—'we're married!'

'Married,' I echoed.

Hugo flushed darkly as Emily rushed on about the wedding and the journey and how they spent an hour searching for the von Holstein villa.

'I'm sorry I didn't warn you, dear Cristabel, but there was simply no time. It happened all so suddenly, didn't it, darling?'

Hugo's gaze had not left my face. Fortunately, I remembered my manners and congratulated them both and Emily insisted they take me out to a 'traditional Viennese coffee-house.'

I refused Hugo's assistance as I climbed into the cab, wishing Emily had warned me about the wedding. Perhaps she deliberately hadn't so she could monitor my reaction to the news? Did my reaction matter to her? More importantly, did my reaction matter to me?

Emily filled the silence with her usual, vivacious chatter. Marriage suited her and she clearly adored Hugo. Hugo I found difficult to read. There was nothing in his manner to suggest he was not sublimely happy with his present situation, though I wondered. He barely spoke in the cab and when he did, it was in answer to his wife's prodding.

With profound relief, we arrived at the coffee-house where Hugo secured a table for us.

I complimented Emily on her trousseau.

'Oh,' she blushed, 'Hugo chose all my clothes. He said he wanted to show me off!'

'Emily, why didn't you tell me?'

She looked uncomfortable. 'I told you: there was no time.'

Hugo had returned and the three of us sat there awkwardly sipping our coffee.

'We called at the villa,' Emily said again. 'What a *beautiful* place. The housekeeper was not very friendly, but I suppose they can be rather frosty. She was about to turn us away when a male voice enquired. It was your Count.' Her eyes rounded on me. 'Why did you not tell me he was so young and handsome? I had expected to find an old man with a gouty foot and instead *Sir Galahad* greets us and invites us in.'

I stared at her. 'He invited you in?'

'Why, yes. He didn't know you had gone out.'

'Did you meet my charge, Miss von Holstein?'

'No, but I saw another lady.'

'Princess Sibylla,' I nodded. 'She's the Count's cousin.'

'And hoping to be more, I daresay.'

'They are both widowers so it's certainly likely.'

Emily reached for Hugo's hand. 'Cousins can make the best spouses, can't they, darling?'

He didn't answer but continued to sip his coffee.

Emily pouted as she slipped her hand into her reticule. 'We'll be staying here for a few weeks. This is the address of the hotel in case I forget to give it to you in the cab.'

I thanked them for the coffee and said I preferred to walk back.

'Are you sure?'

'I'm very determined about it. A walk was my purpose for coming into town.'

She nodded and kissed my cheek. 'Do you promise to come and see me when you have some spare time?'

I promised her, as Hugo and I exchanged a polite, and uneasy, farewell.

\*　　　\*　　　\*

The sun danced on the cobbled street before me.

I was pleased with my efforts and with my reaction to Emily's news. I suspected they would marry one day and had accepted it. Seeing Hugo again hadn't stirred the slightest feeling of resentment within me. I did not love him: I never had and experienced liberation in the fact.

As I approached the wrought-iron gates of the villa, I fervently wished last night had not occurred. Why had I not stayed in my room? Why did I allow him to persuade me to return to the ball?

I decided to walk in through the back entrance. I had no desire to see anyone. Encouragingly, the gardens appeared to be deserted.

Then I heard the wheels of a carriage.

I turned around to see a laden carriage stop at the little villa. I could only make out two forms, but one was unmistakable with her red hair glistening in the sun.

Dara.

Dara and her son had arrived.

# PART 4

# Eye of the Serpent

# CHAPTER TWELVE

I did not see Dara until the following week.

A maid placed a note in my hand one morning. I read the elegant sloping handwriting asking me to come to the villa tomorrow afternoon. *Come alone*, the note insisted and the maid waited to take my answer back to *madam*. I promised her I would come and, when she left, I put the folded note under my sleeve. Dara's return could only mean one thing: *she must be the Count's mistress.*

The certainty of the fact depressed me. I now understood why he rejected me so harshly after our lovemaking on the night of the ball. He *knew* Dara was on her way and no longer needed to amuse himself with the little English governess.

But what could explain the brief intensity flooding his face when he saw the bracelet on my arm? I fancied then it must have been the sight of the bracelet; however, he never mentioned it. Perhaps the memory of Dara, *his mistress*, had pricked his conscience, for he had recovered his equilibrium before anyone else noticed.

I was not so lucky. I had fainted in his arms like a girl fresh out of the schoolroom. This embarrassing truth carried me into the little

247

villa's charming pink and gilded reception room where Dara received me.

She was dressed exquisitely as always, her hair pinned high, and her ears glittering with the diamonds the Count had given her for Christmas. A tiny smile danced upon her reddened lips. 'Do sit down, my dear. I hear you are providing the staff here with an incessant source of entertainment.'

'How was your journey?' I replied coolly.

'Uncomfortably long,' she moaned. 'I couldn't bear to be away another day. The mountains can be so lonely without the family in residence.'

'I would suspect so.'

She examined me archly. 'Something has happened to you since I last saw you. There is colour in your cheeks.'

'The air is warmer here,' I reminded her.

'No,' she insisted, 'there is another reason.'

She rang the bell for tea and, while we waited, chatted on about the various features of the villa and promised to give me a tour if I so wished it. I said another time perhaps as I had to write letters this afternoon.

'Oh, how *mysterious*,' she chuckled. 'Dare I ask who are the recipients?'

'It is no secret. My family and an acquaintance in town.'

'An acquaintance in town,' she murmured. 'Friends of yours?'

'My former charge and her husband.'

'Her husband?'

'That is correct.'

'And his name is . . . ?'

I glared at her impertinence and I think she interpreted the message for she laughed.

'Yes, I'm very rude, aren't I? But as I am, how shall we say, *retired* from the world, I must have something to occupy my time.'

'You do so by collecting information about others?'

She tapped her lips. 'How very derogatory it sounds the way you put it but I suppose, yes, collecting information about people is my forte. Opera singers do hear a vast deal and I still have my contacts.'

'And they bring information to you?'

She clicked her tongue. 'Now *you* are being rude and here I wanted us to have a pleasant cup of tea, or do you prefer coffee?'

'Coffee would be nice, thank you.'

'Coffee,' she smiled, 'is very Austrian. Perhaps this place is growing on you?'

'It is perfectly natural that it should, considering the time I have spent here.'

'The time has flown,' she agreed. 'I remembered when I first saw you. I wagered you wouldn't last a day and here you are, months later, and *such an influence* on the family.'

'I believe you exaggerate my talents.'

'No,' she disagreed, 'you have influenced certain members of the household, one of whom is quite in love with you.'

The heat rose in my face and when she said 'Herr Mendel', I felt an acute sense of relief.

'Yes, Ernst Mendel. I heard he had an altercation with you at the ball. Over a bracelet and you were vastly offended?'

I stared at her, shocked she should know so much. 'Who told you?'

'He did. As steward to the family, I have various business dealings with him, as you understand. He seems quite persistent in his suit of you.'

'He won't take no for an answer.'

'How unfortunate,' Dara clicked her tongue. 'But you *did* encourage him.'

'If I did, it was unintentional.'

'I don't believe you.'

I shrugged. 'It doesn't matter to me what you believe.'

'Oh,' she used her best condescending smile, 'I understand perfectly. There are larger fish more to your liking than our poor Ernst Mendel.'

She was baiting me and I refused to be baited. Not now. Not when I knew there was little hope.

To my relief, she let the subject go and poured another coffee.

'And now I must ask you a favour from woman-to-woman. Would you oblige me?'

I dreaded her question.

'I want to know, has there been any talk of a

wedding between the Count and the Princess?'

'Sibylla?'

'Yes, Sibylla.'

'Not as far as I am aware.'

She seemed relieved. 'You comfort me. Sometimes I fear he may take another wife. He has promised he won't but now I am not so sure. I would like to be sure, you must understand, for Paul's sake.'

I did understand; however, her words stung. Why did she confide in me? I did not want to know her business with the Count.

Or did I? I wanted to blurt out and demand the exact nature of her relationship with him. I had no business to do so, of course. What possible charge could I throw at her? A moment of madness on the night of the ball? An incident he seemed determined to forget?

I left the villa, feeling more profoundly depressed than when I arrived. The depression increased when Dara insisted on giving me a tour of 'her' little villa and the confirmation of her relationship with the Count lay in the splendour of the place.

I avoided the gardens where Ernst Mendel often prowled in the hope of catching me on my daily walk and went in through the servant's entrance.

Sibylla had taken Liesel out on afternoon calls. They had invited me to go along to soothe Liesel's mischievous desire to call on Hugo and Emily at their hotel.

251

'Oh, why not, miss?' she had pleaded. 'I want to meet your Hugo.'

'He is not *my Hugo*,' I reminded her.

'The English Hugo is very handsome,' Sibylla teased Liesel, 'but I do not think your governess will fall in with our plans?'

Liesel tried once again and I firmly refused. Hugo and Emily were on their honeymoon. I would not go to see them unless they invited me to do so.

I half expected a note from Emily reminding me of my promise and had decided to act upon it only upon its arrival. It felt odd seeing them again so far from home. For some unexplainable reason, I no longer associated myself with the young woman who had left England seven months ago. I had evolved in the remote castle on the mountains and its history and its legends continued to entice me. I couldn't rest until I knew all of its secrets, the silent secrets which lay undisturbed in its ancient walls. If only those walls could speak! Perhaps they knew what had happened to Conrad of old, as they had witnessed Fräulein Suski's demise and Countess Malena's flight from the castle.

The Countess. I found it difficult to imagine the Count married—the Count as I knew him.

Or did I know him? He acted so strangely of late, I began to doubt my own conviction. Perhaps *I* had imagined certain moments to be special when they were not. I could be a victim of my own interpretation and the possibility stung with the clarity of truth. He had been nothing more than polite and attentive to me, except for those times in the gardens when he . . .

When he what? What did I have to accuse him of? Being overly attentive? Begging my friendship when he should not? Asking me to stay at the ball? Leading me to the summerhouse . . . the summerhouse I couldn't bear to see again.

*'Fräulein.'*

The stark face of Frau Vetsera towered before me.

'You have a visitor in the parlour.'

I nodded, hoping she didn't detect the cause of the high colour in my face. She would have seen me return from the villa where the Count's mistress resided. I didn't bother to ask the names of my visitors for I had only one acquaintance in Vienna who would claim me.

It was Emily.

Her sunny smile sent my present concerns packing, as did her effusive embrace.

'You *naughty* girl. You promised to come see me. Where can we talk?'

I led her up to my room.

'Very nice,' she commented, inspecting items at her leisure, 'your employer is generous to put you in such a room.'

'It won't be always like this,' I said. 'He will marry and his wife will see the rules of convention are obeyed.'

She laughed. 'How bitter you sound! Your words do not match your beautiful face. What is troubling you? I knew it the moment I saw you and I thought—'

'It's not Hugo,' I interrupted.

She sat down in relief. 'I'm glad to hear it. I feared . . .' She shrugged. 'A silly fear, I know, but I had to be sure. I have a confession to make, well two, actually.'

'One is?'

'I never wanted you to have Hugo. When he made his shocking proposal to you, I made certain he was in his cups for I knew he would get an instant refusal from you. Do you hate me for it?'

What she said made sense when I thought back to his impassioned plea and my repugnance of it. 'No, I don't hate you for it, but thank you for owning up. And the other is?'

She couldn't stop smiling.

*'Emily.'*

'Oh, very well. I never could keep a secret. Guess who came to see me at the hotel yesterday?'

'Not Empress Elisabeth?'

'Stop funning. No, your charge, who is also, if I am not mistaken, the daughter of a princess and a relative of Empress Elisabeth.'

*'Liesel* came to see you?'

'Why, yes, with her cousin, the princess.

Aren't you lucky! Mama will be quite jealous to learn of your connection with royalty!'

I felt suddenly uneasy. 'What was the reason for their visit?'

Emily inspected the remains on my lunch tray. 'Do you have anything to eat here?'

'I could ring for tea.'

'Yes do, for we have much to discuss.'

I did not like to make a habit of ringing for tea unless I was in the schoolroom with Liesel. I could see Frau Vetsera frowning and reminding me of my position in the house. I would prefer to fetch my own tea, of course, but that would be frowned upon also. One could never please in this household.

Emily removed her gloves and eyed me with a speculative air. 'How is your employer?'

'I wouldn't know. I haven't seen him lately.'

'That is a lie for you blush every time I mention him. I can't say I blame you. He is fantastically handsome for a Count. I always imagined Counts to be old men with long moustaches and round bellies. *Your Count is* a pleasant surprise.'

'Emily, he is not my Count.'

'*Yet.* Aha! I have learned your secret and there is no point denying it. I wouldn't be so glum about it. You do have a very good chance.'

'I doubt it.'

She grinned. 'Oh, I know you will grumble and say you have no breeding or dowry, but you have something more than those concerns.'

The tea arrived and I waited for her to continue when the maid departed.

Emily nibbled on a biscuit. 'Whether you like it or not, you attract men. Liesel alluded to one Herr Mendel in the house? Who is he?'

'The Count's steward.'

'You dislike him?'

'Intensely.'

'Good, for a steward cannot compare to a Count. Even if you should end up as the Count's mistress—'

'He already has a mistress.'

'Does he? He's very organized, this Count. I shall have to think on it.'

'You shall be doing no more thinking on it,' I insisted firmly. 'You are here to enjoy your honeymoon, are you not?'

'Yes, but Hugo and I are concerned about you and your future.'

'You needn't worry. When this post finishes, I will find another. It is the life I have chosen.'

She nodded, not very convincingly. 'Whatever you say, you have certainly made an impression on this household. Your charge came to see me out of curiosity and to find out more about you.'

I poured a second cup for us both.

'She seemed very interested in a bracelet of yours— What's wrong? Your hand is shaking.'

'She asked you about the bracelet?'

'Yes. What bracelet? I've never seen you wear a serpent bracelet. Why didn't you show me before? Liesel says it's worth a fortune.'

I collected the bracelet from its hiding place. Its very presence of beauty and danger stirred strange and unexplainable emotions within me. I sensed its power and its power frightened me.

'It's beautiful,' Emily breathed 'where did you get it?'

I relayed the story.

'Your grandmother found it? No, no, no. She would have sold it if she merely *found* it, wouldn't you think? Why keep something valuable like this all these years when your family is struggling to pay the rent?'

Her logic hinted of a truth I had suspected.

'No, this is an heirloom, a very old and precious heirloom, and you are the receiver of it.'

Receiver of what? I thought. An ancient curse? A legend of reuniting lovers?

Only time would betray the secret I feared and yet must know.

Emily handed the bracelet to me. 'Liesel is keen to have it. The princess offered to buy it for her if you would accept.'

I put the bracelet away. 'Emily, they did not ask you to come and see me, did they?'

'Yes, they did ask, and I felt rather awkward because I knew nothing about it. Now I have seen it, I understand why Liesel is eager to have it. The serpent is the von Holstein insignia, is it not?'

'Part of it.'

'They feel it should be returned to their family—not without due compensation, of course.'

'They are very rude to involve you in this business,' I said, 'for I told Liesel I didn't want to sell it and she refused to listen. She thought I would be tempted by the money.'

'And aren't you?'

I couldn't explain to Emily the way I felt about the bracelet. I knew I couldn't let it out of my possession as much as I feared it to stay. 'No, the money does not tempt me. You are right. It must be an heirloom. Why else wouldn't Granny sell it?'

The first thing I did when Emily left was to write to Granny. I wanted to learn her reasons for lying to me—if indeed, the story of her finding the bracelet on the mountain was a fabrication. It still could be true and there could be another reason why she refused to sell over the years.

I feigned surprise when Liesel stole into my room later in the evening. I was reading in bed when she entered after a soft knock on my door.

'I thought you weren't asleep yet, miss.'

'I thought you *wouldn't* be asleep yet,' I corrected, and put my book aside. 'What is it, Liesel?'

She sat down on the side of my bed, still dressed in her evening attire.

'How was dinner?'

She lifted her shoulders. 'Ordinary, except Papa is still very angry. He snapped at Sibylla tonight. He shouldn't have. She was only trying to find out why Miss Quinn is here, for my sake. Why should she follow us here with her brat?'

I had ceased to think of Dara as Miss Quinn.

'You won't answer, miss. You're like Papa.'

'Some things are better left unanswered.'

'Is that your solution to the problem? To be quiet when there is trouble? To accept the unacceptable?'

'Why is Dara's presence so unacceptable to you? Many prominent men keep mistresses. It is a fact.'

'Dara is different. She has a son, a son who can disinherit me.'

'Even if he is legitimized, I don't think he could disinherit you, Liesel.'

'Oh, it can be done. Papa has the ear of the Emperor. He could have anything changed if he wanted to, but I won't let her brat steal my place. He'll die first!' Her violet eyes glittered as she observed me. 'You think I'm mad, don't you? Mad like my mother and my grandfather, but why should a *bastard* inherit anything? No, I won't allow it. Two of my mother's estates will go to me, as in the will, but the title and

259

the *schloss* should go to Karl. He's the next male in line for the title and I don't think he'd like a brat stealing his inheritance either. Can you see Karl as a count? He should make a very romantic one.'

I thought it ghoulish of her to envisage it when it meant her father's death. 'Liesel, estates and titles do not make one happy.'

'Happy,' she echoed. 'You think you know everything, miss, but you don't. You are in the dark.'

'And you are in the light?'

She shrugged, eager to dismiss the subject. 'I came to say I have a buyer for your bracelet if you are interested. Before you say no, will you hear the price first?'

I conceded, only because I had no choice in the matter.

'The price is . . .' She leaned over to whisper in my ear and I stared at her in astonishment.

'It's a price you can't refuse,' she teased.

'An *offer*,' I smiled, 'and any offer, no matter how attractive, can be refused. Who is the buyer?'

She toyed with the book on my lap. 'Me.'

'*You?*'

'Sibylla loaned me the money.'

'You didn't ask your father?'

'No.'

'Why not?'

'For he would think it rude.'

'And it is rude,' I said. 'I told you I couldn't

260

sell it. It's a family heirloom.'

'But it has the serpent face! It belongs to us!'

'Liesel, I think you should leave. I don't want to discuss the matter any further.'

She turned to glare at me from the door. 'Your grandmother probably *stole* it from us! How does it feel, miss, to be a *thief*?'

The door slammed and I shuddered at the exchange. It was not her words which upset me but her desperation. Why did she want the bracelet so desperately? Could her madness be responsible for the intensity? If not the madness, what else?

*     *     *

Liesel apologized the next morning.

I found her waiting in the schoolroom, an uncertain and repentant smile lurking on her lips. She said she could not remember exactly how she had offended me. I reminded her about the bracelet and she nodded sadly and promised not to mention it again.

We moved onto the intricacies of English grammar, something my pupil had to perfect before I could leave the villa. Her pronunciation also needed attention and she tried especially hard this morning in an effort to appease me.

I couldn't be angry with her indefinitely. She was at a difficult age and one mustn't forget the hereditary madness flowing in her veins.

Before our lesson concluded, she touched my hand, her violet eyes pleading. 'You won't tell Papa, will you, miss?'

'I won't lie to him should he ask,' I replied, and this seemed to satisfy her because how else would her father hear about the incident if I didn't inform him of it?

To my surprise, Sibylla walked into the schoolroom as we were about to leave. She glanced at Liesel and Liesel left immediately with a look of fretful anxiety.

'Poor child,' Sibylla murmured. 'I hear she has offended you, Fräulein Brown, and I must accept part of the blame for I agreed to loan her the money to purchase your bracelet.'

'My bracelet was never for sale, your highness.'

'It's an extraordinary piece, and I'm certain it once belonged to the von Holsteins.'

'Have you any proof?'

I said the words before I could retract them and immediately realized my mistake.

'The emblem of the serpent belongs to the von Holsteins and there is a story of a missing bracelet in the family. Ask the Count if you do not believe me. He knows more about it than I do.'

I nodded, relieved when she went to be on my own. Could it be true? Did the bracelet once belong to them? How did they lose it? More importantly, how did Granny get it?

Granny.

I had sent my letter off and now would have to await her reply. I hoped it would be soon for I did not want to be labelled a thief. Perhaps Granny stole it? The idea was absurd, but it might explain why she refused to sell it.

Her words rose to haunt me once again: *I trust whatever you do with the bracelet will be right.*

\*     \*     \*

I didn't seek out the Count until the next day. I had no desire to ask for an official appointment, however, nor did I want to use Ernst Mendel's method of lurking, a method I deplored as much as the man.

I had strategically avoided him these last few days, hoping he would finally desist in his pursuit of me. His advances did not seem normal and hinted of desperation. There was something else about him I didn't like, the insincerity of his words perhaps or the nature of his attachment to me. Every time I moved, I felt his cool grey eyes studying me for a purpose I could not fathom.

It might only be his way of attempting to fulfil the vacant position as his wife, as Dara led me to believe, but I did not like the man or his methods. And this he knew.

Yet he persisted.

I was thinking over this problem when I saw

263

the Count enter the parlour. He was alone. I waited until the servants took his coat and hat before I pretended I hadn't seen him and breezed into the parlour toward the door.

We stared at each other for a moment, disbelief on his part and feigned shock on mine.

'Fräulein . . .'

He couldn't even say my name.

'Cristabel,' I offered coolly.

He nodded as though he understood my anger. 'You are going for a walk?'

'Yes, my lord.'

'Would you allow me to accompany you? There is a matter I want to discuss with you.'

I shrugged and went out the door. When I heard him follow, I couldn't help a little smile. What I had glimpsed in his face was proof enough he did not mean to reject me so cruelly. There was another reason . . . a reason I had yet to discover.

We walked into the sunshine.

'You hate me, don't you?'

'I believe it is difficult to hate one's employer, my lord.'

'So we are back to the beginning. You promised not to call me by my title.'

'Did I? How *clumsy* of me to forget.'

He stopped suddenly and faced me, his eyes searching mine. 'I have not forgotten what happened between us in the summer-house. *If only I could forget*, things would be easier to bear.'

I stood still, transfixed by his intense proximity, the regret in his eyes and in the line of his mouth. I wanted to reach out and touch him, to assure him whatever troubles tormented him I would gladly share the burden.

'You once promised me you would always tell the truth,' he murmured. 'I am asking you now. Will you keep that promise?'

'Yes,' I whispered.

'Then answer me truthfully. Do you believe I murdered my wife?'

'I do not believe it of the man I know.'

'Yet I am a complex man and the man you didn't know could have done it.'

'I suppose he could have.'

'And what makes you believe he didn't do it?'

'A feeling.' I turned away to hide my embarrassment. 'A silly feeling . . .'

He lifted my chin up to face him, a slight smile hovering on his lips. 'I am pleased to hear you say it. It does not signify what the world thinks of me. Do you understand?'

'Then you are innocent?'

His smile disappeared. 'It is a matter of some dispute. Do you believe me capable of murder?'

'Anyone is capable of murder.'

'Then I pose a question. What does a man do when he is shackled to a wife who

265

dishonours the family name at every possible opportunity?'

His cryptic tone filled my heart with joy. He didn't love Malena; perhaps he never had.

'Don't be too quick to judge me innocent,' he warned. 'I am considered a dangerous man, one who murders to get what he wants. You think I do not know what they say about me? Even my own servants whisper amongst themselves. Old Josef is the most successful, I believe. Has he approached you yet with the slaughter of the beloved older brother by the younger wicked brother?'

I nodded; amazed he could treat the subject so lightly. 'Why do you keep him?'

'He is an old retainer. I cannot remove him.'

'Even if he speaks against you?'

'I am very tolerant for a murderer, aren't I?'

'I imagine in medieval times you would have his tongue removed.'

He grinned. 'Don't give me ideas: I may act upon them.'

We started back toward the house. I didn't have to look up at the windows to know we were being observed.

I brought up the matter of the bracelet. He listened very intently as I prattled on, skilfully avoiding Liesel's involvement in the scheme to buy it.

'Sibylla spoke out of turn. The bracelet does not belong to us but to you.'

'Did you lose such a bracelet?'

A mysterious smile touched his lips. 'It is yours in more ways than you can possibly imagine.'

Before I could ask what he meant by those words, a magnificent carriage pulled by four white horses rolled smoothly down the drive.

When the Count paused, I disappeared around the back of the villa. I had never seen a royal carriage and I was certain this one was a royal carriage. Why I should be so surprised I did not know. The von Holsteins had connections with the house of Hapsburg and their own ancient line descended from kings of old.

I hid behind a tree in the garden to watch the procession. Elaborately dressed footmen jumped off the back of the carriage to open the emblazoned doors where three ladies descended. The first two emerged, glittering with jewels and their own self-importance. The identity of the third lady surprised me. Baroness Outten! I had never imagined her to be in the company of such companions.

Curiosity drove me into the house where I heard a supercilious voice say, 'My dear Count, Her Royal Highness, the Empress, is very interested in your villa.'

'Indeed,' said the other, 'the Empress plans to build her own villa like it and has commanded us to gather ideas, if my lord agrees?'

'A royal wish is a royal command,' the Count

replied. 'Would you like me to give you a tour, Duchess Esterhazy?'

'This is only a short visit, Count. Her majesty has heard of your ballroom and wishes me to appraise it.'

'Then to the ballroom it is.'

The Duchess nodded. 'Sophie, you and Baroness Outten shall wait for me here. Is your daughter at home, Count von Holstein?'

'I'm afraid my daughter is out with her cousin, Princess Strecken-buriltz.'

'A shame. The empress is very interested in your daughter, Count von Holstein, since the early death of her mother.'

The Count remained silent.

'An unfortunate affair . . . the Empress has heard the rumours and wishes to speak to you. You are to present yourself at the palace for a royal dinner. An official invitation will naturally be sent in advance . . .'

The voices trailed off and I scrambled to my senses. Where I had developed the art of eavesdropping, I did not know. I think I managed to convince a passing housemaid of my innocence as I headed for the stairs.

'Fräulein Brown?'

I turned around as Baroness Outten approached me with a warm smile. 'I believe your charge is out with her cousin this afternoon?'

'Yes, they are often out in the afternoons.'

'Leaving you for some much needed rest, I

wager.'

I waited for her to explain.

She laughed. 'You must forgive my impertinence. All I intended to imply is I am only too aware of the complexity of your pupil.' She glanced around her. 'Is there anywhere where we may have a private chat, Fräulein Cristabel?'

'The gardens, but your companion—'

'Oh, Sophie! She has restless legs and has wandered off. Don't worry, she will return before the Duchess does. The Duchess is very punctual.'

We strolled through the gardens where the Baroness could see Duchess Esterhazy perusing the ballroom.

'Liesel is a difficult girl,' the Baroness began, 'but I applaud your success with her.'

'My success?'

'Why, yes; you, my dear Fräulein Cristabel, have accomplished an almost impossible feat.'

'And what is that?'

'You have remained longer than any of your predecessors.'

I immediately thought of Fräulein Suski and shivered. Had she simply fallen to her death or had someone pushed her? A vision of Liesel smiling her secret, strange smile suddenly haunted me. She could not remember if she had slashed my dress. Perhaps she could not remember if she had pushed Fräulein Suski over the edge of the mountain?

269

I didn't want to consider it but I must and the Baroness seemed to follow my thoughts.

'She is harmless at times, but she must be watched . . . just like Malena.'

The Baroness stared ahead of her, lost in her own memories. 'I met Malena on her wedding day. She was the most beautiful bride Austria has ever seen. Nobody would ever have suspected what lay behind such radiant beauty.

'I can't blame Max for what he did. If Malena had lived, Liesel would have been corrupted by now and beyond our influence.'

'Are you insinuating the Count murdered his wife?'

'I do not insinuate: I know it. Malena spoke to me the day before she disappeared. Do you know what she said? She said Max wanted to get rid of her. And do you know why? I'll tell you why: Malena was carrying a child, a child that did not belong to her husband.'

She turned me toward the glass doors where the Count and the Duchess exited. 'The man you see laughing there is a murderer. Be warned, my dear. Do not become too involved. The von Holstein men are handsome and passionate, but they do not like to be crossed. You only have to think of Rachel to realize I am speaking the truth.'

I couldn't speak. I felt cold and numb.

'Yes, Rachel was murdered,' the Baroness whispered in my ear. 'Someone had left a coat on the lake and Rachel was drawn to it like a child. The ice had been cut underneath. Only weight was needed to make the trap work.'

'It c-can't be true,' I stammered.

'*It is*,' the whisper insisted, 'and the man you see there knows the truth yet he does nothing about it. Why? Not for the love of his cousin, I can assure you, but *for the honour of the family.*'

'I don't believe it.'

'Then you are a fool and disloyal to your friend. You should leave this place while you can. *Leave* and never return.' She smiled brightly as the Count and the Duchess started toward us. 'Thank you for walking with me, Fräulein Brown. It has been *most* rewarding.'

I stood there in shock as they passed me into the house. The Duchess did not have to acknowledge servants, of course, even if I was an upper-class one.

Relieved to be ignored, I returned to my room in a dare. My hand shook as I reached out to turn the knob on my door. *Rachel murdered, and the Count knew!* It all made sense. He had denounced my accusations against his cousin *for the honour of the family.* The honour of the family came first and only a murderer would know how to make a crime look like an accident. Hadn't he succeeded with his wife? He'd been acquitted, yet the suspicion remained.

So weak and shaken by this news, I did not

notice the state of my room when I first entered. I gazed at my pale face in the mirror and in the reflection saw the emptied drawers, tossed coverlets and letters and books scattered across the room.

Someone had been in my room searching for something. Why? I had nothing of value, except—

I looked around in horror, frantically checking the hiding place where I had put the bracelet. I closed my eyes in relief: it was still there.

But the questions remained. Who would want to steal a bracelet and why?

## CHAPTER THIRTEEN

The warmer days did not prepare me for the darkness to come.

How beautiful the villa looked with its summer blooms in the day and its spectacular lights at night! I knew, as long as I lived, I would never forget this time of endless parties and dinners, where danger seemed as far away as England itself.

The official inauguration of the World Fair occurred on 1 May and since its opening, I had been there twice, once with the family and once with Hugo and Emily. The fair attracted many international visitors including monarchs and rulers as exotic as the Shah of Persia.

I did not forget to write to Lady Gisela and inform her of my impression. I longed for the peace and tranquillity of the mountains and almost envied her being there. It was like another world, a place where dreams could indeed come true.

In Vienna reality reigned as did a sense of unease and a foreboding I did not understand. Perhaps I should do what the Baroness suggested: leave and never return.

But I couldn't leave. I had to discover if the man I loved was a murderer and one who protects murderers. I had to learn the truth for myself as much as for Rachel's memory.

The season excited Emily.

'We simply *cannot* leave yet. *Everyone is* here, even Nasr-ad-Din, the Shah of Persia. Is it true he offered to buy the Empress from the Emperor?'

I smiled at her. Only at Emily's hotel could I relax. Since the ransacking of my room, I trusted no one and carried the bracelet with me at all times. 'Liesel says so. She went to dine at the palace, as you know.'

'The Empress is *so beautiful*,' Emily sighed. 'Oh, I can't wait to write to Mama! Yesterday, we saw the Emperor—at a distance. He's very distinguished but not half as handsome as your count.'

'Emily, I wish you would stop referring to him as *my* count.'

She winked. 'I know your secret. You can trust me to keep it.'

'And what secret is that?'

'You are setting your cap at him, and why shouldn't you? It's a grand scheme.'

*If only you knew.* I'd thought about confiding in Emily and had decided against it. I had no evidence, only suspicions, and my suspicions changed daily.

I attempted to avoid everyone, Dara included. Visits to her villa only depressed me and I sent her invitations back politely. It was an odd arrangement. She never once stepped outside the boundaries of her villa and Herr Mendel and the Count proved to be her only visitors when I desisted.

The Count. I avoided him too, though without detection, I surmised, because he was hardly ever at home. He left early and returned late. I sometimes watched him leave from my window and experienced an intense longing in the pit of my stomach.

I continued my lessons on English grammar with Liesel and wondered about her renewed efforts. She wanted me to leave too. The sooner she perfected her grammar, the sooner I would leave. She knew I would not abuse her father's charity if I had no purpose for being here.

I was not the only one to notice a change in Liesel. She worked very hard at her lessons, but she could not hide the shadow beneath her eyes.

Frau Bruns provided the answer one night when she woke me in a panic.

'Fräulein Brown, come quick.'

I recognized the voice in the darkness. 'Frau Bruns? Is that you?'

'Yes, it's me.'

I put on my slippers and grabbed a wrap. 'Is it Liesel?'

She wouldn't answer any of my questions, but led me to Liesel's room. The moonlight cast an eerie glow on her unoccupied bed.

'I found this in her bed.' Frau Bruns thrust a doll into my hands.

'Do you often check on her at nights?'

Frau Bruns shook her head. 'I put her in bed and give her a drink, like I did with her mother. But Liesel didn't drink what I'd made for her.'

She guided me to a basin where I assumed in the light one could see the evidence that the special mixture had not been consumed. I glanced around the room in the darkness. Where would she go at this time of night? How did she get out?

The window, and a very obliging tree.

I sat down. 'We must wait for her, Frau Bruns. We must not fall asleep, as we want to judge her reaction. Can you go downstairs and make us some coffee?'

She nodded.

'Good, because it could be a long night.'

And it was a long night. Despite the strong coffee, I nodded off once or twice, but when I heard the latch of the window some hours later, my sleepiness suddenly deserted me.

Liesel crawled into the room, oblivious to Frau Bruns and I hiding in the shadows. She must have smelt the coffee for she looked around her frantically and her face paled when she saw the cups left on her dresser.

I stepped out. 'Liesel, where have you been?'

She gave Frau Bruns a withering glance. Frau Bruns lifted her shoulders in answer and I said, 'Won't you sit down?'

Knowing she had no alternative, she removed her dark, hooded cape and sat down, a petulant snarl on her lips.

'You've been spying on me. Are you going to run to Papa like you always do?'

I sat down and faced her. 'Liesel, you know that is not true and you haven't answered my question. Where have you been?'

'I don't have to answer to you,' she snapped.

'Then you leave me no alternative but to wake your father.' I headed toward the door.

'Wait.'

I half turned. 'Do you have a confession to make?'

'I promise I'll tell you everything if you promise not to wake Papa.'

'If it is important, he may have to be told in the morning,' I warned.

'I haven't done anything *wrong*,' she insisted. 'Do you mind if I change first? This dress is terribly uncomfortable.'

I waited as she disappeared into her dressing-room to change. Frau Bruns picked up her discarded cape and frowned. Silently, she showed me the initials inside. OS.

Liesel caught us inspecting it.

'Who is OS?' I asked.

She snatched the cape out of my hands. 'OS is a . . . friend.'

'A friend?'

She nodded, tugging the train of her dressing-gown. She sent Frau Bruns another scalding glance and Frau Bruns quickly disappeared.

'You mustn't be angry with her, Liesel. She thought you could be in danger.'

A low chuckle escaped her lips. 'Frau Bruns is a silly old hen.'

'Even silly old hens can sniff danger when danger is present.'

I watched the candlelight flicker across her face. 'Everyone thinks I'm still a child but I'm not. I hate it.'

'Do you believe it is a grown-up thing to do to sneak out of the house and deceive your father?'

Her face flushed. 'I went to meet a friend.'

'This OS is presumably male?'

'Yes, Odin Smith is a poor musician. I met him at my last school.' Her violet eyes

277

widened. 'Papa would never understand. If he knew, he'd forbid me to see Odin.'

'As well he should. You don't know Mr Smith's motives. He may be a fortune-hunter seeking some easy prey.'

'I'm *not* easy prey.'

I lifted my shoulders. 'He must be very persuasive to convince you to sneak out of your father's house in the middle of the night.'

'I haven't done anything *wrong*, miss.'

'Perhaps not yet, but you must cease this behaviour at once. Consider the harm it could do your reputation if you were caught? Consider your father and how bitterly this news would disappoint him?'

'Father'—a whimsical smile touched her lips—'*hates* me so what does it matter what I do?'

'He doesn't hate you, but behaving like this will not help you.'

She nodded, suddenly solemn. 'Will you say nothing, miss, if I promise to do what you say?'

'I can't make you that promise, Liesel.'

Her hand shot out to grasp mine. She fell on her knees and raised her terror-stricken face. '*Please, miss.* I beg you. I promise I'll be good. I promise to do everything you say.'

And with such an appeal, how could I possibly refuse?

\*       \*       \*

Frau Bruns and I decided to monitor Liesel over the next few weeks. To my surprise, Liesel did not complain about these arrangements, however, nor did she pretend to be happy about it. She was strangely restive and I wondered if this Odin Smith meant more to her than I had originally assumed.

A poor musician? Yes, I could see Liesel being enchanted at the *idea* of such a romance. Someone who understood her passion for music, someone who *declared* his love for her, love she felt her father denied her.

An overwhelming sense of pity for this tortured girl led me to ignore my own judgement on the matter. Of course, her father should have been told. I should have told him. But I could not; not when she promised to give up her secret assignations with the elusive Mr Smith.

Difficult days passed. I constantly felt tired and drawn from my nightly watch as shared with Frau Bruns. We couldn't trust the other servants, however, and it was inevitable someone should discover our plan.

Frau Vetsera summoned me downstairs one morning.

'Miss Brown, what is this charade you and Frau Bruns are playing?'

'Miss von Holstein is . . . suddenly afraid of the dark,' I improvised.

'Miss von Holstein has a maid and a nurse to look over her, does she not?'

'Yes, but she wanted Frau Bruns and me especially.'

Those black eyes bored into me. 'I think not, Fräulein Brown.'

'Oh, I assure you, it is quite true,' I bluffed. 'Ask Miss von Holstein if you do not believe me.'

I endured a moment of panic before I realized she would not dare ask Liesel anything in her current mood.

I went away and immersed in the aftermath of my success, I did not see danger coming.

Ernst Mendel blocked my path in the corridor.

'Good morning,' I said with false cheer, and attempted to pass.

He raised a hand. 'Cristabel . . . I can't let you go. You wound me deeply with your aloofness. I know this is an English trait—'

'Herr Mendel,' I said, as coolly as I could muster, 'please let me pass.'

'No,' he whispered.

I glanced at his impassioned face. Why did he continue to refuse to take no for an answer? I detested the man; could he not see it? 'Ernst, if I have given you the wrong impression, I humbly apologize, but I must beg you again, sir, to please let me pass.'

His hands suddenly imprisoned me against the wall. 'How can I, when you tempt me so? Am I so repulsive in your eyes?'

I glanced down the hall, hoping, *willing*,

someone to find us. 'It's not that, it's—'

'*Him*, isn't it? The Count . . . you have your sights on the lord of the manor. That is why you refuse my humble proposal.'

'I gave you my answer, sir, and it is no. Must I ask you again to release me?'

A terrible smile appeared on his face. 'You deserve to be punished for your incivility. And punished you will be.'

I felt his mouth on mine, hard, unrelenting, wanting to inflict pain. I struggled inside his iron embrace, scratched, bit, and kicked, whatever necessary to escape his mouth for one vital moment.

It happened. I screamed.

So did several maids and the noise brought the Count running down the hall. His gaze swept across us, absorbing the scene, noting the welts on my neck where my attacker had left evidence of his insistence.

He asked the servants to leave before he raised a questioning brow at Ernst Mendel.

'You've an adventuress in your house, my lord,' Ernst smiled. 'I merely attempted to expose her and she attacked me.'

'Attacked you? And how do you explain the marks on her neck?'

'Purely defence.'

'Against a lady?'

Ernst chuckled. 'She's no lady, but a *whore* after your title. Can't you see it, or has she managed to blind you too?'

281

The Count turned to me. 'What happened?'

'I have rejected his offer of marriage and he wouldn't let me pass.'

'She *lies*,' Ernst spat. 'A born adventuress she is, using her pretty face and her *false* modesty to bag you.'

'You must have thought highly of her once to make an offer of marriage?'

'Before I discovered what she really is. You must dismiss her, my lord. She's created enough disruption in this house.'

'It is *you* who have caused the disruption, Herr Mendel,' the Count replied smoothly. 'By attacking Fräulein Brown, as witnessed by the housemaids, *you* are the one who should be dismissed.'

I watched Ernst's face flush, dark and furious, as though he couldn't believe what had just been said.

'Either you apologize to Miss Brown, or you leave this house. I advise you to think over your decision very carefully, Herr Mendel.'

'Why don't we dispense with the formalities, *Brother*. You've always wanted to be rid of me some way or another, but I have no further need of your charity.'

'No? Who will pay your exorbitant gaming debts? Not your fine friends, I'll wager.'

Trapped against the wall, I glanced from one to the other. *Brothers?* Yes, many things made sense now. Ernst Mendel had never been treated as an ordinary steward and how his resentment must have grown over the years, watching the family, knowing he shared their blood but could never share their status.

He turned to me, his face distorted and full of scorn. 'Yes, I am the *bastard* son of the late Count. Do you find this news distasteful?'

I suddenly feared what he might do. Rage like his evolved from a deep-rooted antipathy. 'I do not think of you any less because of it,' I ventured to say.

Blue eyes burned into mine. 'But still you reject me?'

'I do not love you. How can I marry a man whom I do not love?'

He laughed, an awful, dangerous laugh, before he nodded curtly. 'Then I bid you farewell, Cristabel Brown, but I shan't apologize. I know when I am not wanted and I shall leave of my own volition. Good day.'

I watched him stride past. He paused once to look at the Count. I couldn't see his face, but I could guess at the expression on it. He hated his half-brother because his half-brother had everything he desired, myself included.

I could no longer pretend. I loved the Count. I wanted no other. Every other man paled against him. It might be a foolish fancy, but I had formed a habit of dreaming about him at night, dreaming about a knight of old, Conrad reborn into Maximus.

Maximus. I longed to call him my Maximus but I dared not.

'Are you hurt? Did he harm you?'

I closed my eyes at his voice, a voice I lived to hear. 'I am fine. Is it true what he said? Is he really your brother?'

'Yes. Come to my study where we can talk unobserved.'

I followed him there, ignorant of the servants chatting in the corner as we passed and disappeared into the room.

The fire beckoned. I warmed my hands while he poured the wine. When he handed me my glass, our fingers touched, the touch so fleeting and yet it evoked such an intensely alive feeling. I willed him to do it again and might have asked if he had not spoken. I quickly sipped my wine as I listened, needing the spicy liquid more to forget his touch than Herr Mendel's attack.

'Yes, it's true. Ernst Mendel is my half-brother. While my mother lived, we kept the secret of his existence from her. My father left instructions on his deathbed for the care of Ernst and my brother and I have tried to honour his wishes.'

'He resents you bitterly.'

'I can't blame him. He didn't learn of his real father's identity until his tenth birthday, which happened to coincide with mine. His mother, who had kept the secret, drank herself into a state and informed the boy he would never be recognized as one of the family. Instead, he would have to live the lie, or he

284

would have to leave the castle and never return. Ernst decided to keep the secret, but on my mother's death, he made the mistake of approaching my father. My father loved my mother, you see, and seeing the boy reminded him of his one indiscretion which he gravely regretted.'

'Why did he not send them away?'

'It would have easier if he had. But Ernst begged to stay in the castle and agreed to all of my father's conditions. My father was a good man. He didn't want the boy to suffer but neither could he fulfil the boy's demand to be recognized as part of the family. Recognition of bastards does not occur in families like ours.'

I wondered if this applied to Dara and her son or would he make an exception in their case? Of course, if he married Dara, her son *could* be legitimized and recognized as a von Holstein, something Ernst Mendel had never achieved.

'Who was his mother?'

'A peasant girl who developed a nasty habit of drinking herself into oblivion in later years. She died a year after my mother and left Ernst nursing her discontent. On his deathbed, my father made Rudolf and I swear to take care of him.'

I finished my wine. 'He has turned against the hand that fed him.'

The Count stared into the fire. 'It was

285

inevitable. For the past year, I have been honouring his debts, but it shall not continue. He dared to attack you . . .'

I waited for him to say *the woman I love.*

But he did not. Instead, he continued to stare into the fire. 'Cristabel, you should leave this madness. Go back to England, marry some English saint and never return.'

'Do you wish me to leave?'

'No! But I dare not ask you to stay.'

We studied each other for a moment before I found myself in his arms, hearing what I longed to hear and experiencing what I only dared to dream.

He held my face in his hands, a mocking glint in his eyes. 'This is madness. How can you prefer me to a safe English saint?'

'Very easily,' I assured him. 'I don't want a safe life.'

A whimsical smile touched his lips. 'My brave, foolish girl. When I said you should leave, I meant it. You believe yourself in love with a man who doesn't deserve your love and *can never deserve it.*'

I took his hands in mine. 'No one can dictate who we love and who we should not love.'

'Foolish girl. Can you honestly love a man who murdered his own brother?'

'It's not true. I don't believe it.'

'You'll have to believe it, just as I've had to accept it. I should know. I was there.'

The certainty in his voice frightened me. 'What do you mean?'

'I handed my brother the pistol I had checked and repaired. It misfired and he died. Others said I had planned it. Maybe I did. Who will ever know when the truth can't be proved?'

'It wasn't your fault. It was an accident.'

He smiled. 'How quick you are to defend me, but the facts can't be changed. I killed my brother: I know I did.'

I read the pain in his face. 'Perhaps somebody tampered with the pistol after you—before you gave it to your brother. Perhaps somebody who coveted and may still covet your title.'

He laughed. 'If you're speaking of my cousin Karl, he doesn't have the brain for strategy.'

'A shooting accident doesn't require a great deal of strategy. Was the Baron out hunting with you that day?'

'Yes, Karl was there. But he loved Rudolf and mourned him more than I did. Rudolf and I never saw eye to eye on matters. He liked to indulge in a life of idleness and dissipation, a lifestyle which earned him equal amounts of popularity and contempt.'

Yes, I could envisage the laughing, popular Rudolf, surrounded by his elite group of friends, his love of hunting, gambling and women evident in the society he kept. The

287

kind of society I imagined the Baron frequented, the kind of society my Maximus detested.

'You are smiling. What do you find so amusing?'

'You, my lord. You are the younger brother, yet you act as the disapproving elder. Are you certain you have not indulged in a similar lifestyle?'

'Perhaps I have,' he grinned. 'Dare I blame it on the blood? We von Holsteins are said to be cursed with a passion we cannot control.'

'And is the curse true?'

He lifted my chin up to face him as his eyes searched mine. The intensity of his gaze alerted me and for a moment I believed we could have been in another time, another place where convention and the rules of etiquette did not exist. A time where anything was possible, even the impossible.

We stared at each other as though in a trance.

'I knew you would come one day. I've waited for you.'

'And I you,' I whispered. 'What is happening?'

'You feel it too?'

I nodded because I could no longer speak. His lips descended on mine and transported me to that other world where I wanted to be, the world where my home existed.

'Oh, my darling!' He captured my face in his

288

hands. 'How I've dreamt of nothing else but you. My every thought, every minute of the day is consumed by you.'

His confession warmed my heart, dispelling the web of doubts in my mind. 'I—I thought that you . . .'

'No,' he murmured. 'I have not forgotten. How could I?'

'I don't know,' I answered honestly. 'I certainly wouldn't call the night a forgettable one.'

'It was special, unlike anything I've ever experienced before.'

I arched a brow. 'I won't ask how many women you've said that to.'

He looked offended. 'What I say is the truth. I can't explain it.'

Snaking my hands around his neck, I drew up to kiss him, to savour those lips again.

'I hate us being apart.' I buried my face against his chest. 'I hate all this secrecy.'

'So do I.'

A far-away look had come into his eyes. Withdrawing slowly from me, he paced before the bookcase, his hands clutched behind his back. 'I haven't spoken to you because I haven't been at liberty to do so. I can only assure you that my intentions are honourable.'

Why did his voice have to sound so cold? 'Your intentions,' I began, 'are not what concern me at the moment. What *does* concern me is how you feel about me. Am I some passing distraction to you? Or am I what I hope I am to you?'

'Oh, Cristy,' he moaned. 'You must know how I feel about you.'

Perhaps it was the tremble in his voice, the hopeful timbre of emotion in his face that sent me running back to his arms. Enshrouded in the warmth of him, I pressed my mouth to his, drawing from him what I wanted so badly: his soul.

And that is how Frau Vetsera found us.

We sprang apart when she entered, the very unwanted voice of convention jolting us from our delicious, forbidden world.

'Pardon, my lord, but there is a visitor to see Fräulein Brown. A lady.'

Her black eyes scalded me.

'Get out, Vetsera!' the Count barked. 'Get out!'

She closed the door on us, but not before I detected the tiny smile on her lips.

We drew apart and I had to smile. What else was there to do?

She won't repeat what she saw,' the Count said.

I studied him. 'How can you be so sure?'

'Because if she does'—he kissed me one last time—'she'll be dismissed quicker than a red-handed thief.'

I still felt mortified at having been caught in such a compromising position. 'I don't want her to think—'

'Too late, my love,' he laughed. 'Too late.'

*      *      *

Emily discovered my secret, as I knew she would.

'You're in love,' she blurted when we retreated to my room.

I could see no point in denying it. 'Yes.'

'And does your Count love you? Has he proposed to you?'

I sat down with a sigh. 'Not yet.'

'But you believe he will?'

'I *hope* he will.'

'But they say he has a mistress who is here in Vienna. Surely you've heard about her?'

'I have. She's residing here in the small villa with her son.'

'And this does not bother you?'

'Oh, Emily! It is so hard to explain what I feel, but I know he is the one. It might be an impossible dream, especially when everything appears to be against us, but I love him.'

Emily frowned. 'And what if he does not propose to you? Will you agree to be his mistress?'

'He will propose. He is honourable.' The words left my mouth and I hoped they convinced Emily.

They did not. 'How can he be honourable with a mistress and son living on his estate?'

'I don't believe she is . . . or has been . . . for

291

sometime.'

'Has he told you so?'

'No, we have not discussed her yet. There have been other concerns.'

She nodded. 'Like the murder of his wife and brother? Cristabel, I must beg you to be careful. He is handsome and charming, to be sure, but the rumours about him are monstrous.'

'They are all untrue.'

She sighed. 'I can see you're in love with him and it's a credit to you to believe he is innocent, but I just want you to be careful. Hugo and I want you to be careful.'

'I will be,' I promised her. 'When do you leave?'

'In another week or two. We have been invited to several parties so we have decided to extend our stay. Are you still coming to the opera this evening?'

'Yes, but I shall not be attending the Shooenberg soirée afterwards. Princess Sibylla is most kind to invite me to the opera but I will not trespass on her generosity by following them there. I shall return to the villa.'

Emily examined me. 'Not with the Count, I hope?'

'No!'

'Ah, you blush and thereby admit the thought is delicious.'

'*Emily.*'

'Don't you Emily me. I am a married

woman now. Let us hope you shall soon be one too. Hugo is ready to defend you should this Count offer you a *carte blanche.*'

'I'll never accept a *carte blanche.*'

'So said the last woman who became a mistress. Are you sure you'd be strong enough to leave this man if there can be no honourable future with him?'

'Yes, though it would break my heart, I would.'

She embraced me. 'Then I am satisfied. Just remember you are welcome to return with us if it does not go as planned with this Count.'

I nodded and watched her go, confident of a proposal in the next few days.

\*      \*      \*

Dara was accompanying us to the opera.

I did not believe it when Liesel told me. 'Are you certain?'

'Yes. Papa informed Sibylla and I at breakfast. He said he could not have you return to the villa by yourself so invited Miss Quinn to come and would hear no argument against it.' Her mouth set in an ugly line. 'I hate Dara and her stupid son. I wish they'd go away or die.'

'Liesel, that is a horrible thing to say.'

'Is it? Why should one pretend? You hated Herr Mendel and arranged his dismissal. Am I wrong to want the same?'

I asked her how much she knew of Herr Mendel's dismissal.

She smiled. 'It's supposed to be a secret, but you can't keep a secret from me. Why didn't you tell me?'

'It only happened this morning.'

She studied me thoughtfully. 'I didn't think you would accept him. Ernst Mendel has nothing to recommend him, does he? He might be a von Holstein but he's a *bastard*.' She laughed. 'I told you, you can't keep a secret from me. And now I must ask you something, miss. Are you in love with my father?'

'Y-yes.'

'You came here to set your cap at him?'

'No, I came here to teach you English.'

'But when you saw him, you decided to trap him?'

'I don't believe your father can be trapped into anything.'

A whimsical smile appeared on her lips. 'And does my father love you?'

'You'd have to ask him that question: I cannot answer for him.'

'So he hasn't declared his love for you yet?'

I shook my head.

'But you wish it?'

'Yes, I wish it.'

'And you want to marry him?'

'That is the general progression when one is in love.'

Her violet eyes scanned my face. 'You are honest with me, aren't you, miss?'

'Why wouldn't I be?'

She shrugged. 'Many people lie when they are afraid, but you do not, miss.'

'There is little to gain from lying. One is always found out.'

'Not always. Some people are very what is the word?—*skilled* at it. So skilled they can even murder and get away with it.'

Her face suddenly paled as she glanced out of the window. Did she know something? She had been mulish ever since Frau Bruns and I had discovered her nightly escapade. But had we mistaken her defiance for fear? 'Liesel, if you ever need to confide in someone, I am here.'

She nodded and quickly asked what I intended to wear to the opera. Her former childish excitement returned and she followed me to my room where we sifted through my garments.

'Wear this, miss.'

The green dress.

'With your bracelet. Have you heard from your grandmother yet?'

'Not yet and I really must persuade you to forget about buying it for I will never sell it.'

Her hand seized my arm. 'And I must *persuade* you, miss, to *sell* it. If you do not . . .'

I glanced at her frenzied face. 'And if I do not?'

She forced a smile. 'I will be very upset! It belongs to us, but I suppose if you do marry my father, you'll become one of us, won't you.'

'Liesel, you go too fast.'

'It is funny to think you could be my stepmother.'

'You would resent me?'

She considered. 'Maybe, but at least you may be consoled in the fact I do not hate you as I hate Dara.'

And I had to be content with that.

\*　　　\*　　　\*

As I dressed for the opera, I couldn't dispel an unpleasant premonition. Something would occur this evening. I could feel it.

The feeling only intensified when I slid the cool bracelet on to my arm. The eyes of the serpent mocked me as they glittered in a silent warning I did not understand.

I glanced at my reflection in the mirror. The exquisite cut of the dress did little to humour me. I knew I should stay but I could not. Something propelled me to go.

Liesel stood at the door. 'You look nice, miss.'

I returned the compliment and she nodded as she sat on the edge of my bed. I studied her face in the mirror. She seemed strangely preoccupied. Did she feel it too? Or did she know?

'Miss—'

A maid came to advise the carriage awaited us. I thanked her as I went in search of my reticule. 'What were you going to say, Liesel?'

She left my bed. 'I suppose we must go. We don't want to miss the beginning of the opera, do we?'

I sat beside Dara in the carriage. I had never seen her look more beautiful. She wore a deep purple satin gown with the Count's diamonds glittering at her ears. I felt very insignificant in my green dress, however, the bracelet could not be called insignificant.

'Very unusual,' Dara commented on the way there. 'It belonged to your grandmother, did it not?'

I nodded and she glanced at the Count. I could not interpret the silent exchange between them. It was an awkward journey. Liesel remained curiously silent while Dara prattled on and I believe she experienced the same acute relief when we finally arrived at the opera.

'Oh, it's sure to be a memorable night,' Dara gushed, as we alighted. 'Look at the carriages! I daresay there'll be a crush inside.'

Her assumption proved to be correct. Men and women crammed the reception room. Dara, Liesel and I disappeared to the cloakroom where we found Sibylla taking off her fur coat.

Her eyes sparkled. 'What good timing! I

297

never would have found you both out there.'
She pointedly ignored Dara as she squeezed
between Liesel and I. 'Come, Karl is waiting
for us outside.'

The Baron smiled when we approached.
'Max has gone up and I have been given the
commission of escorting you ladies to the
family box. Unfortunately, I can only take two
on my arm.'

Liesel immediately claimed one while
Sibylla claimed the other, leaving Dara and I
to follow.

'I believe he offered his arm to *you*, not to
them,' Dara whispered to me, as we walked
along the carpeted corridor. 'Confess now,
what is your secret weapon where the men are
concerned? They are all madly in love with
you.'

I felt the colour rush to my face. She must
have guessed my feelings for the Count, for
her lover and the father of her child.

We reached the box. 'I have to warn you,'
she smiled, as her gaze fixed on the Count, 'I
do not intend to lose.'

'Nor do I,' I smiled back, gliding past her.

Pleasantries resumed in the box. The Baron
sat beside me while Dara sat beside the Count,
much to the annoyance and, I believe,
astonishment, of Sibylla and Liesel.

'Resourceful girl Dara,' Karl whispered in
my ear, 'I daresay her efforts will soon be paid
off when she becomes the new Countess.'

I stared at him and he shrugged in apology. Could it be true? Had the Count let her sit next to him in order to prepare everyone for an announcement?

Liesel looked equally confused and I could not see Sibylla's face, but I imagined she wondered the same.

The opera began and I tried to suppress the hurt and anger welling inside me. How could he make love to me and then flaunt his mistress in front of me? I had never felt more of a fool.

I left halfway during the second act on the pretence of going to the powder room. I walked along the corridor, angry, confused. I would not cry. I *refused* to cry over him. I had to collect my senses and quickly, before anyone noticed.

When I felt well enough to return, I turned around, only to meet the source of my frustration.

He seemed surprised to see me. I noticed the card in his hand and nodded bitterly as fresh tears sprang to my eyes. I had been foolish to hope he had come out here looking for me.

'Cristabel, what is the matter?'

I angrily wiped the tears from my face. 'You don't care?'

'Don't be foolish.' He seized my arm and escorted me outside. He nodded politely to one or two people we passed on the way, explaining the 'lady' needed some air.

'Some air?' I lashed at him when we walked out on to the street. 'How it must amuse you to see me like this. This was your plan, wasn't it? To *humiliate* me in front of your mistress?'

'My mistress?'

'Dara!'

He laughed.

'How *dare* you laugh? Yes, it must be a great joke between you and her, the naïve little English girl who believed herself . . .'

'Who believed herself?' he prompted.

The faint mocking glint in his eyes urged me forward when the shot fired. I meant to slap him and instead fell into his arms, a strange burning pain in my shoulder. I saw blood on his sleeve . . . and the last thing I heard was the alarmed cries of onlookers on the darkened streets of Vienna.


# CHAPTER FOURTEEN

I awoke to the sound of humming.

Frau Bruns' face appeared before me, a little blurred. 'She's awake!'

I felt someone's hand touch mine.

It was Liesel. Tears of relief glistened in her eyes. 'Oh, miss, how are you feeling?'

'My shoulder hurts and I have a terrible headache.'

'As well you might,' said the voice I wanted to hear.

The Count sat in a chair by my bed and monitored my pulse. 'Much better. What year is it and who is the Queen of England?'

'My brain isn't injured.' I rolled my eyes. 'Must you insist?'

'Yes, I must.'

I sighed. 'The year is 1873 and Victoria is Queen of England. There, are you satisfied?' He had not yet released my hand and I felt elated because of it.

Liesel sat on the other side of my bed. 'You saved Papa, miss. If you hadn't stepped forward, he would have died?'

I glanced at the Count for confirmation.

'A little melodramatic, but it's true.' He frowned, though he remained smiling, 'You foolish girl. What ever possessed you to save my life?'

'I mustn't have been thinking correctly.'

Liesel grinned. 'Her brain is fine, Papa. I don't know what you were worried about.' She translated for me: 'Papa thought you might have woken up with amnesia.'

'*Hoped*,' he clarified. 'I fancied the idea of keeping you a prisoner in a vulnerable state.'

'*Papa*,' Liesel groaned. 'Shall we go and tell the others now? They're still waiting downstairs.'

I watched them go, happy to note an improvement in their relationship.

301

Frau Bruns remained and I asked her all the questions I needed to know. The time, had they caught the villain, and who waited downstairs.

She shook her head. 'There's evil here. I felt it and when I saw the Count carry you in with blood all over your dress, I thought they'd killed you.'

'So they don't know who fired the shot?'

'No, unfortunately.'

I examined my nightdress and blushed. 'Who . . . ?'

'The Count,' Frau Bruns advised. 'I helped and all the work was done by the time the doctor came.'

'You still don't believe ill of the Count, do you, Frau Bruns?'

'I don't know, but something is very wrong here.'

'Liesel seems very happy.'

'Liesel is false. She's tortured in her mind.'

'Has she tried to escape again?'

Frau Bruns nodded. 'She tried last night, but I caught her.'

'Oh dear. I suppose we will have to tell her father. I had hoped—'

Someone knocked at the door.

Frau Bruns went to answer it and Sibylla and Dara entered the room. They were both very distressed over the incident and Dara first mentioned Herr Mendel as a suspect.

'He left the villa in a bitter rage; he could

have done it.'

Sibylla shook her head. 'Poor Ernst. He was never content. His mother never should have told him he was one of us.'

'Whoever fired the shot,' Dara continued, 'had a good reason for wanting to harm the Count. What of your brother, Princess? He's next in line.'

I couldn't believe the audacity of Dara.

Nor could Sibylla. 'Karl! How dare you accuse him?'

'I hear his debts are rather pressing,' Dara observed.

'Karl would never do anything unethical, no matter how pressing his debts. And who are you to judge? A poor Irish girl who climbed up the ladder from the sewer!'

'Better a poor girl from the sewer than a penniless princess—eh?'

Dora smiled at me before she left the room.

Sibylla was still in shock. 'She shall be punished for that outburst. *Who* is she? A sewer rat, nothing more! I don't know why my cousin keeps her.' She glanced apologetically at me. 'I should have behaved as a genteel lady and not answered her charge. Poor Karl. He is so wronged by the world. You believe in his innocence, don't you?'

'I would like to think so.'

'But you don't. You believe he killed his wife, but you are wrong. He still mourns her, you know. You shouldn't think so badly of him.

303

He values your good opinion.'

I closed my eyes.

'You are tired and must rest. You did a very brave thing, my dear.'

Frau Bruns saw her out. She had become my nurse and insisted I sleep. I gratefully conceded, overwhelmed by the visitations, as well meaning as they had been.

I drifted off, aware of a cloud of danger gathering around me and knowing I was unable to prevent it.

*       *       *

Hugo and Emily came to see me.

'I can't *believe* it. I thought Vienna a safe place. It's terrible someone should want to murder the Count.'

Hugo asked after my wound. I assured him I felt little pain thanks to Frau Brun's administration of laudanum, and I would make a full recovery.

'It's monstrous,' Emily cried. 'Hugo and I are quite determined you should accompany us back to England. If someone really wants to kill the Count, you could be in danger just by being here.'

'Emily, you know I can't leave yet.'

Hugo studied me in silence, his handsome face gravely concerned. 'I must insist, Cristabel. It is too dangerous.'

'When do you leave?'

'Friday next,' Emily answered. 'By then, you should be well enough to travel.'

I appreciated their concern and said as much.

Emily frowned as she glanced at her husband. 'Perhaps we should take her back to our hotel. Then we'd make sure she is safe.'

'You truly are special friends,' I smiled, 'but I am quite settled here and Frau Bruns is very good.'

Emily still didn't seem convinced.

'I thank you for your kind offer but please trust my judgement.'

'I will . . . for now.' She leaned forward to kiss my cheek.

'Do send word if you change your mind,' Hugo said.

I agreed, with the realization nothing but utter despair would make me leave the Count now.

*       *       *

My resolution strengthened over the next few days. The Count himself monitored my recovery and though no words had been spoken, a silent understanding existed between us.

Others had noticed, including Dara.

She brought Paul to my room as I rested one afternoon. I had ventured out for a walk in the morning and the exercise had tired me. I thought perhaps the laudanum had been a little too strong for I constantly felt sleepy and at times had drifted off into a snooze when someone had come to visit me.

I needed coffee to endure Dara's visit. She brought her son as a reminder to me of *her* understanding with the Count.

He showed me some pictures he'd been drawing.

I melted at the child's innocence. Seeing him made me feel homesick for my own family. For mother, Granny and Tommy. My letter would distress them when it arrived and they would insist I return home.

'He's such a good boy,' Dara whispered. 'Would you rob him of a father, Miss Brown?'

I was unprepared for her question.

She stared at me directly. 'I want to know what is between you and Max. Are you engaged?'

'We are not engaged.'

'And will you promise not to become engaged to him?'

'I will promise nothing of the kind.'

She smiled. 'You are a worthy rival, I must say. We both love the same man but whom will he choose?'

'If you are asking me, you cannot be confident he will choose you.'

'How very astute you are. The accident has not dulled your brain a whit.'

I seized the opportunity to change the

subject. 'Do you really believe the Count is in danger?'

'I don't believe it, I know it. When one has lived as I have lived, you learn to sense danger as you sense hunger. I know many people in Vienna. My friends at the opera houses keep me informed. They all expect something to happen to Max. This is why I have come. Between us, we must persuade him to leave Vienna. He will be safer at the *schloss*. While he remains here, he is in danger of losing his life.'

'What have you heard?'

'Someone wants him dead and it can only be Karl or Ernst. Ernst has little to gain, unless of course he is working with Karl. Don't you think it is ironic only days after Herr Mendel is dismissed, an attack is made on the Count?'

I nodded. 'He must be very bitter.'

'Yes . . . you were partly the cause, I believe. The von Holstein men are very passionate.'

'Herr Mendel was more than passionate. He was obsessed with the idea of marrying me.'

'Why do you find that so unbelievable? You are quite beautiful, you know.'

'I can't explain it . . . I just feel there is something odd about him.'

'Listen to your instincts then, for you may be correct.'

\*     \*     \*

The next day I discovered my bracelet was missing.

Frau Bruns had removed it on the night of my accident and had presented it to me when I awoke. I'd kept the bracelet under my pillow until the first time I left my bed and I had hidden it amongst my underwear. Not even the maids touched my underwear.

I pulled out the drawer, frantically searching through with one arm. My shoulder pained me but I had to keep looking. It must be there . . . it must.

It was gone. Someone had taken it, just as they had attempted to take it before.

I felt sickened, horrified and sank to the floor in despair.

Frau Bruns found me sobbing on the floor. 'What's wrong?'

'My bracelet, someone's stolen my bracelet.'

I did not want to cry like a baby but I felt the loss acutely. I couldn't explain why but I felt as if I'd lost my soul.

We questioned Liesel first.

She seemed genuinely surprised about the bracelet. 'I didn't take it. You can search my room if you don't believe me.'

I leaned against the wall.

'You look very pale, miss, you should rest.'

'How can I rest when my bracelet is missing?'

She nodded. 'I'll help you. We'll question all the staff.'

She did do this; however, I believed her efforts to be in vain. She knew very well where my bracelet was, she only *pretended* she didn't.

I mentioned my concerns to Frau Bruns. She listened intently to my plan and nodded silently. We would allow Liesel to sneak out tomorrow night and I would follow her, I suspected Liesel held the key to my missing bracelet.

*　　*　　*

The long-awaited letter from Granny arrived.

I saw it on my dresser when I returned to my room. I held it in my hands, wanting to open it and yet dreading to do so. The familiar handwriting prompted me to read what lay within.

> *My dearest child*
> *I received your letter with some concern. You must not sell the bracelet. I thought you would have realized its importance by now but since you obviously haven't, I must enlighten you.*
> *The bracelet is more than a bracelet: it is a legend. Those who seek it must never possess it. But in your hands, it is safe. Why, I cannot yet say, but you will learn the truth in time.*
> *Guard it well, my child, and return to me when you can. Then we will discuss it.*

309

*Your loving grandmother who misses you,*
      *Frieda*

I hugged the letter to me, wishing Granny could be here now. She would know what to do.

I went down to see the Count. I found him in the armoury, categorizing the swords and weaponry of a by-gone era.

He grinned as I approached. 'Conrad would have used such a sword. It appears I have been born in the wrong era. I would have loved charging off into battle with such a sword.'

'It's in your blood,' I murmured wryly. 'The warrior of old.'

He returned the sword to its place on the wall. 'The past has a curious way of affecting the future. An old woman once told me a woman would enter my life wearing an unusual bracelet. I never believed it until you arrived at the ball wearing it. Do you remember that night?'

'How could I forget?'

'I could no longer ignore my attraction to you. Should I blame the bracelet? Does it hold a secret power?'

A thread of humour echoed in his voice and quickly faded when I remained silent.

He came toward me. 'You are unwell. Allow me to carry you to your room.'

'No, I'm fine,' I assured him.

'Then we should proceed as planned.' He grimaced. 'I have longed to do so.'

'The bracelet is missing,' I blurted.

He paused. 'Missing?'

'Yes, I'd hidden it in my underclothes—'

*'Lucky bracelet.'*

'—but it's not there. I've searched everywhere for it.'

'Have you questioned the staff?'

'Liesel did,' I murmured. 'I can't lose it . . . not now.'

He drew me into his arms. 'It belonged to your grandmother, didn't it?'

I nodded miserably. Better to have him think it special because of that than because of its legendary power.

He summoned Frau Vetsera to us. She arrived within minutes, her pinched face paling at the sight of me clasped in his arms.

'You called for me, my lord?'

'We have a thief in the house, Frau Vetsera. A bracelet has been taken from Fräulein Brown's room.'

The black eyes studied me. 'And what does the bracelet look like, *fräulein*?'

I looked at her and thought: *she knows very well the answer to that question.* Why pretend she'd never seen or heard of it? Was she protecting Liesel? I didn't want to consider the likelihood of Liesel's guilt.

The Count explained it. 'It's very valuable to Fräulein Brown. I charge you with the responsibility of finding the culprit.'

'Yes, my lord.'

When she left, I said, 'I don't trust her . . .'

'My dearest love, she is only a housekeeper. You aren't afraid of her, are you?'

I closed my eyes at the wonder of his voice. 'No, I'm not afraid of her.'

'There's my brave English girl.' He held my face in his hands. 'She should be afraid of you for you will soon be her mistress.'

'Oh, will I? And why should you want to marry me?'

He kissed me. 'For countless reasons, one of them being I quite enjoy the idea of an English bride.'

I had dreamed of this moment and now it had arrived, I wanted to savour it forever. The murmur of his voice in my ear, a lover's voice murmuring things I could never repeat, the strength of his arms around me, holding me to him as his mouth explored mine in wondrous discovery.

I asked him about Malena and her unborn child.

'Yes, I knew about the child. She threatened to run away with her lover and create a scandal. I challenged her to do so because I hated living a life of deceit. I hated her, I wanted her gone, and I felt nothing but relief when I found her dead in the mountains. She'd been strangled, possibly by her lover, but for the sake of the family and for Liesel, we thought it better to say the cold had killed her.'

'Did you know who her lover was?'

'No, but Malena found his identity amusing. I don't even think she knew who the father of her child was. She had so many lovers and often liked to string along two at a time. It was her way; it made her feel alive, she said.'

'And what about Dara? Won't she be upset by our news?'

His thumb caressed my lips. 'I don't love Dara . . .'

And I forgot to ask any more questions.

*     *     *

We decided to keep our engagement a secret until I could talk to Liesel.

I returned to my room with a feeling of exquisite elation. I couldn't wait until we solemnized our vows. How wonderful it would feel to be his wife, a man whom I admired, respected and adored. A man whose simple touch consumed me, as though we had been separated in another life and found each other again.

Could life be more perfect?

The secret smile showed on my face when I looked into the mirror.

Frau Bruns noted it. 'You're very happy today.'

I nodded because I could not trust myself to speak.

313

'You love him, don't you? The Count.'

The impassioned murmur caught at me. I turned around and clasped her hands. 'He didn't hurt your Malena, Frau Bruns. I know you knew more about Malena than he did. She had a lover, maybe two, at the time of her death. Do you know who they were?'

She shook her head. 'Malena told me about the baby he didn't want. He killed her because of it.'

'No, he didn't. He found her strangled in the mountains. Her lover must have killed her. You must think very carefully, Frau Bruns. Try to remember with whom she spent her time before she died. It's very important.'

Her brown eyes scanned my face. 'Why do you care what happened to my Malena?'

'Because I believe the man who hurt Malena to be the man who tried to shoot the Count.'

Frau Bruns sat down, startled by this news. She had never considered there could be a connection.

'Did Malena say anything before she left the castle that night?'

'She gave me something. "Keep it safe, Frau Bruns", she said, "until I return". But she didn't return, did she? She was dead.'

I sat down beside her. 'What did she give you? It might help us to learn who hurt her.'

She thrust her hand into the pocket of her skirt and placed the small package into my

314

hands.

'You open it.'

It had never been opened. I tore the paper to reveal the missing miniature of Elaina, the one Conrad had cherished and the one which someone had supposedly stolen from Malena.

I held history in my hands. The miniature was very old. The painting was encircled by a row of emeralds and tiny seed pearls. The workmanship was faultless and the painter had preserved the likeness of the tragic Elaina.

I suddenly felt very ill as I looked at her face—and what lay on her wrist.

'Your bracelet,' Frau Bruns pointed.

'Yes, it's my bracelet,' I echoed, my fingers touching an engraving on the underside of the miniature. I turned it over to reveal the entwined E & C, surrounded by a circling of words in the old tongue.

'What does it say? I didn't know it had words on it.'

No wonder, I thought, for the words were very tiny. 'It says: *Eternity . . . cannot part us . . . I entrust . . . the power . . . of the . . . serpent.*'

Frau Bruns glanced at me in confusion. 'How can she be wearing your bracelet?'

'Because it was hers. The bracelet was made to symbolize their love, to reunite them should they ever part.'

My own voice sounded foreign to me. 'Whoever has taken my bracelet is under the mistaken belief its power will work for them.'

315

'An evil power,' Frau Bruns whispered.

I wrapped up the miniature and gave it back to Frau Bruns. 'We must find the source of this evil. Liesel will lead us to it.'

Frau Bruns seemed confused. 'She goes to see her lover.'

'I'm not so sure about that. There is something else worrying her. I have to find out what it is. We'll continue with our plan this evening. No one must know. I don't want to alarm the Count until we have some proof.'

'You're not well enough,' Frau Bruns frowned.

'I didn't take the laudanum today,' I confessed.

'You shouldn't go out,' she insisted. 'You're too weak. Let me go.'

'No.' I was adamant. 'I must do it and I must go alone. I'll be all right if you revive me with some hot, strong coffee.'

Frau Bruns still didn't look sure. 'You must be careful.'

'I will,' I promised, wishing I felt as confident as my tone implied.

\*       \*       \*

Dressed in Frau Bruns' cape, I followed Liesel. She hurried across the lawn, slipped through the gate and headed down the street.

It was nearly midnight. The occasional light from a lantern did little to illuminate the

316

darkened streets or my mood. What mischief was Liesel up to? Where would she lead me?

She rushed down a maze of streets until, at last, she disappeared into the overgrown hedges of what looked like an abandoned manor house.

The moon cast an eerie light on the weathered stone structure, partially hidden by tall cypress trees the leaves of which rustled in the breeze. Keeping to the shadows, Liesel walked around the side of the manor and vanished. I followed her steps in my weak, tired state, trying the series of locked doors until I found the unlocked one. Stiff with age, I pushed it enough to squeeze through and found myself at the top of a flight of stairs. A sole burning torch was fastened to the floor and beneath it a ledge filled with candles. I lit one and started below.

The stairs descended further and further into what I imagined must have been a well-functioning dungeon in the Middle Ages. Remnants of former terrors remained as I passed cells with torture instruments, all decorated with hideous gargoyles. I felt as if I had found Hell and expected the Devil to greet me at any moment.

I knew I should turn back. It had been foolish to come on my own. Foolish, yes.

Reaching the final step, I clung to the shadows and followed the faint glow of light at the end of the corridor.

317

Voices greeted me . . . familiar voices. I knew I should have stopped then; I should have not come here on my own but I went on, seduced by the deceiving power of curiosity. I had to find out the truth and here was my chance.

My heart thumping inside my chest, I came to a half-open door where I glimpsed a part of Liesel's profile.

'I won't let you kill her!' Liesel's shrill voice echoed.

'Shut up, little brat'.'

Through Liesel's screech, I strained my ears to register the owner of the voice. Herr Mendel?

'Let's get rid of her. She knows too much.'

'She doesn't *know*, she suspects. Like her unfortunate predecessors.'

Mesmerized by the commanding feminine voice, one I knew so well, I inched closer and closer until I stood plastered behind the door.

Terror gripping my throat at the discovery of the killer, I watched Ernst Mendel capture Liesel in his arms.

'Ah, my sweet, will you really kill an innocent girl?'

Sibylla gave him a bland smile. I had never seen such coldness in her eyes before and I shuddered. A person hardened and determined to carry out a purpose. I feared for Liesel, and I feared for myself.

'Pig!' Kneeing Ernst in the groin, Liesel

318

wriggled out of his grip and fled, tearing past me to freedom.

'Damn,' Sibylla muttered. 'I'll have to get to her later.'

'Will she go to her father?'

Sibylla considered. 'Probably.' Her thoughtful gaze slid over Ernst and she withdrew a pistol from under her skirts. 'Sorry, Ernst, but I have to protect myself.'

The blast terrorized my ears.

Sibylla stood over the body with a laugh. 'Well, it was either you or me.'

Imprisoned behind the door, I swallowed. I didn't dare move an inch. I couldn't move even if I wanted for the shock had set my limbs in ice. I'd just witnessed a murder. I couldn't believe it. Ernst dead by Sibylla's hand. I gulped again, wishing I'd stayed back at the villa, wishing I could shrink to the size of a pebble.

My hands wouldn't stop shaking. I gripped the wall, the urge to cough looming like an unstoppable giant in my throat.

Shoving my face in my hands, the muffled sound exploded and before I could run, I found myself dragged into the room by Sibylla.

'How very obliging of you, Miss Brown.' Sibylla beamed. 'Here I was contemplating how best to dispose of you and you have saved me the trouble. *Do* come in. Sit down.'

Thrown into a rickety old moth-eaten armchair, I faced the unusual calm of a cold-

319

hearted killer. I did not expect to live. Sibylla would kill me as she had killed Ernst Mendel and I would never see Max again.

'Follow Liesel, did you?' Sibylla clicked her tongue. 'How stupid of you.'

'Are all your victims stupid then?' I asked, noticing the glimmer of my bracelet upon her wrist.

'Yes.' She twisted her wrist under the light. 'Liesel stole your bracelet for me. It wasn't hard to convince her to do it . . . almost as easy as tearing up your dress. We had to make you leave, you see. We had to stop your developing little romance with Max. Ah, I tried so many devices to get this bracelet. I think you have enough intelligence to perceive the attempts through Liesel, Ernst and Baroness Outten and in the end it was so easy. *Hidden in your underwear-drawer, was it?* I would have expected something a little less obvious from you, Miss Brown.

'Poor Ernst,' Sibylla smirked at the bleeding corpse on the floor. 'He didn't suspect he was next on my list. Oh, yes, I have a list. I like to plan everything out. One has to treat these concerns with a degree of professionalism.'

'Why are you doing this?'

'Oh, the usual reasons: money, title, castles. 'Tis why this'—she paraded the bracelet before me—'is such a rare find. The legend has it uniting lovers. I couldn't allow that to happen, now could I?'

320

'Are you saying that Max and I . . . ?' I could scarcely believe it.

Sibylla shrugged. 'I don't know, but I couldn't take the risk. Do you think I am blind? I saw you return from the gardens and I knew what had happened. Do you think I could allow Max to take a young wife? I won't. I won't allow a little penniless upstart like you to steal away Karl's inheritance. *My* inheritance.'

'Karl! Is he in this too?'

'Dear Karl,' Sibylla sighed. 'He inherited too much of the family pride. He'd have us starve in the streets rather than take matters into our own hands. It's why I had to do it. I had to ensure our preservation. My first husband cheated me. He told me he was rich and he wasn't. So I had him killed. After that, it became easy to eliminate the others.'

'The others?' My voice sounded shaky, barely audible.

'I couldn't have distractions in my way, so dear Malena and Rachel had to go. Ah, Malena . . . the Countess whore. She had two lovers at the time of her death, but rather than name Ernst the father of her bastard brat, she chose my brother. She wanted to blackmail him into running away with her. She loved him in her stupid way. Karl doesn't know it was I who followed her up the mountains on Christmas Eve. Malena was mad and did mad things so I knew if she was found up there, the

321

truth would be hushed.'

'You strangled her?'

Her eyes glittered in triumph. 'Remarkably easy, strangling. I'll give you a choice: the gun or a squeeze of your neck. Which do you prefer?'

A glaze settled on her face and I thought her ambition had driven her mad. *She* has the von Holstein madness, not Liesel. 'You wanted Karl to become the Count,' I went on, knowing the longer I delayed her, the longer I would remain alive. 'Did he tamper with Rudolf's pistol?'

'No, I did. Rudolf was a fool and easy to kill. Max has been a little more difficult. If you hadn't saved him, he would have died on the night of the opera and Karl would be Count now.'

I prayed someone would find me. 'Why does Karl being the Count matter so much to you?'

'When I am mistress of the oldest, richest castle, I shall be happy. I did think about *marrying* Max, of course, but he wouldn't consider me, not after you came.' Her cold blue eyes studied me. 'It's very odd . . . I don't know why men find you irresistible. I thought you would be too *pure* for Karl's taste, even Max's.'

I glanced at her laughing face, desperately searching for another question to ask. The pistol remained steady in my direction and escape impossible. I could attempt to fight her

322

and maybe I would when the moment came, but how could one fight against the strength of a diseased mind?

'And Rachel?' I lifted a brow.

'Rachel,' Sibylla smiled. 'You know, I applaud your intelligence and your efforts to alert Rachel's family, Cristabel. That letter never reached them, of course, and I knew I would have to watch you—the snooping governess who fancied herself a countess. You are foolish, just like Rachel when she fell into my trap. I watched her drown and beg for mercy. It is rather pathetic when one begs for their life. I hope you're not going to beg, Fräulein Brown?'

'Beg from you?' I spat. 'I'd rather die!'

She flicked the trigger. 'Yes, show me a sample of the good English courage.'

'You won't get away with it!'

A smile of triumph touched her lips. 'I already have . . .

A gunshot fired.

Smoke clouded the room and I tumbled back with the chair. Its crash jolted my senses. I thought I was dead until I heard Liesel cry out, 'There she is, Papa!'

The Count stood beside her, a vision of fear and authority, his pistol aimed at Sibylla. 'Drop your weapon.'

A low chuckle escaped Sibylla's lips. 'You think you can order me?' To prove it, she lifted her pistol with a brazen smile. 'Are we to duel then?'

'*Drop* it, Sibylla. I won't ask you again.'

In answer, she flicked the switch and fired.

A pall of gunpowder smoke flooded the room. I couldn't see anything, but I could hear Sibylla cackling to herself. The too-near sound burned in my ears.

Speechless with terror, I pushed myself off the floor. Max . . . Max, I wanted to cry out, to alert him, but the smoke in my lungs prevented it. I tried to cough, my water-filled eyes fixing on the bullet hole in the armchair. So Sibylla's aim wasn't as good as she believed.

Crawling out from the chair, my head collided with Sibylla's. She thrust her fist into my face. Stung by the intensity, I lunged at her and we rolled across the carpet.

Her teeth gnashing above me, we both grappled for the weapon. Kicking, scratching and biting, we rolled on. I heard the others trying to work out when to shoot. Sibylla recognized it too, her black, merciless eyes jubilant as her hands imprisoned my neck and squeezed.

Her face blurred before me. I struggled against her hold, to remove her icy grip from my throat, but she was too strong for me. In the fading light, I prayed to see Max one last time . . .

Another shot fired and Sibylla's grip loosened around my neck. She rolled off me, her nails slashing down my arm.

Sliding down to his knees, Max gathered me in his arms. 'Are you all right, my darling?'

'Yes,' I whimpered.

'Shhh, it's over now.'

I closed my eyes, filled with the knowledge that he loved me.

'Look out, Papa!'

Too late, I saw Sibylla hurl a dagger at him.

And too late, I realized how much I loved him.


## CHAPTER FIFTEEN

'Miss, wake up!'

Liesel's cold fingers gently slapped my face and the events of last night came rushing back to my mind. I could barely ask the question.

'He's sleeping . . . she nearly killed him, miss.'

I nodded and decided to get up. Liesel needed me now, more than she had needed anyone before.

She shuddered. 'Sibylla, she . . . Karl wants to see you. Shall I help you dress?'

I nodded. 'You're very kind, Liesel.'

'No, I'm not. I'm wicked. I stole your bracelet and I slashed your dress.' Her haunted eyes studied mine. 'Can you ever forgive me?'

I hugged her. 'Dear Liesel, I always believed

in you.'

'D-do you still think I'm mad?'

'No, I don't. You saved me and that required love and courage on your part, not the traits of a mad person. How did you know where I was?'

She grinned. 'Frau Bruns confessed. She was worried, weren't you, Oma?'

Frau Bruns stepped forward to claim the honour. 'I listen and I watch. I knew someone killed my Malena, but now the evil one has gone and Liesel is free.'

Yes, indeed, Sibylla had left us and a sense of peace overcame the villa.

Karl struggled with self-guilt. 'I am to blame. I'd read the signs with Sib. Her ambition, her *determination* to see me the Count. True, I didn't comprehend the scope of her plan, but I knew something and I did nothing. I could have saved so many.'

'It's not your fault,' I said softly. 'People do strange things sometimes.'

'You don't understand. Max didn't kill Sibylla. He shot her in the leg. We locked her up for the night. In the morning, the room was empty but for a great deal of blood and a paperknife. I think she cut her wrists and escaped to die out in the forest somewhere. Sib always liked the forest. She'd want to die surrounded by green things.'

I held his hand. 'Perhaps it's better this way.'

He shook himself free. 'Sibylla did all of this *for me*. She didn't want me involved in her dirty work. She *sacrificed* herself for me. She didn't want my name coming out in the investigation.'

He looked wretched, bewildered. 'I still can't believe she murdered Rachel. She wrote me a letter before she died confessing all. Poor Rachel. She was barely a child. She didn't deserve to die.'

'No, she didn't,' I murmured. 'But the past *is* the past, Karl. We can't change it. The best thing we can do is learn from it. Tell me, what will you do now?'

'Since I've lost you to our Max,' he said, grimacing, 'I'm thinking of going to Egypt. A friend of mine there is undertaking an excavation. I wager a little time in the sun might warm these cold realities.'

'I almost envy you. I would love to go to Egypt.'

'Perhaps you will one day,' he smiled. 'Baron Karl von Lichtenburg could entertain you with tales of ancient curses.'

'Yes, perhaps, but I believe I've had enough of ancient curses for the moment.'

He nodded gravely. 'If you change your mind, a honeymoon in Egypt is very desirable. Oh, I almost forgot. I believe this belongs to you.'

It was the serpent bracelet.

'And now, I suspect you'll want to see him.

Go on, you have your future to make.'

'Goodbye, Karl.'

'Goodbye.' He lifted my hand to his lips. *'Countess.'*

Liesel returned my room after Karl left. 'He won't come back, will he?'

'Not for a long time, I should imagine.'

She nodded. 'Perhaps it's just as well. The papers will not be as understanding as we are. They are already printing things like: MURDEROUS TWINS and BLOOD-BATH IN VIENNA. They don't believe Karl had nothing to do with it. Papa had a difficult time trying to convince the police of Karl's innocence. They were prepared to hang him even without Sibylla's confession!' Liesel shook her head. 'How like her to run off when there's trouble. She'll be dead somewhere out there. When they find her body, I don't think she should be buried in the family crypt, do you?'

I felt the colour drain from my face. 'Where is your father, Liesel? I have to see him.'

'I'll help you dress, but first you must eat something. You're as pale as a ghost.'

'I can't rest, not until I know he is safe.'

An impish smile touched her lips. 'I've never seen him so angry when I told him what they were trying to do to you. He reminded me of an ancient warrior, ready to defend his lady from the lair of the dragon, if need be. There.' She finished lacing me. 'It's all done. You mustn't worry, Miss, Papa is not seriously

328

injured. I daresay in a few days, he'll be able—'

'Able?' I prompted, catching the hint of mischief in her eyes.

'Able to marry you and resume new duties.'

'Thank you, Liesel.'

She shrugged. 'It should be fun having you for a mother.'

*    *    *

I didn't expect to see Dara sitting at the Count's bedside.

'He's sleeping,' she whispered, her gown rustling as she moved toward me, 'but we can talk in here.'

She closed the door to the dressing-room. I looked around at the evidence of male clothing worn by Max. His scent lingered in the air, as surely as the determined look on her face.

'The doctors are confident of a quick recovery. The dagger missed all his vital organs but came terribly close to achieving its object.'

She had arranged his care, something I should have done if I had not fainted and slept the night away. My own weakness clawed at me like an unrelenting pest.

'I long suspected some bitterness on Ernst's behalf. We were waiting for him to make his move.'

I realized she was so much more a part of

the family than I could ever be.

'I've wanted to talk to you for a long time,' she murmured. 'It's very difficult for a woman like me to have to beg, but begging you I am, Miss Brown, would you deprive Paul of a father?'

The question startled me.

'Oh, I know Max is in love with you, but he would have married me if you hadn't come here and my Paul would have his father. Paul *loves* Max and Max adores him. You've seen them together and I can't bear to think of the slur on Paul's name if he remains a bastard. You've seen the damage being a bastard can do with Herr Mendel. And I confess I have encouraged Paul to believe he will be acknowledged as a von Holstein one day. He wants nothing more than to be Max's son. Would you deprive him of his dream, Cristabel?'

'I . . . er . . .'

'I know this is hard for you and we have little time. Once Max wakes up, he won't let you go. You know that. But if you stay, you shall have cheated a little boy from having a father.'

I returned to my room in a daze, the opposite of how I imagined myself exiting from the Count's room. As I left, I stood at the door and willed him to wake, to prevent what I now felt I must do.

I couldn't look at Dora. I could only pack

330

my bags and run to Emily.

*     *     *

Emily and I sat locked in her bedroom for more than two hours. On my arrival at their hotel, Hugo had been quickly dispatched outside on an errand.

'Oh, my poor darling!' Emily embraced me when I finished apprising her of the events of the last twenty-four hours. 'What unimaginable horrors you must have suffered only to feel you must run away at your moment of triumph!'

'Triumph,' I echoed. 'Emily, it will break my heart to leave him. He means more to me than life itself. Ohl' I turned my tortured face away from her. 'I should go back. I should tell that woman I don't care what happens to her son. I don't, you know. I don't care if Paul remains a bastard for the rest of his life.'

'Then go back,' Emily urged. 'The Count will be expecting you.'

I paced to the window. I knew I had to make a decision and soon. 'But the son!' I sobbed, hating myself for my own weakness. 'If I leave, he'll marry her because she is the mother of his child.'

'He hasn't married her all this time,' Emily reminded me.

'Because he was under suspicion of Malena's murder. He thought it discreet to wait.'

'You are impossible!' Emily flung her arms around my neck. 'Impossible, headstrong and brave.'

'Brave?' I echoed.

'Brave to leave the man you love,' Emily smiled. 'It takes true courage to do that.'

'I am a coward. A jealous coward. Oh, Emily, if it wasn't for that *stupid* child!'

Emily laughed. 'He's stupid now, is he?' She pressed a finger to her lips in sudden thought. 'Did you confide any of this to Liesel, or did you fly the house in tears?'

'Fly the house in tears,' I grinned through my sobs. 'I left her a letter, but it's no use hoping. I have to get away for a few days. I have to think.'

Emily pressed my hands. 'You're coming back with us to England.'

'No,' I smiled through my tears. 'I'm not. I'm going back to the *schloss.*'

'The *schloss!*'

'I know it's stupid but I have to go back there. I have to find this missing book with the legend—'

'Oh, you are insane!' Emily wrapped me up in her arms. 'I know how this story ends. Even if you don't.'

'That's just it, Emily. I don't know how it will end.'

\*　　　\*　　　\*

332

I booked the first train to Salzburg.

Weaving through the ticketing line at the station, I couldn't help glancing around, hoping to see Max, praying for him or someone to stop me.

But no one came and soon I was speeding off, back to the *schloss* and the feeling Vienna had just been a dream.

# CHAPTER SIXTEEN

The journey proved to be tedious. I didn't like travelling alone and when faced with courting couples or run-away lovers, I inwardly groaned. I wanted to believe in the legend. I wanted to believe in the bracelet but uncertainty and doubt clouded my mind.

Dare I believe the legend? Dare I assume Granny Frieda and Granny Hannah had misled me on purpose? Had I known their plan was to reunite lovers, I couldn't have fallen in love with the Count as I had. What bond existed between us now was one forged of our own making, not of some ancient charm.

The long drive up to the *schloss* filled me with a haunting melancholy. I thought of the untried girl who'd come here with Herr Reimann, intent on starting her new post as governess. Now, the woman was returning to her fate.

Fate. I was becoming as fanciful as Liesel but who could not be surrounded by such ancient woods, mountains older than time, a castle whose fabled history enchanted one as much as its beauty?

I waited for the moment where the sun passed through the trees, the turn in the road where one saw the castle for the first time. I

334

remembered my time and it seemed like a lifetime ago.

And there the cream-coloured towers rose out of a clear blue sky.

'Do you want me to pause, *fräulein*?' the driver asked.

'No,' I smiled. 'I've been here before.'

He shrugged and nudged the horses along for the final ride up to the top. Passing the bridge with the stream below gave me no qualms, instead I felt a sense of peace overcome me. The birds chirped in the woods, the stream gurgled and the grand *schloss* awaited.

'*Die Burg der Träume*,' the awed murmur escaped my lips. 'I am home.'

The servants were surprised to see me.

'It's the English miss!' I heard one cry, soon followed by a sharp query, 'Fräulein Brown is *here*?'

They were wondering why I'd come back alone. I wondered why, too. It had been foolish to leave Max. I should have stayed in Vienna and talked to him. I shouldn't have left without saying a word to the man I loved.

I decided to deliver my story to Lady Gisela, the lady of the castle in the absence of the Count.

The servants wasted no time accompanying me to Lady Gisela's apartments.

I found her exactly where I'd left her: in her room, eating from her bed and reprimanding

335

Ingrid on her 'woeful' reading voice. I entered the room, discarded my bonnet and gloves on a vacant chair. 'Lady Gisela!'

'Dear child!' She dropped her plate of cheeses in delight. 'You've come back, have you.' She peered behind me. 'Alone?'

'Yes, alone,' I answered, giving Ingrid a smile of welcome. 'I needed to see you on an urgent matter.'

Lady Gisela read my meaning and immediately dismissed Ingrid. When the door closed, she tapped the edge of her bed. 'Needed to see me, eh? What's to do? You've fallen in love with Max, haven't you, and don't know what to do about it?'

'Oh!' I buried my face in my hands. 'So much has happened! I hardly know where to begin.'

'May I suggest you start at the beginning?' Lady Gisela propped up her pillows. 'And if we're going to be here awhile, let's call for some refreshment, shall we?'

She rang the bell and Ingrid soon had our order of hot coffee and whatever delicacy came with it.

'I brought you chocolates.' I laid the gift box on her bed. 'And news.'

'Oooh.' My lady ripped open the box and began sampling the goods. 'You know how I *love* news.'

And while she ate, I talked. The strong hot coffee helped wash away some of my weariness and two hours later, I had emptied my heart.

'Sibylla cut herself, did she! Well, that'll put an end to her ambition, won't it? Good and proper. I can't say I'll mourn her. She was much too fake. Too bossy with Karl. I daresay most of his problem was having to deal with his sister! And the scandalmongers got wind of it, eh? That's a shame, but can't be avoided now. At least Karl's in the clear. I like the boy. He's not a devil and he'll suffer enough. The shame of Sibylla and poor little Rachel. Liked that gel. Shame, shame . . . what a waste of young, lively blood?'

She had less kind words to say about Ernst Mendel.

'That man. Never liked him. I'm glad Sibylla shot him. Best thing she ever did.'

For Liesel, she nodded in deep thought and even put the box of chocolates aside. 'This experience will do her good, I say. Make her grow up. What's Max got planned for her?'

'I don't know.'

Lady Gisela looked at me shrewdly. 'You missed a part of the story. About the bracelet and Max.'

I stared at her. 'You *know* about the bracelet?'

'Of course. I knew you had it before you arrived.'

'I don't understand.'

A softness came into her eyes. 'You weren't meant to, child. You came back to unravel the legend of the bracelet, didn't you? Try and find the missing book of secrets?'

'You *have* the book?'

'The book is lost, but who needs a book when one has a brain as sharp as mine?'

I was brimming with anticipation.

Lady Gisela chuckled. 'I think I'll keep you on a string a little longer and we'll discuss it over dinner.'

'Oh, *please*, Lady G! I've travelled long and far.'

'Humph. Convincing plea. But this kind of thing should be done over an evening meal, wine and candles. Perhaps I'll give you half now and half later? Will that satisfy you?'

I crossed my arms. 'You're going to leave the best 'til last, aren't you?'

'I won't hoard everything!' she promised. 'Now, send for some tea, would you? Tea with lemon. I need to revitalize my brain.'

I sat cross-legged on the floor before her, a hot cup of tea with lemon in hand, as the story of Conrad and Elaina tickled my ears. I interrupted her. 'I know all this. Liesel told me.'

'Ah,' she smiled, 'but I wager Liesel didn't tell you about *Sabeen*.'

'*Who?*'

Lady Gisela made an I-told-you-so face. 'Sabeen, the daughter of the forest lord, Hagen. Sabeen, the ex-leman of Conrad. Jealous Sabeen, who informed the castle of

jump out of the window like Elaina had jumped to her death. 'You pushed Fräulein Suski to her death, didn't you?'

She shrugged. 'Merely an accident. She overheard Ernst and I talking. I had to kill her.'

'You delight in murder.'

'Only when necessary.' She smiled, her keen gaze searching my body for the bracelet. 'Good, I rather fancy that bracelet. They shan't find it on your body. Throw it to me.'

'Never!'

Sibylla lunged at me. I drew to one side, desperation prickling up my spine. How could I escape? 'You won't get away with it, Sibylla,' I tried. 'Max will come back. So will Karl. Karl loves you. He feels wretched. He wants to help you.'

I had confused her. That was good. Now, *how* was I going to escape? I'd have a fight on my hands and one of us was going out of that window. I hoped it wouldn't be me.

'You are trying to save your skin.' She smiled thinly. 'It won't work.'

'Wrong, Sibylla. Its not too late. Forget your hate. Karl wants you to forget it.'

My farce was working. Doubt flickered a moment in her eyes but soon recovered with hardened purpose.

'Good try.'

Sibylla seized my neck, squeezing hard. Her eyes glazed over. 'Die! Die! Die!'

343

I choked against her might. Like chains of steel, her fingers gripped and squeezed and we stumbled across the room. I fought to remove her hands off my neck but my strength deserted me. I was tired and hungry, and now I felt like weeping bitterly.

Sibylla shepherded me to the window. I spluttered when the hard stone grazed my elbow. The cold wind tore through my hair but the force of it didn't stop her. I latched on to the curtains in a desperate bid to keep inside.

Sibylla laughed, grabbing my legs and forcing me out of the window.

I clung to the curtains for dear life, my legs dangling in the night air. Up above, I could see Sibylla's face peering down at me, triumphant.

I swallowed and closed my eyes. I prayed. I called for Elaina's help. Anyone's help. I didn't want to die. I was too young to die.

My fingers slipped with the movement of the curtain. Sibylla must be cutting it free. A little wail left my lips. Soon, it would be over.

Someone shouted from the window. I heard a scream and then Sibylla's yelp as she was thrown out. Her startled blue eyes hurtled past me. She tried in vain to latch on to me. Her hand caught my left ankle but a gentle shake of my leg sent her spinning down to her death. I felt no remorse, only innate relief, and joy.

For there, in the tower window, was my warrior of old pulling me up to safety. He didn't rest or dare to look at me until I was in his arms.

'I'm here now,' he said. And I won't ever let you go.'

I buried my face in the warmth of his chest. 'How did you know?'

Aunt Gisela. When you failed to arrive for dinner, she rang for Ingrid to search for you. Ingrid heard the two of you up here and went for help.'

I nodded. 'Take me away, Max. Take me away from this room.'

He carried me in his arms to the great hall where Lady Gisela took charge of my recovery.

'You'll have to let her go at some point.' She smiled fondly down at her nephew. 'What the girl needs is *food*, not wine. May I suggest the pork in apple sauce?'

I was grateful for Lady Gisela's nonchalance that night. It made me forget, though I refused to leave the security of Max's arms. He ended up spooning the food down my throat, determined I should eat.

He didn't offer to carry me to my room, but instead carried me to his. With heartbreaking tenderness, he undressed me out of my gown and into my nightdress brought to him from my room. Then he unpinned my hair, brushed it, and put me in his bed.

'Don't leave me,' I begged. 'Not tonight.'

He was only going to fetch a drink, but I wanted him close. I wanted his arms around me.

Cosseted by the love and emotion in his face, I soon fell asleep, the nightmare of the night slipping away with each gentle stroke of his hand down my back.

## CHAPTER SEVENTEEN

In the morning, I was able to dissect the terror of the night.

'Who would have thought Sibylla would come back?' Lady Gisela pondered aloud. 'Did she say what she did with the book?'

Liesel's room was searched and the book found in her, yes, underwear drawer. I recalled Sibylla's critical sneer and had to smile. It appeared my hiding place wasn't so stupid after all.

Max and I were married the next day in a quiet ceremony at the *schloss* with Lady Gisela as witness. Her eyes sparkled mischievously and only afterwards would she supply the reason 'over cake'.

'One must have a wedding cake and I had yours ordered the moment you arrived.'

I looked at her in some confusion. 'The moment I arrived?'

'Back here. I knew Max would come charging after you. It was fated.'

We were sitting in the great hall. 'Fated?'

Lady Gisela gave me a meaningful look. 'The second half of the story is this: after the tragedy of Conrad and Elaina, three guardians were given the duty of protecting the bracelet and the legend throughout the ages.'

'There were three?' Max joked.

I squeezed his hand under the table.

Lady Gisela glared at him. 'This is serious.'

Max raised my hand to his lips. 'Forgive me if I appear a little distracted, I have an enchanting bride waiting, you know.'

'Well, you can wait another ten minutes,' Lady Gisela said in an unsympathetic tone, turning back to me. 'Did you note my lack of concern when you told me the bracelet had been stolen from you?'

With Max holding my hand to his lips, it was difficult to concentrate. 'Y-yes. I thought it odd at the time but there was so much we discussed that day.'

'I knew it would return to you,' Lady Gisela explained, 'even when it had been stolen from you. Have you not yet guessed? Did you learn nothing from Granny Hannah?'

Max dropped my hand. 'How do you know Cristy's relations?'

Lady Gisela savoured her moment of triumph. 'Cristabel, what was Granny Hannah's reaction when she saw you?'

I searched my mind. 'Joy, I think. And a little surprised, maybe?'

'Surprised, yes, as well she should be. My

dear child'—Lady Gisela paused for emphasis—'*you* are the exact image of Isador, Isador the sister of Elaina, the Elaina who married Conrad von Holstein. There is an old painting of Isador in Mittenwald. Hannah wouldn't have shown it to you when you came because we knew you had to fulfil the prophecy.'

'What prophecy?'

'The one engraved on the back of Elaina's miniature. You said you found it.'

The words came rushing back to my mind. *Eternity cannot part us. I entrust the power of the serpent.* 'Does this mean . . . ?'

'Yes, there is a connection between your family and ours. Isador removed the bracelet from her sister's body before they buried her. She loved Elaina and wanted to keep something of hers with her always. And so the bracelet has passed from mother to daughter throughout the generations, waiting for the time when Elaina would be reunited with her Conrad. The guardians have kept all secret; always two from Elaina's family and one from Conrad's. *I* am the guardian for Conrad. Granny Hannah and Granny Frieda are the guardians of yours.'

I stared at her in utter amazement, disbelief, wonder. 'It certainly explains Granny's secrecy . . .'

Lady Gisela nodded. 'She's clever, your Granny F. We knew the power of the legend would lead you to Max. We only worked to make it happen a little more . . . naturally. I pray we succeeded.'

Max answered for both of us. 'We don't need an enchanted bracelet. I fell in love with Cristabel the moment I saw her.'

I didn't dare to think it could be true.

'It's the truth,' Max confirmed, drawing me to him.

In his arms, I believed. I had decided not to believe in this nonsense, but I sat there, numb and bewildered. Everything suddenly made sense . . . I had *felt* the power of the bracelet, I had *felt* its eye upon me, a true descendent of Elaina, searching for her Conrad. It explained the miraculous way I'd won the post at the remote castle in the mountains, I, a woman of little experience and no connections.

Lady Gisela had a confession to make on that score.

'I'm sorry my dear, but you didn't win the post out of the blue. I arranged it with the help of your grandmother. Oh yes, we've been corresponding for some time. I have a complete account of your childhood, Miss Brown. Even down to when you lost your first tooth.'

Max and I shared a look. *'What?'*

'It's our job,' Lady Gisela shrugged. 'What is the good of a title without meat? I wouldn't be a *true* guardian if I wasn't conspiring in the dark to put you two together.'

                    *           *           *

The amazement of Lady Gisela's confession accompanied us back to the bridal chamber where Max and I spent the remainder of the week. We had much to talk over and to discover about one another.

'But your wound—' I protested.

'What is a wound to keep me from devouring you?'

I laughed, savouring the dream of my lover's voice in my ear. 'Please tell me I'm not dreaming.'

'You're not dreaming,' he murmured obediently. 'I plan to love you thoroughly, truly and completely the rest of my days.'

'And royally,' I added. 'Don't forget about the grand tour of Europe and our trip to England.'

'Our *leisurely* trip to England.' He placed a kiss on my bare stomach. 'After a deliciously long Mediterranean cruise. You've finally returned to me at last. I have a great deal of catching up to do.'

The mocking glint had faded from his eyes and in that moment, I truly believed the bracelet had united us.

Max frowned. 'You created so much disruption in my life, I should have recognized the connection earlier. I was drawn to you from the moment I saw you standing there in the light. How could I have known it was you?'

I dared not smile as I had experienced the same feeling. 'Could the legend be true?'

'I don't know.' He captured my hand in his. 'But I do know I have never loved a woman as I love you.' He pulled me into his arms and kissed every inch of my face. 'You don't look like Elaina, do you?'

'We have to see the portrait of Isador in Mittenwald.'

'We will,' he murmured in promise. 'But after a year-long honeymoon.'

'A year long?'

'Then I'll know every inch of you and I'll be able to judge if the likeness is true or not.'

'It'll take you a year?' I queried in delight.

'One has to do things . . . thoroughly,' was his answer.

Much later, I gazed at his face in the moonlight. 'I thought you wanted to marry Dara.'

'Dara! Whatever gave you that idea?'

'She is the mother of your child, is she not?'

There was a long pause. 'Did she tell you I'm Paul's father?'

'Not exactly but she implied—'

He laughed. 'My dear, sweet Cristy! Is that why you ran away?'

'Partly,' I admitted.

'You were foolish to doubt and you've given me a great deal of trouble.'

I lifted a brow, my recently dressed wound

paining me. 'Oh?'

'Yes,' he frowned. 'There's only one thing I detest more than lies and deceit, and that is a long ride in a carriage.'

'You fool,' I flung my arms around his neck. 'My own lovable fool. I scarcely dared to hope . . . I loved you so much.'

'Loved?' he queried.

'Love,' I amended, giving him a reproachful smile. 'You were telling me about Dara.'

'Yes.' He collected my hands. 'It appears she played us both for fools. Dara was my late brother's mistress and Paul is my brother's son. She insisted on keeping Paul's identity a secret because she thought he'd be in danger after Rudolf's murder. And he was murdered. We know that now.' He studied me in amusement. 'Dara must have persuaded you to believe otherwise as she almost succeeded in persuading me that you didn't love me.'

'What changed your mind?'

He held my face in his hands. 'Faith . . . and an old legend, it would seem.'

'How did Dara take the news?'

'Curiously well. She asked me to pass her regards on to you when I raced off to catch the last train.'

I felt a great fool.

'And now, my Elaina, the night is young and you have kept me waiting long enough.'

'An eternity,' I reminded him, wrapping my arms around his neck in an aura of ecstasy I knew would be often repeated.

I don't know how long we stayed inside that bridal chamber, but it seemed like an eternity before we finally did emerge.

Time did not signify: we had found each other again.

I imagined Granny smiling at us from England.

The eye of the serpent had its legend.

# Chivers Large Print Direct

If you have enjoyed this Large Print book and would like to build up your own collection of Large Print books and have them delivered direct to your door, please contact **Chivers Large Print Direct**.

**Chivers Large Print Direct** offers you a full service:

◇ **Created to support your local library**

◇ **Delivery direct to your door**

◇ **Easy-to-read type and attractively bound**

◇ **The very best authors**

◇ **Special low prices**

For further details either call Customer Services on 01225 443400 or write to us at

**Chivers Large Print Direct**
**FREEPOST (BA 1686/1)**
**Bath**
**BA1 3QZ**